Sherlock Holmes and The Arcana of Madness

A Horror Mystery

John Linwood Grant, Angela Yuriko Smith, and Naching T. Kassa

BOOK 11 IN CRYSTAL LAKE'S DARK TIDE SERIES

Let the world know:
#IGotMyCLPBook!

Crystal Lake Publishing
www.CrystalLakePub.com

Follow us on Amazon:

WELCOME
TO ANOTHER

CRYSTAL LAKE PUBLISHING
CREATION

Join today at www.crystallakepub.com & www.patreon.com/CLP

If you are at all familiar with the reminisces of Dr. John H. Watson, you will recall that he kept a tin dispatch box within the vaults of Cox & Co. at Charing Cross. This unassuming box with the words, "John H. Watson, M.D. late Indian Army" painted across the lid, contains a veritable treasure trove of untold cases. Cases both solved and unsolved by the Master, Mr. Sherlock Holmes.

It may come as a surprise to the reader that shortly after the discovery of the box, the vaults of Cox and Co. were breached by a person or persons unknown. The only vault which showed any disturbance was the one belonging to Dr. Watson. The box had been opened and it was clear that several manuscripts had gone missing.

Until a few years ago.

During the redevelopment of Broadmoor Hospital in 2019, three manuscripts were found within the grave of the artist, Richard Dadd. Each of these manuscripts had been carefully preserved and seemed to have been prepared for publishing by John H. Watson himself.

Watson made several notes on each story, and it seems that he wished them to be published in a certain order and not chronologically. For example, the adventure, "A Promise of Blades," was to be published first, even though it occurred in the year 1896—eleven years *after* the case which follows it. "A Promise of Blades" was also set to be published in The Strand Magazine, while the other stories. "The Adventure of the Tarot Card Prophecies," and "The Riddle of the Red Tower," were to be published in the American magazine, Colliers Weekly. (Perhaps this is why "Blades" features British spellings while "Tarot" and "Riddle" feature American.)

There is no reason given for this strange chronology. And no reason given as to why these cases did not see the light of day. Were they suppressed by Watson's literary agent, Sir Arthur Conan Doyle? It hardly seems likely considering the nature of the cases, all of which contain a strange and occult bent. Perhaps, Holmes himself forbade the publishing of these accounts. Or was it someone else entirely? The cases were stolen and hidden in Dadd's grave. It may be the answer lies there. Whatever the reason, I fear it is a puzzle whose solution lies far beyond our ken. Only Sherlock Holmes could find the truth. Just as he must find the truth within these three cases, all connected by The Arcana of Madness.

A Promise of Blades

John Linwood Grant

If she drifts into that half-world between sleep and waking life; if she allows him come to her . . .

Catherine shudders upon her disordered bed, one hand knuckle-white as it grips the counterpane, the other thrust out in impotent denial. She must not let it happen, not again. Is her discipline so easily broken, her defence so weakened by the years?

If . . .

But it is not him!

Relief. Puzzlement. This is not him, but a woman who walks through her mind, a stranger. There is sinew there, and dark hair, the cheekbones high and sharp; those eyes of sullen brown are lifeless coals, waiting for fire to come to them. It is a face of command, requirement. All around her are books, stacked, shelved . . . tumbled.

From a handsome reticule, this woman draws forth a pack of playing cards. She sorts through them, withdrawing three.

"Sept, huit, le roi," she says. And at last, a flame of pleasure glints beneath her brows . . .

The scene shatters, images afloat on a red and shoreless sea, until Catherine can take no more. The bedclothes tear, her legs spasm; her scream is inside her, as silent as the man who slumps amongst his precious books, his throat a smile which does not end.

She does not understand. Why, after so long, does murder once more speak to her?

Part One

It may be some time before I play cards again. When such invitations are made—the usual "I say, Watson, will you make up a fourth this evening?"—my reply is brisk. No, I will not. And my friends, slightly puzzled, murmur that I work too hard, and go to seek another player.

As for solitaire, to sit alone, and deal out the things—the spread of the cards, the sly array of numbers, of hapless knaves and knowing queens, and that urge to stare at the backs of them, at even the most commercial of patterns . . . it cannot be done.

For there is madness there, and blood, though it began with nothing more than the opening of an envelope . . .

There are times when I must give the impression that my friend Sherlock Holmes has only two moods—bored and enervated for lack of challenging cases, or intense and electrified by his latest conundrum. The truth is less dramatic, for there were many weeks, occasionally months, when moderately interesting crimes came to light and were solved or referred back to Scotland Yard with clear pointers as to how they should proceed. During these periods, Holmes displayed neither manic excitement, nor sulked and shot holes in the wall; he merely did what he did best, cementing his reputation as the world's sole consulting detective.

So, it had been throughout the first half of that year—a robbery in Chelsea, a minor political affair involving the Italians, an unpleasant murder in Hampshire, and so on. A dozen cases were set aside as tedious; a half dozen were solved to the degree to which Holmes had any interest.

I myself, having fewer excuses to rush from my practice than usual, saw many boils, alcohol-hardened livers, and infected cuts—until one particular item arrived at Baker Street, on the morning of June 17th.

"What have you there, Watson?" Holmes murmured from his armchair.

I was trawling through the first post, as I often did—I knew by now which enquiries would be of no likely interest—but had paused at the last in the pile.

"This final envelope . . . there's something inside it. Not a letter, I mean."

He came over and took it from me, unopened.

"Hmm. Stiff, too large to be a calling card. The envelope is nothing special, a standard 'extra' for larger enclosures. Scentless. Postmarked . . . Wokingham. A formal invitation, perhaps, though I know of no function or event of any importance related to that area."

He placed it back in my hand, and I slit the end of the envelope carefully, slipping out its contents.

"A playing card!" I exclaimed.

"Of a sort, Watson."

As I turned the card over in my fingers, a smile played at one corner of his mouth. The card was larger than one from any normal pack, some six inches by four inches, with an intricately patterned back in dark blue and grey. The device on its face was a disembodied hand wielding a strangely curved sword which pierced a crown. The finer detail of the reverse I could not make out, but my dislike of the object was visceral, instinctive. I let it fall to the desk, face up.

"It is the Ace of Swords," said Holmes. "A Tarot card. I happened to make a study of the styles currently in circulation after that Weeping Child episode, as you fancifully recorded it. Not that the Tarot aspect there was any more than a deception. Now this card—it is not of any design I have seen before—does not bear the usual straight sword. Furthermore, if I am not mistaken, this is hand-painted. A unique item."

"Best kept away from, if you ask me," I sniffed. Why a single card should bother me so, I could not explain, but as for such things in general—Tarot cards, planchettes, and hovering trumpets—I saw them as paraphernalia designed to deceive.

Should you condemn me as one with his eyes closed to higher matters, you would be wrong. It was not spiritualism itself which irked me, but the astounding degree of fakery and profiteering which the field seemed to have accumulated. For every potentially genuine seeker after truths, there were ten stage acts and a hundred private sittings, which had been assembled for the single purpose of bilking the bereaved and walking away with their coin.

Holmes chuckled. "Oh, come now, old fellow. The Ace of Swords is, if my memory serves me, representative of intellect, mental clarity, and penetrative thought. Besides, it was once merely a card game."

He picked up the card and envelope, examining them further.

"There is no note, no return address, but someone has written two words under the gummed flap. 'Albert Smith,' in capitals. A man's script—right-handed, moderate education, but it betrays little else. Too common a name to begin chasing down without further information."

"Could it be a warning of some sort?" I mused. "Or a clue in some case which has not yet reached us?"

"Always possible. As I have no idea as to why I might be warned in such a manner and know of no misdeed to which this refers, all we can do is place it aside and continue with our usual work. Time, Watson—time will no doubt tell."

And he slipped the card, almost absently, into the old toast-rack on the mantelpiece, a place where many idle notes and unanswered letters slept.

The following afternoon we had a visit from Inspector Lestrade, who was in his usual huff about several matters in Holmes's hands. He accepted a cup of tea but was in no mood for niceties.

"Mr. Holmes, the commissioner really must hear if—"

"The pearls are with Ma Humble's people, in Wapping. Lady Mellin was indiscreet, and a fool to herself, but the situation may be recovered. Put pressure on Levitt, by Swan Wharf, and he'll give them up. Ma Humble has other matters with which to deal. She will not intervene."

Lestrade looked down at his cup of tea, the wind drawn from his sails. "Ah, well, much obliged, I'm sure."

"Indian," I said.

"The thief is Indian?"

"The tea, Lestrade."

"Ah."

Holmes tilted his head back, hooded eyes regarding the policeman.

"You have something else, inspector. Something which vexes you."

Lestrade's sallow, rather sour features went through several reorganisations before he spoke.

"Josef Becskei. Murdered yesterday afternoon in his shop, not far from Primrose Hill. No suspect, no witnesses. I was told not to mention it unless Lady Mellin's situation was . . . resolved."

Holmes shrugged. "Lord Mellin has influence—Mr. Becskei presumably does not."

"Not with the commissioner, or anyone I'd care to meet," said the inspector, looking uncomfortable.

"And were there unusual circumstances to this crime, ones which made you consider my assistance?"

"I . . . yes, Mr. Holmes. Well, not circumstances, but evidence of an odd nature. If it is evidence at all."

"Go on."

Lestrade reached into one of his inner pockets and drew out a small package of folded waxed paper. "They have been photographed. And subjected to one of your 'fingerprint' techniques, as we had so little else on which to go. Nothing there, so I reckon they wore gloves."

My friend nodded appreciatively and took the proffered package. The contents made me blink, and I was about to speak out until I saw Holmes's warning look. For inside were three playing cards! Ordinary things, as you might find in any club, and nothing like the card received in the post, but still . . .

"The king, seven, eight of spades," Holmes murmured.

Seeing that he had piqued the detective's interest, Lestrade added what he knew.

"Mr. Josef Becskei was a dealer of rare books and occasional *objets d'art*, especially those which pertained to mysticism, occultism, and what were apparently Kabbalistic studies, a term with which I was not familiar. A man in his fifties, without obvious enemies, he was discovered by a patrolling constable, who noticed the shop door slightly ajar. The constable was quite shaken, for the corpse was found bound to a chair with marks of violence upon it. The throat was cut wide open, cards in the lap."

Holmes held up the king. "Yes, a spatter of blood. This one, at least, was in the vicinity when your man was killed. Was anything obviously missing?"

"We have no idea. The shop is a series of small rooms piled high with old books and nonsense. I doubt that even the late Becskei could have known what was in there."

"We will have to visit the scene of the crime before any more damage is done. Watson?"

I got to my feet. It was a fine day. I had no patients booked, and it had been some time since I had been of any real use to my friend.

"At your disposal, Holmes."

"Good man."

We were fortunate that there was an unoccupied cab standing at the end of the street; Lestrade had business elsewhere but gave the cabman directions. The constable on duty at the shop would let us in if we mentioned his authority.

On our arrival, Becskei's establishment presented a small, grimy frontage between other shops; the sign above the door said "Curios." But no one had called, said the fresh-faced constable outside, who was excited at meeting Holmes. Passers-by had gawped, curious as to what had occurred, but that was all.

Inside, the shop extended way back and contrary to what I had expected, it was not all decrepit. Cluttered, yes, with shelves bowed under the weight of many elderly volumes, and without apparent system, redolent with the smell of aged paper and foxed leather.

"Becskei did not welcome passing trade, though he kept up an appearance." Holmes gestured. "The least interesting books occupy the immediate vicinity—Parish records, mouldering sermons, and poor novels—but as you go further into its depths, there are some genuinely rare texts. Collectors' items, uncommon religious texts, Rosicrucian pamphlets. He knew his business, and his true business revolved—I am sad to say—around the arcane and mystical, not the rational world."

It was in a disordered side-room that we found the chair to which the victim had been bound, rope left dangling from its arms. My friend ignored it at first and spent some time investigating the nooks and crannies.

"A cash drawer and an expensive German fob watch, untouched; same for a copy of Merveille's *Indices*, worth a pretty penny. Neither a common cracksman nor an informed bibliophile was here, but someone with a distinct purpose. We can assume that the cards, or a pack of them, came with the intruder. And look, by these shelves—the faint footprints of a woman, or possibly an adolescent, where the floor is dustier."

"It could have been a customer, earlier that day?" I suggested.

"A reasonable suggestion, but there was blood on the sole which made these prints. The woman trod here during or after the event. And made no attempt to, or did not think to, obscure her passage."

"Perhaps she did not think that Sherlock Holmes would apply his talent to the case."

Holmes smiled. "There is that. Still . . . " He turned his attention to the single straight-backed chair in the centre of the cramped room. "Of no importance in itself. The rope is instructive." He took out his pocketknife, and with difficulty cut free a knotted section of the bindings, placing it in his jacket pocket.

Above the shop, Becskei's living quarters were Spartan, almost entirely free of books, papers, or personal frippery beyond hairbrush, razor, and soap. A single large ledger lay open, with one page torn out, missing. I looked at the preceding pages.

"This would have covered sales or acquisitions in, um, January of this year."

"Good, good," said Holmes. "We may assume that whatever the intruder was after, it was purchased during that period—and we are not supposed to know what was sought, hence the missing page. So, a tangible object or objects, not information alone. Did Becskei give up his prize before he died, I wonder? And why the playing cards, eh, instead of letting it seem a common burglary? For whom were they leaving a message?"

Outside, the constable begged my friend's attention.

"I should have said, sir—there was a caller, very early this morning, but I didn't let her in. I thought maybe she was a neighbour."

The officer described someone in her thirties, with untutored black hair, large grey eyes, dressed in a heavy fur coat—of East European origin, he had assumed. "A Roosian, maybe, sir."

"A Russian woman!" I said, looking to Holmes.

"We shall see. Becskei was Hungarian, a quite different matter, if that was what you were thinking, Watson. What did she say to you, constable?"

The young man frowned. "She asked . . . she asked if any cards had been found. Well, that made no sense to me—I was just set on to watch the shop, and no one told me nothing but that a bloke had been killed. And then she up and left, she did.”

Holmes seemed disappointed. We went then to see Becskei's body. I knew the doctor on duty at the police morgue, a sturdy fellow named Roe, and we discussed his findings so far. Dr. Roe was happy to oblige.

“Straightforward, really, Mr. Holmes. Your man was tied up, probably after a blow to the left temple, and subject to various assaults—a bruised cheek, split lip, and cuts to his upper arms.”

“During questioning?”

“Quite possibly. After these were made—not long after, I'd say—a sharp blade was used to slash open his throat.”

“Slash?” Holmes.

“Absolutely.” Roe gave a cheerful nod. “One sweeping blow. I've seen a number of assaults over the years, and this wasn't done with your usual cut-throat razor or knife. From the depth of the wound and the skin at the edges, I'd say a sizeable—and unusual—blade was used.”

My friend pursed his lips and took up his hat. “I must be homeward bound, Watson. I need to give some serious thought to this case.”

“You believe it to be more than robbery with assault?”

“We shall see. But I do believe it to be far from over.”

“Why so?” I asked as I hailed a hansom.

“Because,” he said, his face grim, “I have not yet fathomed the relevance of those particular three cards. And because there are thirteen spades in the suit . . . ”

I heard nothing more from Holmes concerning the murder of Josef Becskei for some days. I was not currently at Baker Street at all for part of each week, for I was helping out an ill colleague, and had to sleep in the rooms over his practice on occasion. Every time I intended to ask Holmes about Becskei, or the cards, something else intervened.

In the middle of the following week, however, he himself took me aside after lunch—and his eyes held that gleam of excitement which I knew so well.

"Sir Richard Cleves is dead," he pronounced.

I did not know the name. "Should I be commiserating, Holmes? Or loading my revolver?"

Holmes snorted. "He was killed last night, in his mistress's rooms; such was the uproar that he could not be removed without the papers finding out. And on his body were found . . . "

I was clearly expected to have an answer.

"Cards of some sort?" I hazarded.

"Quite. The jack of spades, and the cards two to five in the same suit. Lestrade is bringing them in an hour or so , to add to our collection."

"But no more Tarot cards?"

He looked annoyed at my reminder. "Not yet, Watson."

Cleves, a well-heeled—as the Americans say—art collector, had been discovered by Maisie Evans, a dancer, in the Chelsea flat where he maintained her. She herself had been chloroformed by persons unknown, and had awoken to find her "benefactor" tied to a chair, his wrists sliced open. There was considerable bruising to the man's body, inflicted to it in the seated position.

Others in the building heard nothing of the assault on Cleves, but could not ignore the young woman's extended series of screams when she came round to find the man murdered, as she seemed to have almost lost her wits. Her only coherent words, the papers said, were "Richard," "dead," and "Thoth."

We had more on this when Lestrade arrived, around two in the afternoon. He had the harassed manner of a ferret which had been forced down too many rabbit holes to no effect.

"Take heart," said my friend affably, as Mrs. Hudson let the inspector in. "Only a few cards left now. The affair cannot go on forever."

"Take 'heart'? Very amusing, Mr. Holmes. It'll be clubs and diamonds next." He leaned by the window, peering out into the rain. "I don't think this Evans girl knows anything. The affair with Sir Richard was of long standing; the wife knew, I am told, and considered that it kept her husband out of trouble whilst she attended to various good works."

I gave an awkward laugh. "Funny arrangement."

"More common than you think with our 'superiors,' doctor," said Lestrade, shaking his head dolefully. "Anyway, Miss Evans was attending to refreshments whilst Sir Richard slept, heard the front door open—"

"It was not locked?" Holmes interjected.

"She'd not thought to bother. For all the private goings-on there, the neighbourhood is respectable. Someone came up from behind, and a pad was placed over her nose and mouth. That's all she remembers."

"Were there other sounds . . . smells?"

"The girl is a goose. Easily alarmed, little sense. She could offer nothing more. I might say that there are several politicians watching what we do over Cleves—he had no real influence, but plenty of friends."

"We will have to speak to her when she is recovered. The scene of the crime?"

"Much as the other, and yes, I did take pains to do your 'observations' for you, Mr. Holmes. I can learn, you know. Sir Richard was tied to an armchair with ship's rope, exactly the same as with Becskei. No obvious sign of burglary, and no other playing cards. See? Scotland Yard is not entirely useless."

Holmes blinked twice, and I believe he was holding back a laugh.

"Why, Lestrade! Would I suggest such a thing?"

The inspector pulled another face. "Well, anyway, much though it pains me, Mr. Holmes, I would beg that you give this case your full and urgent attention."

"I assure you that I am doing so, inspector."

"And your conclusions thus far?"

"Minor points, naturally, but of limited value. I expect the knots in both cases to be similar, and the rope itself to be a common sort from any small ship or wharf-side. There will have been at least one man present, perhaps two, in addition to the female. One man at least will have a maritime background. As for the playing cards, they are easily obtained from McCluskey's Assortments in Piccadilly and many neighbouring gentlemen's clubs. The woman at Becskei's is most likely French; the 'Russian woman' is a mystery. They are not the same person, for the latter's boot imprints, slightly larger, were clear on the muddy pavement outside the shop."

"French?"

"The shoes were made to a pattern common in southern France. They are not currently fashionable here. There is some wear to the heel and scoring of the sole, so she is fond of them, or has had them long enough for them to be comfortable."

"Or can't afford to replace them?" I said.

"Possibly, Watson. However, she wears *Eau d'Lys-blanc*, a very expensive French *parfum*. The scent lingered at Becskei's. Those two facts are suggestive."

Lestrade's cheeks had a red flush. "Oh, come now! How can you possibly know of such small details as Frenchie shoe styles and perfumes, Mr. Holmes?"

"It so happens, inspector, that I spent time in and around Marseille, after Reichenbach. One never knows when the 'small details' might be of use."

The inspector humphed but could find no quick response.

"This woman is the killer, then?" he asked.

"It may be so, but I have no idea who she is, or why she commits her crimes. We know she is seeking something tangible. Once again, we are back with the cards—the suit is still incomplete."

"Marvellous." The inspector jammed his damp hat back on his head and stood. "I must search the whole of London—or even farther afield—for a Frenchwoman with money, without any knowledge of her name, residence, motives, confederates, or anything really. And she searches for something which none of us can determine."

"A suitable job for a consulting detective, I would suggest." Holmes lit his pipe. "Do have patience, Lestrade, my dear fellow. I have set wheels turning."

"So you say, Mr. Holmes, so you say."

Although flustered, he did leave us the cards from Maisie Evans's rooms, with the address of those rooms and where Sir Richard's body was being held.

After Lestrade had gone, I looked at my friend. "Should I go to the morgue, and . . . ?"

"Please do, Watson. In particular, you might confirm that the wounds could be made by a reasonably healthy woman—let us suppose—and make sure that there are no more subtle aspects which the typical police doctor might miss."

I hesitated. "'Richard,' 'dead,' and 'Thoth'? What do you suppose that last word means, Holmes?"

"A mishearing is not inconceivable. But otherwise . . . Thoth, the Egyptian ibis-headed god of mathematics, intellectual knowledge, and learning in general. You see the correspondence with the card I received, Watson?" He picked up and opened a pamphlet by his side. "After Becskei, I had one of my acquaintances obtain a few relevant publications from the more peculiar societies that abound these days—in case they might suggest lines of enquiry. Much is nonsense; many articles are deliberately obscure in their attempt to pretend at wisdom. But listen to this, Watson:

"'Hermes Mercurius Trismegistus, a conflation of the Egyptian Thoth with the Grecian Hermes . . . is symbolical of the function of understanding. He has four implements: the rod, the wings, the sword, and the cap, denoting the science of the Magian, the courage of the adventurer, the will of the hero, and the discretion of the adept . . . it is curious to notice the rapport which seems to exist between the four suits of the Tarot cards, sometimes called 'The Book of Thoth,' and the symbolical attributions referred to.' There seems little doubt that this is relevant to our problem."

I duly returned to the police morgue and examined the corpse of Sir Richard on Holmes's behalf. Cleves's naked body, on the morgue slab, was a testament to claret, heavy puddings, and little exercise. I had the unkind thought, looking at his swollen face, that his money must have been a factor in any young woman's interest in him. Or perhaps he had been a kind and witty man?

Whatever his nature was once, it had fled the flesh. The gashes across his wrists and inner forearms were more than would have been required to make him bleed to death and, as with Becskei's throat, there was that sense of savagery. Yes, a woman could have done this, though not any I believed I had ever met.

The other injuries did seem—as Holmes suggested—to be ones which would be painful but not life threatening, acts which might be done to encourage disclosure or cooperation. There was nothing else of note, and I felt little wiser.

More satisfying, though, was my encounter as I left the morgue. For across the street was a figure I recognised—not from a previous meeting, but from the young constable's description outside Becskei's place.

Looking directly at me stood a woman of around the right years, slightly taller than average, with somewhat wild black hair and clear grey eyes, a fur overcoat in the East European fashion obscuring her frame. I made to cross, but a packed omnibus intervened, and when it was gone, so was she.

I had seen the Russian woman, of that I was sure.

A glance down adjoining streets, packed with many pedestrians, proved futile, so I went on to my second destination, a request from Holmes as I had taken up my hat and coat.

Maisie Evans was not a goose, by her neighbours' brief accounts, but she was in shock. I visited her to discover if she was well enough to be questioned, and found her disturbed, driven almost mute by discovering her lover's body so cruelly dealt with in her own—or their—bedroom. She was swaddled on a settee, sleeping fitfully. Cleves's wife had, to my astonishment, hired a nurse to attend to her.

"Lady Mary is one of them Rum Christians," said the nurse. "Thinks evil of no one, and busies herself with missions, but cares little for convention." The old woman came close, imparting what she clearly saw as a confidence. "I can tell you, doctor, even though she was saddened at Sir Richard's death, her next thought was for this girl here, and for his office staff and their futures."

When I mentioned that I was working on behalf of Mr. Sherlock Holmes, the nurse was as forthcoming as anyone could wish.

"*The* Dr. Watson. Well, I never," she said as she boiled the kettle for tea. And whilst she shared much tattle which was of no use, she was informative on Cleves himself, having been nurse to his son some years ago.

"Oh, he collected such things as you wouldn't never want in the house, Sir Richard did. Hindoo and Mussulman books, and all manner of nonsense. That 'Gyptian stuff, too. A nice man, he was— you wouldn't have thought it of him. But that's learning for you, though I shouldn't say it, you being a medical man . . . "

Of alchemists, Rosicrucians, and the like, sadly, the old nurse knew as little as I. She did, however, show me the dressing room next to the main bedroom, and there stood a large oak bookcase of oddities—religious books and Egyptian statuettes, that sort of thing. Very much the sort of works which would suit the back of Josef Becskei's shop.

On the nurse's return, I thanked her and said that I or Mr. Holmes might call in a day or so.

I had much to recount at Baker Street and took a hansom back immediately, only to have my excitement at my encounters somewhat spiked, for Holmes was waiting for me with other news.

"We have an evening engagement, Watson," he said, holding up a piece of thick, cream paper.

"You have, you mean, Holmes. But you would like me to accompany you."

"Not at all, old chap. You are specifically named herein."

And he handed me the folded paper:

Madame Rostov requests the presence of Mr. Sherlock Holmes and Dr. John Watson.

8pm, the 27th inst. We must meet, before the blades are complete.

The address was across the river, in Southwark.

"A bit imperious," I muttered. "That is tonight. Who is the woman, and what does she mean by blades?"

Holmes raised an eyebrow at my tetchy tone. "The writing is by an older—perhaps elderly—woman, left-handed, who originally wrote in the Cyrillic script but has since learned the Latin equivalent. Russian, most likely, from the painful formation of the letters, and—" "I have seen the Russian woman, and she is not elderly," I interrupted, describing my chance encounter.

"Nor is Madame Rostov. I recall that the woman was briefly *en vogue* in 'polite' society as a spiritualist, not half a dozen years ago."

"And 'blades'?"

"That reference will prove to be either worrisome or most useful." He took up one of the playing cards from the table next to him—the king of spades. "The *spada*. The Italian name for a sword or blade, and hence the suit is called, in English, spades. The etymology is quite simple and has been on my mind."

I sat down. "That Tarot card you were sent—a Sword. The cards left on the bodies, and thus the murders—all spades. They are connected."

"So it would seem, Watson. That single card is surely linked to what has occurred since I received it, and what may be to come."

"You may be in danger."

"A possibility in a number of the cases I undertake. Come now, we have faced many a risky situation together over the years, have we not?"

We had, though in truth those dangers had been mostly directed at Holmes. But it flattered me to be included, and I went on to describe what I had observed at the police morgue and at Cleves's rooms. That Holmes was taking this matter very seriously was evident by his lack of any criticism, even trifling, of my actions or my observations.

It was clear that he had been struck by a sudden thought. "I did say 'what may be to come,' Watson, but can we be sure that nothing occurred before Becskei's death? I have been assuming that we enter at the start of the play, as it were. I must send a telegram to Lestrade. What else might have been missed, eh?"

I was unsure as to his meaning.

"So she, our proposed criminal, has obtained at least part of that which she seeks, taken from amongst Sir Richard's possessions. But why then should he be tortured and killed, if the item was in plain sight on his shelves and easily retrieved? And a Russian—or Russians—have a stake in this, somehow. I fail to understand what this mysticism and occultism is really all about, though, and how it relates to the killings."

Holmes was scribbling notes for the telegram office.

"The field, if I can call it that, is really too wide to comprehend, Watson. You might read a dozen books on that subject and form a dozen views. Spiritual reformers, alchemists, an esoteric brotherhood . . . one of those movements which blend Eastern wisdom, Biblical and Koranic texts, the Talmud and more, to present some tradition of hidden mysteries. Benign, in general, but a fine furrow for lunatics to plough as well. It seems clear that Becskei and Cleves were involved in studying, if not practising, something of the sort."

My heart sank.

"Brotherhoods, conspiracies, and madmen, then."

"Or madwomen," said Holmes. "Perhaps we will find out tomorrow."

The Southwark residence named was a modest end-of-terrace house with badly pruned roses around the door, so unprepossessing that I had to check with the cabman to see if we could be mistaken. But there was no similarly named street nearby with which it could be confused.

"Hardly a St. Petersburg palace," I remarked as I knocked on the door.

Within a few moments, we heard the rattle of a door-chain, and were greeted by a short, round-faced old woman in widow's mourning clothes. I took off my hat, confused.

"I'm sorry—we were seeking Madame Rostov, and—"

"*Da*, is here." Her small, deep brown eyes appraised us as if we were ducks hung outside a stall. "You come in." And she stepped back.

In the hall I smelled freshly baked bread, coffee, and—I believed—sauerkraut. The interior of the house was in far better condition than the exterior, the walls adorned with a clutter of religious icons, embroideries, and shelves of copper artefacts, from ornamental kettles to small bracelet charms.

"I collect," she said, noticing my interest. "I am Mrs. Bessovitch. Is my house."

There seemed no doubt that she was East European, though only Holmes would be able to place her in any particular country or region.

"A recent bereavement?"

"My husband. Many years ago."

"I am sorry."

"So is he."

This peculiar exchange saw us through to a large front room, whose sole occupant was instantly recognisable.

"Madame Rostov," said Holmes, bowing his head an inch or two.

She really was a quite striking woman. Her clear grey eyes might have been cut from some semi-precious stone, and her hair was surely true black, not dark brown or any result of dyes or preparations. The silk dress she wore was of a purple hue, and simple, almost stark, in cut.

"I did not want to invite you, gentlemen. I did not want you to come. But we are sometimes players in greater games. Please, be seated."

Before we could speak, Mrs. Bessovitch returned with a tray on which were four wine glasses and a stoneware bottle.

"*Medovukha*," she said, and filled all four glasses with an amber liquid. "From a sailor friend who owes me."

Madame Rostov smiled, which quite altered the hardness of

her face. "Everyone around here owes Mrs. Bessovitch something. She has been my landlady, and my mother-hen, since I came to London."

I took a sip from my glass and gave a cough. It was some sort of wine, but the taste—sweet, with a sour tone.

"A Slavic variant of mead," said Holmes, seeming appreciative. "Unusual to find here."

"*Da*. I have pastries, if you stay long."

And there the two of us sat, the old woman remaining on her feet by the door, the younger one standing in front of an unlit fire.

"I will add," said Madame Rostov, "that Mrs. Bessovitch is far sharper and more resourceful than most people you will ever meet. Anything you might say to me, you can say to her."

It was Holmes's turn to smile. "I suspected as much. But one deception should be stripped away, I think, before we continue. Do you return home to West Yorkshire often, Madame? You return a certain Bradford flatness beneath your assumed accent."

The landlady chuckled. The younger woman remained straight faced.

"Keighley, and my true name, sir, is Catherine Weatherhead— though I do not wish it repeated outside these walls. For the famous Sherlock Holmes, I make allowances. Madame Rostov suits me for most roles, and it is Madame Rostov who needs to speak to you so urgently."

"You are a medium, a spiritualist."

"Not as you would understand it. I could no longer be so definite, even to myself. The Madame has been engaged as such, but this is not the time for a performance."

"I am pleased to hear it. What *is* this the time for, though?"

"You are known for your logic, your pragmatism, and for your poor opinion of the ab-natural—or supernatural. I have information you require, but how I obtained it will not suit you, so we must leave that element for another evening. Do you agree?"

Holmes sipped his *medovukha and* rolled it around his tongue. "If I do not?"

"Then you have my leave to return to your Baker Street."

I could almost believe that this woman was truly a scion of some Russian imperial line, used to command from birth.

"Pray, proceed," said my friend.

"Very well. There is a woman in the city who kills. She takes pleasure in doing so, though that is not her ultimate purpose. I do not know her name, but I have seen her bring death—"

Holmes held up one hand.

"You have *seen*? What does that mean, Madame? You were there?"

That earned him a scornful look. "I am hardly such a fool as to call you here, Mr. Holmes, and admit that I had stood by whilst murder and theft were done. I had heard that you were a detective of note, but . . . "

I thought Holmes was about to rise and walk away, but he remained where he was, face expressionless, eyes almost closed.

"Carry on, Madame."

"A man was recently murdered in what I imagine is a bookshop of some sort, or a library." She described Becskei and his immediate surroundings quite distinctly. "More recently, my night was disturbed by images of an older man, overweight, in private quarters. Both were killed with a type of long, curved blade I do not recognise."

"What was left with the bookseller; what with the latest victim?"

"The king, seven and eight; the jack, two, three, four, and five, all spades," she replied without hesitation.

"And what was taken? What message was meant by the playing cards?"

"There is no message. Each replaced a Tarot card of corresponding value, from the suit of Swords—cards which were in the victims' possession. What that in turn means, or why they were wanted, I have no idea, as yet. Oh, and Mr. Holmes, she knows of you. She has stood on Baker Street within this last week and stared at your door. Pondered, planned."

"Has she, by God!" I exclaimed. "Holmes—"

"It is not there," he said quietly. "I have taken photographs and sent the original elsewhere."

"It?" Madame Rostov sighed. "You hold one of the Tarot cards?"

"The Ace of Swords."

She turned, ran her hand along the mantelpiece, and turned again.

"This woman will find it. She will feel it."

I put my glass down with a rather too forceful clink. "Dash it, will someone tell me what we're talking about? Spades and swords, playing cards, this Tarot nonsense . . . "

Holmes put his hand lightly on my arm. "If—if I give credence to what Madame Rostov has imparted, then the woman in question is seeking certain cards from a Tarot pack. A very particular Tarot pack, presumably. Becskei had three of them, Cleves five, and I was sent the ace. There are fourteen cards in a Tarot suit, not thirteen as in the common packs. Either she has the remainder already, or they are held by another who has an interest in arcane matters."

"Extraordinary."

"The replacement of one for one is easily explained," said the woman. "Following the alchemical law of equivalence—or some madness peculiar to her—she gives a blade for a blade."

"But—"

"I am neither a scholar nor a collector. I sense things, Dr. Watson, and believe me, I would often rather not do so. I am not clairvoyant, nor do I have conversations with dead great-aunts about where the family silver went. As Madame Rostov, the spiritualist, I had some success utilising my sensitivity." A faint blush touched her pale cheeks. "And by employing certain other means."

"Planchettes? Palm reading?" I said, and possibly my tone was somewhat disrespectful.

Her eyes were hard as she came closer and crouched before me.

"Dr. John Watson. Let Madame Rostov see . . . "

She gripped my hands, her unadorned nails sharp and the rings on her fingers digging into my flesh.

"Yes, yes . . . he worries about what lies beyond the Veil, the dead of his past. He scans the papers for news of former comrades, and here . . . a letter—a man has fallen in a place called Kumasi, a captain turned colonel, brought down by sickness. Another soul who has fled this world. Do they wait for him? He crumples the letter, throws it from him, and his lameness from old seems heavy on him . . . "

Madame Rostov stood up, breathing heavily; I sat there, stunned.

"You cannot . . . " I stuttered. "I mean, how?"

She looked at Holmes, who seemed fascinated.

"Our daily lives betray us," she said.

He narrowed his eyes, then laughed. "Oh, well done, Madame." He turned to me. "Take heart, Watson. Madame Rostov does not mean to toy with your feelings."

"But how did she know that? I did receive a letter, three days ago. Laird Rogers was taken by swamp fever, on policing duties in Ashantee territory last month. We were hardly close, but I did discard the letter, and pace, thinking on old days."

"She spoke to your daily woman as, I imagine, Miss Catherine Weatherhead."

Madame Rostov nodded. "Miss Weatherhead was in the area of Dr. Watson's surgery, and was open to that constant chatter which underlies most households. Servants observe far more than their masters and mistresses realise. And the letter was in your waste bin, from where your help retrieved and read it."

"Keen observation, a knowledge of human nature, logic . . . " Holmes bowed in his seat. "I am almost tempted to listen to you further, Madame."

"I am not of concern here. This woman, whoever she is, has Swords she yet requires. And what happens next, I do not know. Could I be sure that she did not have further plans—and was I to be silent if Sherlock Holmes was one of the victims along the way? Believe me, gentlemen, I ended up placing the matter before a higher power."

"You prayed?" I asked.

Madame Rostov looked at me with reproach. "Really, doctor? No, I asked Mrs. Bessovitch what I should do."

More *medovukha* flowed, and the younger woman fixed my friend with a hard stare. "Then you believe me, Mr. Holmes?"

"I do not know," he said. "But I will be honest with you. I remain here because it so happens that I knew Eden Mallick." He glanced at me. "A police inspector, Watson, retired now. Not a man given to fancies. I sent him a telegram as to your standing and trustworthiness, given that he was a Southwark man, and had a reply before we came here. In essence, he wrote: 'She is a handful. But yes, trust her with your life.'"

"It was an honour to work with him. I miss his company, truth be told."

"If Mallick has such trust in you, Madame, it is hard for me to have less, despite my deep reservations as to anything related to spiritualism. Is there more you wish to tell us?"

"I will tell you what I know—what I have seen."

And so it was that we heard in detail of Josef Becskei's murder, and of Sir Richard Cleves's—in such detail that astounded me, and obviously troubled Holmes. We received a precise description of the Frenchwoman; Madame Rostov did not seek to adorn her tale, nor could she offer anything outside such specific events.

"If I could have seen any other way, gentlemen, we would never have met, never have spoken. Mrs. Bessovitch wrote the note to you on my behalf, precisely because I could not bring myself to do it. I have seen murder before, Mr. Holmes, and it has never left me. Do you think that brings me any pleasure, any satisfaction?"

"I believe it does not," said Holmes, looking grave. "A fact which gives additional weight to your testimony. You mentioned previous 'visions,' well before this year—those were similar?"

"I do not wish to speak of them. Suffice it to say there was a man—perhaps a monster—once, who came to my mind against my wishes. That is long past."

"Very well. I will not press you, Madame."

We parted that evening with guarded assurances of cooperation, and as Holmes and I took a stroll in the cooler air, I felt as if a most unusual event had taken place.

"I am confused, Holmes. Do we accept her words?"

He twirled his cane in the air as he walked.

"I understand that Madame Rostov has worked with the police before, in the late eighties, being of apparent value to the Southwark division. She even helped find the man who shot and wounded Mallick in '88. She is said to be a capable woman.

"This business jogged my memory—I *had* heard the name Rostov elsewhere, in passing, and although I should not have done, I enquired of Superintendent Swanson at Scotland Yard. His response was terse, but intimated she was not a fraud. Beyond that, he would not speak of her."

I could not understand why he 'should not have done,' as Holmes had rarely shown any great sensitivity about disturbing authority. I let it pass.

"Maybe she was some agent of theirs at the time? But as to her spiritualist talents, how else could she have come about the degree of detail she provides?"

"I can conceive mundane possibilities. For example, there might be a turncoat in the Frenchwoman's entourage, or perhaps another person, as yet unknown, working against that woman's interests—one who passes what they know on to Madame Rostov. If so, she could well consider it safer not to name them. Whatever the situation, it is difficult to ignore such a source in this muddy case."

"So you do not, at heart, believe she has visions."

The cane stilled. "My prejudices are—for now—irrelevant. And I am more impressed by her reticence than by the usual recitations of past successes and encounters. Whether that is female modesty or intelligence—well, I suspect it more likely reflects the latter."

"A striking woman, anyway. What did you think of the imposture, over her name and so forth?"

"Theatrical, I imagine, and inspired—even tutored—by her Mrs. Bessovitch."

I had no rejoinder to that.

Part Two

Above; below. Pale, warped timbers, forming some mockery of a vaulted ceiling; an altar table spread with light. Candles burn around a bowl which contains many colours—oil, perhaps, its surface sheened by the candlelight?

It is the same woman, bearing a curved, almost twisted blade, yes, the same sword. Hoods and robes obscure figures in shadow, figures who murmur, chant . . .

Off Kensington High Street, in a well-furnished dining room, Catherine shudders. She grips a glass filled with blood-crimson, a heady wine, holding it too tight; the others in the room look concerned.

"Are you . . . unwell, Madame?" asks a mere girl, no more than fourteen. The girl wears her best dress, a modest but pretty affair in soft, pleated linen. "Should we postpone the sitting—"

She gestures, no, wait, but cannot speak. Gaslights hiss, indifferent; an older man takes the glass gently from her hands before it shatters, and people around her talk of spirits upon the Aether, as if this is a wondrous thing.

"Has Father come to talk with us?" asks a homely face by the harmonium . . .

The blade is being anointed from the bowl and given its own fire.
"As with the Swords of Kerubim, so this is our Weapon of Light."
Renewal of its consecration. That is the word. Dedication to a purpose. But that purpose is not what the congregation believes.
The woman who bears it knows better.

For two days, Holmes buried himself, almost literally, in reference books and obscure manuscripts; in monographs and in membership lists compiled from various associates or sources provided by his brother Mycroft. He sent letters and telegrams, scanning the responses with varying degrees of annoyance. I, on the other hand, after transcribing everything said by Madame Rostov, was set to scour Holmes's old correspondences.

"There was an incident in Paris last year, Watson. Fraud, involving a Frenchwoman. The letter would be from . . . let me see, *le comte* duVilliers, in the 16th arrondissement. I believe it arrived in November."

My friend's filing system was erratic, keyed to his own mode of thinking, but I did, at last, locate the letter he required.

"November 24th," I said, handing it to him. "Your French is better than mine."

"Yes, this is it. The ageing *le comte* duVilliers had been gulled that summer, persuaded to lend a large sum to one Eliane Gueret, a widow from the Avignon area who had fallen on hard times. She charmed him, entertained him, and then . . . "

I chuckled. "She ran off with his francs, of course."

"Indeed. Not an uncommon occurrence. Some said her destination was America, others England. I recall that we had just concluded the affair with the German agent, Oberstein, and there were political ramifications of that case, as you know. I sent a note to *le comte*, regretting I was not free to assist him. But take a look at this."

He handed me a photograph which depicted several evidently wealthy people at a dance. *Le comte*, moustachioed and rather rigid, was easily identified. The woman on his arm appeared to be trying to turn her head from the camera, but enough of her face was visible.

"She looks . . . yes, I see it. She is very similar to Madame Rostov's description of the woman we seek."

"She is. I wonder—coincidence or happy circumstance? It warrants at least a brief communication with Paris. Our old friend *Inspecteur* Lebrun will no doubt oblige us with more background on the woman."

"Madame Rostov could confirm they are the same person."

"Possibly—but not the many details which authorities choose not to release to the newspapers. Let us first see what Lebrun has to offer."

I saw that he still had reservations about our visit to Southwark, and that in one matter he had misled the psychic, or whatever I should describe her as. He had retained the Ace of Swords at Baker Street, for I saw him staring at it a number of times. When I asked him why the deception, he admitted that his initial doubts had spurred him to it.

"If Madame Rostov were working for another, even benign, element in this game, I wanted to hold something 'in hand.'"

By this time, I had begun to find myself arguing in favour of our Southwark friend. Not only was her information precise, but she had surprised me with some of her comments. Before we had left her, she made it clear that she thought the whole field of spiritualism and mysticism was littered with fanciful, invented schools of thought, and outright deception.

It was fortunate that I had warmed to her, for it soon seemed that we would be in close company. Holmes arrived back at Baker Street one morning, looking pleased with himself.

"I have been to see Maisie Evans, who is much recovered. She did not say 'Richard,' 'dead,' Watson," he announced, throwing his cane across the room. "She was misunderstood."

"Then . . . ?"

"She said 'Richard Dadd.' The late artist—you remember that we have crossed paths with his work before?"

I did indeed. And although I preferred not to dwell on those disturbing cases, I remembered the nature of Dadd's life well enough—the tragedy of a talented painter who became mentally disturbed whilst in Egypt when young. After returning to England, he killed his own father, sought to travel to France, and in the process, wounded a fellow passenger. Thus, he was confined for the rest of his life—Bethlem first, then Broadmoor, where he died in '86 after many years within its walls. But his painting never stopped; was indulged, in fact, by his physicians. Therapeutic, they hoped. And as is the way with art, his work was never more in demand than after his death.

"Miss Evans," continued Holmes, "now remembers that Cleves once told her, when in drink—he was searching for more work by Dadd. 'The painted blades,' he said to her, a few days before his death. 'Soper's gone, poor devil; the Hungarian has certain of the others but will demand a stiff price.' His very words, she affirms."

"And remember, Watson, the Ace of Swords was sent to me from Wokingham, not far from Crowthorne and Broadmoor Criminal Lunatic Asylum. We have another lead, it seems. If this is one of Dadd's strange creations, who knows what secrets it holds, even if imagined ones?" He looked gloomy for a moment. "I should have recognised Dadd's work far earlier."

"Can't say I did, Holmes, and I too have seen paintings of his before. But who is this Soper?"

"Excellent question. That is something I am seeking to establish, and why I wish you to visit Broadmoor Asylum whilst I work. You have an associate there, do you not?"

"Gerald Laws, the neurologist."

"This American bullion case occupies much of my time at the moment, and the Government is somewhat insistent. Ask if Madame Rostov will accompany you. Offer her expenses, if that is an issue."

I did not waste time questioning his choice. Holmes always had good reason for any charge placed upon me.

"What am I to look for? Any trace of Dadd creating a Tarot set, and so forth, how it was disposed of when he died—and any odd dealings with outsiders which might have occurred?"

"You have it, old chap. Find me a scent to follow."

"Ten years have passed," I pointed out.

"A man like Dadd is hardly likely to have been forgotten, and some staff of his time must remain."

I wrote to Madame Rostov in the same hour, asking if she would accompany me to Broadmoor, for the purpose of unravelling more of this mystery; she, in turn, wrote back that afternoon, agreeing. We were to meet the following noon at the local railway station, curiously named Wellington College for Crowthorne, after a nearby public school (as my gazetteer informed me).

The day was bright, with Madame Rostov waiting as promised, in a grey dress and a simple wide-brimmed hat. As there were traps waiting for visitors to the asylum, we were soon before the great studded gates of the establishment, and Laws was waiting to escort us. A short, pleasant man, he was far more intellectual than I, and more a keen student of the human nervous system than of humanity. His role at Broadmoor was as a visiting doctor who established if organic damage was a component of an inmate's condition.

"You know we are interested in Richard Dadd's time here," I said, after introducing my companion as an art aficionado. I doubt that Laws really noticed that she was female.

"Only just before I took up the position," said Laws, sweeping us past the stations from which wardens observed the comings and goings of the day. Over three hundred inmates, at least one hundred and fifty attendants, I understood.

There was an incongruous air about Broadmoor—its red brick bulk were tastefully done, atop a ridge outside the village, and the terraces at the read flowed down into the tranquil countryside; inmates potter and garden, amused themselves at cards and with musical instruments.

But in some of the blocks to either side, the more deeply disturbed sat and rocked, cried out coarse imprecations, or muttered to the voices they imagined they heard. And here and there were the convicts, marked out by uniform, who had committed dreadful crimes and later lost their minds, transferred here from some of the worst prisons. I looked to Madame Rostov, who seemed unaffected.

"I have seen madness, doctor," she said, under Laws's recitation of the layout as he strode ahead of us. "I doubt there is much here that could disturb me."

"There," announced my medical associate as we emerged onto the terraces. He pointed to a white-haired attendant on a bench, smoking an old-fashioned clay pipe. "Joshua Carlin probably knew as much about Dadd as the doctors. He was in charge of ensuring the artist received his materials."

The attendant's rheumy eyes observed our approach, and he lowered his pipe.

"Carlin," said Laws, "I wonder if you would speak to my friends of your old friend Dadd? May I present Dr. John Watson and Madame Rostov."

Carlin rose. Laws said he would see us later in the smaller waiting room for professional visitors.

"Rare to be asked to address a lady," said the attendant, "except those who are bound here as sheep or shepherdesses."

By which he presumably meant the female wing. "We do not wish much of your time, Mr. Carlin—our enquiry is rather specific, and may seem odd."

"Odd, in Broadmoor?" He laughed. "No such thing, sir. And I am Joshua to them with honest intent."

"You have been here long?" asked my companion.

"Thirty years, ma'am. Thirty years and a week. I seen 'em brought in, and I seen 'em put gentle under the sod, God grant us all such mercy. But what might I be helping you with?"

"You were—are—familiar with Mr. Richard Dadd's work whilst he was here?"

"I am, though I have days of forgetting, being older now, troubled with my joints and so forth."

"It comes to us all," I said. "Can we see where he worked?"

"Block Two, sir, where the trustier folk are let employ themselves."

Laws had made a good choice, for Carlin was well -known by all and acted as a passkey in his own right. We faced no hindrance in being taken into the block where Dadd had been, and even to the rooms, currently empty, which had served one as his bedroom, the other as his studio.

"I'm no painter," said Carlin, "and a whitewash brush is as much as I choose, but Mr. Dadd was a gentleman, a quiet one, who set himself to many a fine piece in his time. The superintendent had me provide his needs: oil paints and watercolours, canvasses, and suchlike; they all went through me. He had requirements, see—a type of paper as would take the paint right, brushes as small as one of 'is own elves might wish."

"Yet he cut his own father's throat and attacked another man." Madame Rostov stood apart from us, staring at the walls.

"Part of him did, ma'am, only the deluded part of him, and that was quiet for the most part." The old man clucked his tongue. "He was right gifted, poor Mr. Dadd."

He showed us some of the man's paintings, still hung here and there in the asylum. They were fine works, with astonishing detail— many far smaller than I had expected, and a marvel in their intricacy.

"These small ones—do you know if he ever worked on any sort of cards or gaming pieces? Playing cards, for example."

Carlin stiffened and rubbed his thin fingers together as if nervous.

"Why would you ask that, sir?"

"Because Osiris may have appeared again in such works," said Madame Rostov. "And we fear these cards carry the taint of madness. At least two men have died because of them."

I described the Tarot card I had seen, the Ace of Swords. The old fellow leaned back against a wall, silent; an inmate passed down the corridor, lost in some fantasy, humming to himself.

"Mr. Carlin, if you have any—"

I saw a slight gesture from my companion that I should be quiet for a moment.

"The Aether is disturbed," she said. "Joshua Carlin, I see that Richard Dadd was kind to you in return for your care with him, but his work is being misused. Good souls must be strong now, and open. The false child must not prevail."

"The false child." Carlin started. "That was how he put it, more than once."

"Then . . . ?"

"Albert Smith found them. I remembered bringing Mr. Dadd some sheets of stiff card, not cheap, but knowing naught of what he did with the stuff—that would be in his last year, poor soul. Anyway, Albert had been in a storeroom, rooting around as always—he turned a coin or two from what was no longer needed, selling it in Wokingham. Most knew, none cared much. This was after Dadd had passed on, of course, maybe eight or nine years after. Yes, '95 it was. Last year."

Albert Smith! Common enough, of course, but that was the name on the envelope received by Holmes. This was surely the sender.

"Another attendant?"

"Yes, ma'am. And he said as how he'd found some cards, with painted swords and suchlike which he thought were my man's work. Albert showed me one, and I said as it were surely Mr. Dadd's, but they seemed to have been thrown away, for they were in a box of emptied paint tubes, torn sketches, and the like. I reckoned as they were some of the last pieces the old gentleman worked upon, and I said they belonged to the family. Albert, he agreed that were like to be the case."

"What happened?"

He shrugged. "I can't as rightly say. Albert was a touch sly—not wicked, mind, but always seeking opportunity. Only he would know. And he has gone, left his post this fortnight past, without a word."

I could no longer restrain myself.

"Will the superintendent have an address for this Albert Smith, Mr. Carlin?"

"I have it," he said, and looked straight at Madame Rostov. "You spoke of the false child."

"Yes. The one inside Richard Dadd, the one who slew his father, who listened to what he thought was Osiris. You understand, Joshua, and so do I."

"I didn't care for that other woman who asked me such questions . . . "

"A Frenchwoman, I presume." Madame Rostov appeared entirely in control.

He looked surprised. "That's her. Called herself Miss Dorcas, and said she was with the board, but I doubted that. The superintendent did not know her, he admitted to me later."

"She is our enemy and will do no good with your late charge's works. Her intent springs from madness, not healing."

He released a long breath. "Let me fetch my pocketbook from my lock box, ma'am, and I shall give you all I know of Albert."

When we said farewell to Carlin and returned to Dr. Laws, who was leafing through patients' charts in the waiting room, we had as much as I felt we could—an address for Albert Smith, and descriptions of both Smith and the mysterious Dorcas woman. The latter was described much as my companion had previously described.

There followed only a light tea with Laws on the upper terrace, served by inmates. As I was sure that neither I nor my companion could have held a conversation on art for long, we were relieved to discuss lighter matters, interspersed sporadically with Laws's views on neuropathology, addressed to me.

Back in Crowthorne village, Madame Rostov was pensive.

"We should find Smith."

"I would usually report to Holmes at this point."

"And I would usually be considering what to have for dinner. Are either relevant, considering that we are a few minutes from

Wokingham, and have an opportunity to find out what has happened to Albert Smith?"

Our compromise was that we took the next train up the line to Wokingham, and at the post office there I telegrammed Holmes with the basic details.

"What was that about a 'false child'?" I asked after I had consulted a cabman on the addresses. We were in only a small market town, and Smith's house was within easy walking distance of the railway station.

"It was in the paintings, doctor. Did you not see? Dadd's children have faces which are masks, almost adult masks. There is something false there."

I slowed my stride, thinking. "Observation, eh? Madame Rostov is a formidable lady. Is her other persona so commanding?" I meant to tease, but her expression did not soften.

"Few people know Catherine Weatherhead, doctor. Such knowledge must be earned. Madame Rostov is my name, my face, for most of the world."

Chided, I begged her pardon—though whether the faint smile I received in return came from Yorkshire or from Russia, I did not know.

The small house on Denmark Street was empty—and by this, I mean that it had been emptied, not only of occupants but of furniture too, as was obvious by a glance through the window. My peering attracted the woman from the house next to it.

"Morpeth & Son are to handle the letting," she said, pushing strands of hair back under a mob cap. "Smithy upped and went days ago, but he had the place cleared out."

"Smithy?" I dared to enquire.

"Mr. Albert Smith, the owner, sir."

"Did he move to . . . " What was I to say? "Better surroundings" would seem rude. "Nearby?"

"None know, sir, not even the agents, who await his word."

That seemed to be that. I knew that there was a train within the half hour, and felt I had done sufficient gallivanting for one day.

"Did you find your work as a psychic satisfying?" I said as we walked, for I confess that her ability to adapt to each situation we met had impressed me. "When you were most active in such circles, I mean."

"I needed money, and I needed to gain recognition in a field of lies and shadows. I did what was necessary."

"But you do have some sort of gift. That must be most advantageous."

"Advantageous? For a chronicler, doctor, you do not always seem to listen. I see death, murder, and I have no choice in the matter. Shall I hand you this gift? Do you believe you would relish such an ability?"

We stood on the platform and stared at each other.

"I was a soldier." I took off my hat and turned it in my hands, remembering the feel of an army cap. "Officially a medical man, but the heat of war allows for little distinction. I did what was necessary, and no, you are right—these things do not fall upon our shoulders for the sake of amusement. Those who take any pleasure in murder are Broadmoor's meat and drink."

"And your Mr. Holmes?"

It took me a moment to realise what she meant.

"Holmes?" I replied. "He is a creature of the mind. His understanding of pain, of violence, is more . . . cerebral, less visceral. And he has a habit of seeing people as puzzles to be solved. But injustice stirs him."

"I do not care for puzzles."

A curious woman, Madame Rostov.

Lestrade was present when we arrived at Baker Street, as was his narrow scowl.

"This is Madame Rostov, a . . . an associate of ours. Madam Rostov, Inspector Lestrade," I said, not sure what else I should disclose.

"Madame." The inspector rose, but his interest in her seemed minimal. Holmes had that keen expression when a chase was afoot.

"Three men have died, Watson. My suspicion was correct. There *was* a relevant incident before Becskei."

Lestrade's face soured even more. "Gregory Soper, described as a wealthy, eccentric artist from Chelsea. The constables found his body in his home, in late February, and assumed an interrupted robbery. The idle devils ignored the presence of playing cards next to the corpse, assuming they were part of the general disorder.

Rooms ransacked, no idea if anything was taken. The local sergeant recalled the cards, and yes, when I pushed him, they were spades."

"What state was the body in?" I asked.

"Beaten and bled to death from—" He stopped. "I beg your pardon, Madame Rostov. I will supply the details to Mr. Holmes. You won't wish to hear them, Madame."

Holmes flashed her a glance not to rise to that remark; she duly faked a grateful smile at Lestrade.

The inspector had not seated himself again, but stepped nearer the door. "On that other matter you raised, Mr. Holmes, you were also correct. There *were* a number of odd burglaries, more intrusions, I'd call 'em, in London area at the start of this year. Antiquarians, collectors of fine art—and nothing taken, only stuff disturbed, disordered. We put it down to prank and dares. Some of these bright young gentlemen and their clubs—"

"Or might it have been that someone was searching, unsuccessfully, for a particular item or items?"

"Yes, that would also fit."

"I do. Thank you, Lestrade."

"I must report to the Yard. We shall speak again soon, no doubt. Gentlemen, Madame." And he swept out of our rooms.

"Not the worst of our police officers," said Holmes. "And we are at least used to him. Now, I can see you have much to tell me."

Mrs. Hudson provided coffee; I provided a summary of what we had gleaned, building on the bones of my telegram—and my travelling companion was unusually quiet.

"Very well," said Holmes. "You will be interested to know, then, that I received a further communication whilst you were conducting your enquiries."

"Another Tarot card?" I asked.

"No, but an arrival of great significance to this case." He held up two or three sheets of writing paper. "It is in the same hand as that on the envelope containing the Tarot card . . ."

And he read out what he held in his hands:

> *I meant no ill to anyone, yet I am feared of what may come. It is a woman who plagues me, one as she calls herself Miss Dorcas, but if this is her true name I do not know. I say woman, but by my measure, she is most unwomanly. I am sure it was at her bidding that*

Soper was done for, and I set it down here for others to know.

I will not take blame for this. All my crime was in picking up them cards of old Dadd's, which had surely been thrown away, and making sensible coin from them, as any man might. They were all neat wrapped, and I saw the old man's hand in them clear enough. As he was no more and could have no use for them, I had it to sell them. The first couple I shifted myself, without giving my name, to Soper, and thought of offering the rest entire, like, but then I spoke to a fence in Limehouse—I did not say as I was a spotless soul—and we agreed that to portion them out and tease would fill our pockets better.

So we told these wealthy coves Becskei and Cleves that I had one or two cards—all genuine, like—and would sell what I had, but that there were more to be found, which was in the manner of a truth. Both paid keenly, and I was set with a finder's fee on top. Every so often I would "find" another card for them: neither man knew what was said to the others, so each hoped for the full suit in time. I thought myself clever.

I did read that Soper had been killed, but thought little of that. Now my man in Limehouse has been beaten brutal, and is not to be found. The cards he held are gone. Dorcas must have a sniff of me from one of them, and has placed questions at the asylum.

She is a Godless Frenchie, and all I can find of her is that she seeks to play with them men as are obsessed with the Cabbala, the Rosy Cross, and something called the Golden Dawn. I heard Dadd speak of those first two, but put it down to him being disordered.

I will not be taken as a murderer, nor a man who lays knife or cudgel on another, and so have written this that my name is not reported as such. I am soon likely to find my way to the Netherlands or Belgium, and lie low, and maybe it will end, but this is my testament.

I have sent the last card, the Ace of Swords, to Mr. Sherlock Holmes the famous detective, for if I do not have it, I am no use to her. He will have this letter too, through a lady friend of mine, if she does not hear from me. He will see that I am an innocent and God-fearing man, who only went astray. I do blame the cards for that, for they were made from madness, and can bring nothing but evil.

"Signed Albert Smith, the sixteenth of June, in this year 1896." Holmes sighed. "If he had come to me earlier . . . Well—two cards with Soper, three with Becskei, five with Cleves, and now we can assume that she has three more from the fence Smith mentions. He, too, may have been killed. That leaves the Ace of Swords, whose whereabouts we know. The fourteen cards of the suit."

"Can they be genuinely evil, these Tarot cards?" I asked, thinking on Smith's testimony, and what had happened even since he composed his letter. Clearly, he had not known that Becskei and Cleves were also dead.

Holmes snorted.

"Consider those great jewels looted from temples and the palaces of maharajahs, Watson. How often does someone ascribe some romantic 'curse' to these things, yet the only inherent evil, it transpires, is what men will do to possess them? This case, I suggest, is no different." He looked at Madame Rostov. "Or would you disagree, Madame?"

She sat staring at her rings.

"In sittings, the game is to work not on what you yourself believe, but on what the sitters consider to be true. If they consider that dead sisters speak to them, that spirit guides bear messages of comfort, you must attune yourself to their beliefs—must develop a kind of sympathy for their views . . . "

"But if—"

"And thus," she interrupted him, "the more crucial issue is what this *Dorcas* believes. If she considers that the Tarot suit of Swords holds some important mystic secret, it colours her thinking, her actions. We do not have to share her view, any more than Mr. Holmes needs to consider me a genuine psychic—it is my information and my understanding of the situation that he requires."

Here, in our rooms, her feigned Russian accent was fainter than ever, her expression grave.

"You are holding something back, Madame," said Holmes. "You tap your fingers against the chair arm, and do not look directly at me."

"My sleep was disturbed some nights ago. Given the emotions that recent events have aroused, I dismissed it at the time as a nightmare, turbulent memories from other days. But now . . . you said, Dr. Watson, that the attendant at Broadmoor gave you a description of Albert Smith."

"Carlin? He did." I checked my notes. "Smith is of average height, forty-five years old, dark brown hair, brown eyes, with a florid face and greying sideburns."

I am no prude, but I will not repeat her next words, which would have suited an army barracks. Even Holmes raised his eyebrows.

"The description means something to you?"

"It means, in all likelihood, that Smith is already dead."

"Pray continue."

"I was half-asleep, Mr. Holmes, confused. I thought that I saw a man being dragged into a narrow alley-mouth, a knife at his throat—no other face was visible in the darkness. As I say, I pushed it from my mind. But that description—if it was a vision, and not a nightmare . . . "

Holmes paced to the window and stared out onto Baker Street. "Where?" he asked.

"Where in London or its vicinity might one find an alley-mouth? I might be able to remember more detail, given time."

"Something, Madame!" he said, the frustration evident in his voice. "Give me something with which to work, not dreams forged of indigestion and 'visions' from your Aether!"

"I did not say it *had* to be Smith." She looked no more pleased than my friend. "Only that it seems logical."

"Logical? Hah! French women and Russian women, mad artists, and esoteric mumblings. Bodies everywhere, and now more vague conjurations!"

Madame Rostov stood, taking up her hat and bag.

"I am done here," she announced, and out she stormed, adding another swear word or two as the door clattered behind her.

I lit a cigarette.

"Well done, Holmes."

"What?" he snapped.

"You have successfully driven away our most useful source of information in the case." Why I spoke thus, I could not be sure, but I felt rather angered. Perhaps the day had left me in more sympathy with our female associate than I had realised. "One who has proved—so far—entirely accurate and reliable. So, as I say, well done."

Bold speech earned me utter silence for the rest of the afternoon. He applied himself to various monographs, texts, and papers, all related to the terms which Smith had used; I retreated into an article on blood disorders.

Halfway through a decidedly muted dinner, Holmes looked up.

"You know, Watson, the psychological sciences are fascinating in their way, with new discoveries about the human mind each year. Diagnoses and treatments for conditions which our ancestors ascribed to demons, the moon, the vicissitudes of Fortuna . . . "

I left off exploring my breaded cutlet and waited.

"Purely organic reasons for insanity," he continued. "The development of hypnosis as a tool, the concept of telepathy . . . what genuine scientific phenomena might lie a little way down the road?"

Suspecting that I knew where this was going, I fell in with him.

"I read that certain instances of telepathy have been proven in the United States, under circumstances rigorous enough for many doctors. Identical twins, for example, are said to demonstrate an exceptional link in their cognitive and emotional states, one we do not yet fully understand."

He nodded, his lips permitted to form a brief smile.

"I may have been too harsh."

"She has never made any pretence of speaking to ghostly ancestors or Indian Swamis. Hardly a purveyor of the supernatural nonsense you so dislike, Holmes."

"I suppose that I must apologise, for the sake of the case, at least. This entire matter is all . . . most vexing."

"Why did you wish her to accompany me to Broadmoor?"

"That you might observe her. I may chide you occasionally on technical aspects of our work, Watson, but I value your insights into the human character."

"Madame Rostov is . . . formidable. Hardened by experience, I would say. I do not understand her, but I find no reason to doubt— or mistrust—her."

"So be it."

That evening's post brought a brief letter from the very woman we had been discussing. As it was addressed to both of us, I took it and opened it before showing Holmes.

Sirs. I do not guide what I see. As best I can recall, there is a pitted iron bracket by the alley-mouth, some eight feet off the ground, and a yard or two along, a broken street sign on a brick wall. NSIGN is all that remains. The area has the look of a wharf-side area or similar, with rope coiled nearby. Thick, heavy ship's rope. Please do not trouble yourselves to reply.

KR

Katerina Rostov, undoubtedly—and in her own hand. When I read this out to Holmes, my friend was further sobered.

"A generous offering, under the circumstances," he said.

"Can you make anything of it, Holmes?"

The prospect of utilising his mind seemed to cheer him.

"Let us assume that the location is in London; we might as well, given that Smith sought quick passage, and Wokingham certainly has no wharves. Apart from indications of the riverside, which help little, considering the length of the Thames, we have those letters, Watson, which are fortuitous in their combination, offering few options. If it is the remains of a notice, such as CONSIGNMENTS, we are in trouble, but otherwise, we have possibilities such as MONSIGNOR and ENSIGN. On the basis of our country's seafaring traditions, I would favour Ensign Street, Lane, or Road—something of that nature."

A London street guide quickly identified that there was an Ensign Street, but that was in the middle of Whitechapel. Ensign Lane, on the other hand, appeared to be an old thoroughfare which wound behind former naval docks, now used for trade, just beyond Wapping. Even though it was growing dark, Holmes insisted that we take a hansom to the spot there and then.

With the cabman paid handsomely to wait, Holmes and I made our wary way through a district which might have been the same a century before. There were a few domestic buildings. Ancient warehouses loomed on either side, and the one public house we saw seemed—from a glance through the open door—a veritable thieves' den.

There were many alleys, and a singular shortage of streetlamps, but I had brought a bull's-eye, and by its light, we found our destination—the beginnings of Ensign Lane with its half-sign, and a dismal alley-mouth within five paces of that. By the alley, a rusting bracket was fixed, part of some arrangement for hauling up goods.

"The scene, at least. Let us see if there are signs of the crime." Holmes edged forward.

As the alley itself was too small for two abreast, I followed, holding the lantern high and with my revolver in my other hand. Above the background odours of decaying wood and rat urine, another smell came to us, one with which I was only too familiar.

We did not need to go far. The corpse, slumped in an alcove, had been subject to exploration by the local rodents, but it was still quite recognisable. He had been beaten, and his throat cut in a brutal, jagged manner, not cleanly as Becskei's had been.

By lifting the edge of the jacket with his cane, Holmes managed to retrieve various items from the pockets, and then we withdrew, relieved to be out of that charnel alley. Watch and pocketbook only confirmed what we already suspected—Madame Rostov's "'nightmare'" had been entirely accurate.

We had found the late Albert Smith.

Part Three

She watches an old woman who boils sauerkraut and liver in her kitchen, and will probably die not of sickness, but choking on a thick, glutinous dumpling. And happy.

"Is this what it comes to?" Catherine asks. "Do I leave them to their pompous talk, to their infuriating pride in 'reasoning' and 'common sense'—or do I stay the course?"

Mrs. Bessovitch shrugs. A handful of caraway seeds goes in the pan, and liver sizzles by its side, crusting, its juices bubbling. A dubious organ transformed into art.

"You are Katerina. You know what is to do."

Catherine smiles. "Which is to say, 'This is your problem, not mine.' It is, of course."

A second shrug is more dramatic, expansive. Mrs. Bessovitch's generous bosom quivers under her apron.

"Is ours, maybe. But, oi, they are not so bad. The doctor, he hears you, and the other listens to him."

"Is that enough? I do not need them; I could rid myself of it all and leave them wandering, half-blind. But there must be a reason why I have seen the Frenchwoman, a purpose . . ."

"Your hawk-nose—tell me, what is this Watson, to him?"

Catherine hesitates. "I don't know. The bond is deep, I see that. Only a remarkable man could tolerate Holmes."

Laughter, deep beneath the smeared, stained apron. "Katerina, Katerina . . . without doctor, Holmes is salt without cabbage—he is needed, but on his own, he leaves bitter taste. Maybe he knows this."

"Is that another of your great-aunt's sayings, or words from some wise babushka in your village, far away?"

The old woman scowls. "Is Mrs. Bessovitch. Now, find plates. I am hungry."

The meal is good, very good.

Catherine's decision has been made.

I do not know what my friend wrote to Madame Rostov the following morning. It must have been uncommonly generous—for him—as the lady herself came to our front door a little after noon. Her manner with me was amiable; with Holmes, a touch wary.

"Madame, I have confidence in both your information and your intelligence," he said, without rising from the sofa. "Let us put any previous disagreements behind us."

"I am amenable." She removed her hat and settled in the chair I had proffered.

"Then I feel it is only reasonable to share what we have with you." He reached for a letter which had come with the first post. "Marie Dorcas Archambault is the Frenchwoman—or, I should say, that is the name she currently uses, when she is not 'Miss Dorcas.'"

He summarised his letter from *le comte*, and showed her the photograph. She stared at it for a second and looked away.

"Yes," she said, displaying no satisfaction.

"She was Eliane Guerin when that was taken," added Holmes. "But I am convinced we seek only one woman. I have uncovered vague talk of this Archambault, who appeared in London, the August of last year. A month after Guerin defrauded a French count. She was soon involved with the Hermetic Order of the

Golden Dawn—possibly she had already had contact with them in Paris at some point. After that, she seems to have kept herself well concealed."

I poured myself a whisky. "The Hermetic Order . . . what is that, Holmes?"

His expression soured. "Yet another secret society."

"One of these criminal gangs, you mean?"

"No. If it is relevant, Watson, I can instruct you in further study. For the moment, I will merely say that this Golden Dawn is a secretive gathering of those who seek to make modern disciplines of ancient and medieval beliefs—the supposed mysteries of Egypt, the writings of various rabbis, and the Qabalah. They spring from theosophy and the Rosicrucians, but profess more intimate knowledge of magical ceremonies."

Madame Rostov frowned. "You seem to be well-informed, Mr. Holmes, if these are supposed secrets."

"It is my job to be well informed, Madame. And it so happens that Watson's question came to my own mind during a far earlier case—it was necessary that I established the Golden Dawn was not a criminal enterprise. What little I could learn satisfied me. I give no heed, naturally, to their so-called magicks."

"And you have a source on whom you can rely?" she added.

He smiled in appreciation of her touch of irony.

"I do. Much of what I knew before was pieced together over some time, but at this point, I have availed myself of a particular source who has little choice, one William Westcott."

"And he is involved how?" I asked. The name seemed vaguely familiar.

"He is, as it happens, a coroner for East London. But more pertinently, he is a founding member of the Order, along with two other men, one of whom died some time ago, Dr. William Woodman."

I was shocked. "Woodman? I knew him, in passing. He was a police surgeon."

"The Golden Dawn is an eclectic business, Watson. So two men, Westcott and a man called Mathers, now run the Order, not— again—that this is widely known. Mathers is currently in France, where, I learn, he has established a temple to the goddess Isis; Westcott, in London, is an Adeptus, one who has attained a high level by their standards, and a member of almost every so-called esoteric organisation you can imagine. We are fortunate that some in authority already considered Westcott's role as coroner to be incompatible with his Golden Dawn activities. Questions have been asked. I merely tightened the noose, and made it clear that there might be further consequences . . . "

Our companion raised one finger to pause him. "Richard Dadd believed that he had been possessed by Osiris. So we have Isis, Osiris, and now Thoth."

"Well said, Madame. And Thoth, in his role as Hermes Trismegistus, a mythical source of great wisdom, may be the most important of them. Westcott admits that Mlle Archambault has great pretensions of arcane knowledge, so great that the Golden Dawn may admit her into their inner circle. She claims to have access to the knowledge of Thoth, and to a 'Secret Master,' some nonsense about voices which transcend humanity. Westcott both dislikes her and fears her a little, I believe. She demands, rather than persuades—"

"Women's reasonable requests, and their stated hopes, are often called 'demands,' Mr. Holmes." Madame Rostov narrowed her eyes. "If a man asks, his request is considered, and receives a measured response; if a woman does so in the same situation, she is considered forward and her views dismissed."

To my surprise, Holmes gave her a sympathetic glance.

"I am not entirely bound by the worst habits of my own gender, Madame, though Watson will probably tell you that I can be impossible—in my own way—at times. I observe humanity, be it male or female, and your comment is not without merit." He looked to his pipe, but left it where it lay. "I imagine you yourself have experienced such unwarranted responses from time to time."

"I have."

"Then please tolerate me for a moment. From what I have learned so far of Mlle Archambault, and from the singularly brutal murders which lie in her wake, I do not believe her to have been 'dismissed' in any common way on account of being female. The evidence points more to either wickedness or delusion. She claimed—to Westcott—that her own aunt died in pursuit of 'hidden' knowledge, and that her father is confined to a madhouse in southern France, the result of what she called revelations.

"He describes her as intelligent and well-financed, but of such a manner that makes both men and women instinctively wary. He would not give me names but admitted that another member of his organisation, a woman, apparently welcomed Mlle Archambault in the early days, and within a week, had warned the entire inner circle that the Frenchwoman was a danger to them all, a manipulator, a possible fanatic."

Madame Rostov looked to me. "Might there be tea to hand, doctor?"

"Um . . . of course. Do forgive me, I should have offered." And I went to find Mrs. Hudson.

When I returned with the tray, the two were deep in a discussion of Freemasonry and various obscure movements, as if there had never been contention between them.

"Ah, capital, Watson. Darjeeling for the brain. And I feel prompted to add a small admission. Madame Rostov, I do still possess the Ace of Swords, but was unfortunately unsure of your allegiances when we first spoke."

This did not seem to bother her. "May I see it?"

"Of course."

He reached for the large Persian slipper in which he kept his tobacco and, to even my surprise, slid the card out from its hiding place between lining and soft sole.

Madame Rostov took it from him, staring intently as she turned the card over a few times.

"The secrets, if secrets they are, are on the reverse, are they not?" she said.

He seemed pleased. "My own conclusion exactly. Initially, I considered the hand, crown, and peculiar nature of the sword. I looked at permutations of what they might mean, but could make nothing certain of it. Then it struck me, and I used a magnifying glass on the card. As an accomplished miniaturist, Dadd incorporated various symbols into the complex design on the back of the card.

"There may be a code therein, but many of the tiny symbols are entirely unknown to me, nor do I believe they represent anything so common as a simple message. Alchemical formulae, possibly. We might consult over them, but we have no way of knowing what is on the other thirteen cards. I am inclined to think that each will be unique, and thus the need for the whole suit. And now I believe that I can trace the Frenchwoman's progress in her search."

Madame Rostov and I sat back, listening.

"In December or January—it does not matter which—she learns that Soper has some most unusual, hand-painted Tarot cards, all in the suit of Swords. She sees them and recognises what they are, or how she might employ them to further her path with the Golden Dawn. She embraces a ritual involving the type of blade represented on the cards—"

"As I said, attunement, correspondence of objects or symbols," said our companion. "Like speaks to like."

Although I knew he disliked being interrupted, I saw Holmes briefly tip his head to her.

"Most likely, Madame. But she does not learn from Soper where the rest of the suit lies. We may assume he does not know. Her search begins, and weeks pass; you will note a gap of three and a half months between Soper's murder and Becskei's. She enquires of other occultists—cautiously, I imagine—and of antiquarians, art dealers, the like. Certain burglaries take place, but are fruitless— and by accident or cunning, she crosses paths with Albert Smith's fence, who gives up details of not only Becskei and Cleves, but also Smith himself. All three men are, at that point, lost."

"I am persuaded," said Madame Rostov.

"Thank you. You say you are not an aficionado of the Tarot?"

"Nor of reading tea leaves or staring into lumps of crystal. You gathered that I have reservations about the tricks of the spiritualist world." She grinned, unexpectedly. "After all, I have employed a number of them to, shall we say, augment a reading which was not going well. But I seek to do no harm, and to avoid falsehoods. A Tarot card representing sudden change, for example, serves as the focus to raise a particular issue, and so on. But the card itself means no more to me than a seven of hearts in a game of whist. I may be able to use it towards a trick; I may not."

I had been silent for some time, but clinked my cup against the teapot as if by accident, drawing their attention.

"Yet you *do* receive impressions of genuine events," I said. "I do not think anyone in this room could doubt that, not after Albert Smith."

"Unfortunately, doctor, what I see is never pleasant. I have never seen lovers meet, or children take their first steps. Never touched on episodes of joy or tenderness." She glanced at Holmes, as if trying to decide something. "Let me offer a specific example. When I was twelve years old, I witnessed a woman being strangled in the house next door. Yet I was in bed, in our attic, at the time, half-asleep. This sight and others came to me unwanted, unasked for, and they have never left me."

"Extraordinary," I murmured.

Holmes closed his eyes and leaned back. "So . . . I imagine that you were bright, perhaps brighter than your peers, and being subject to these inexplicable events, you were often viewed with suspicion by the people around you."

"Up there I was called Mardy Cath, the unnatural girl who 'saw' things—and it made me no friends, nor pleased my family."

"And so," he said, "you spent much time alone, and perhaps read quite widely. After some time, you conceived the notion that you might capitalise on this ability, rather than let it further ruin your life. But Keighley was hardly the place for a career as a psychic, for you would not be able to reinvent yourself there, being known to local people. Opportunities there were limited; you came instead to London and its pavements of gold. Here, with Mrs. Bessovitch's assistance, you created Madame Rostov."

"You are correct, Mr. Holmes. Despite certain dark and troubling . . . incidents, the imposture succeeded."

"But now . . . ?"

"As the years passed, my appetite for such activities diminished. Most private sittings were too dull, or too sad; I was exposed constantly to the small sorrows of every human being. Working with the police was a little better, for those cases were often sordid or brutal."

Holmes opened his eyes. "I recognise those limitations, though I satisfy myself that I serve justice along the way. I note that you contacted us not as Miss Catherine Weatherhead, but as your other self."

"A considered ploy," she said. "I retain Madame Rostov to sit for very select groups of people now and then, such as,"—she named three or four clients whose high rank in society surprised me—"In our present situation, it seemed best that Madame step forward once more."

"I cannot disagree." He stood at last and came to the table to retrieve his cup of tea. "I mentioned the sword depicted on our card. It is a *khopesh*, a very ancient and odd Egyptian blade with a sickle end, the inner edge of the curve being sharpened. Sir Richard Burton's useful 'Book of the Sword' includes the form. From the wounds on our victims, I very much suspect that a *khopesh* was used for the killing blow or blows. An unnecessary embellishment, unless . . . "

"Ritual," said Madame Rostov. "As with the exchange of cards. The affair must be measured by the Frenchwoman's beliefs, not ours."

Apart from being tea-boy, I was unsure as to my role here.

"What are we to do next, Holmes?"

"Given what we know, her single intention at this point must be to recover the Ace of Swords. Ideally, I imagine she wishes to leave its current owner—myself—with a corresponding Ace of Spades upon or beside my corpse. That would no doubt fully satisfy this ritualistic approach she favours—"

"Is obsessed by." Madame Rostov shook her head, looking weary. "The few times I have crossed the paths of such types in the spiritualist world, I notice that if they settle on a particular approach, they will repeat it again and again. Regardless of logic."

"A monomania," said Holmes. "There are many less esoteric criminals who will do much the same. I must send Mrs. Hudson away for a few days, for safety's sake. We would not want her harmed by someone seeking information on our household and its habits, or by an intruder."

I thought that wise and agreed. "Though Maisie Evans was only chloroformed, not otherwise hurt."

"True, but with the killing of Albert Smith . . . there were no Tarot cards in his possession, and no spades left beside him, yet he is most decidedly dead." His face grew graver. "Normally, I might make further general enquiries over the weeks, seek experts to tell us more of what is hidden in Dadd's designs, even try to unravel this tangle of societies and movements to clarify matters, but here, time may not be our ally . . . I suspect Archambault will now do whatever she deems necessary to complete her quest."

"But why?" I asked. "I mean, Holmes, gathering and owning a unique set of cards, the domain of the obsessed collector or the antiquarian certainly . . . but to kill for them? To use such damnable rituals? What on earth possesses this madwoman?"

He shrugged. "The murders I understand. The men in question had seen, and could describe, her. Some, such as Becskei, may have known her. As for the rest, the manner in which these things have been done—that I shall no doubt ascertain with time."

Frustration set a tremble to the leg I had injured so many years ago. "We should take the initiative."

"A fair point, old fellow. I do see an endgame which must be played out, preferably on our terms. Madame Rostov, you have provided invaluable information, and for that, I am most grateful—but Watson and I must now take steps to corner Archambault and her associates."

For a second it seemed as if she would bridle at that statement.

"Not," he added quickly, "because I mistrust you, nor because you are a woman. But there are both practical and legal problems to consider, and Scotland Yard will have its opinions. Inspector Lestrade will sniff and sour at any hint of the esoteric or 'ab-natural.' I must couch this in purely mundane terms for him."

His point was taken, and our parting from Madame Rostov was more genial than before. When she had left, Holmes turned to me.

"From the increase in tradesmen and loiterers on the streets outside these last few days, I imagine that, as Madame Rostov thought, our rooms are being watched. What I cannot know is if Smith gave up the location of the last Tarot card. Are we watched because we are involved in the case, or because she suspects I have the Ace of Swords?"

"Lestrade could post someone to watch the watchers," I suggested.

"Oh, the more constables involved, the clumsier things become, Watson. We would end up with a music hall show."

A sudden fear struck me.

"You mentioned Mrs. Hudson—but what of Madame Rostov? Is she not in danger?"

"She may well be."

"Then we must do something, Holmes!"

"I have. A reliable private agent is following her and observing her Southwark address when she is in residence."

That was some comfort, at least. "These legal problems, Holmes . . . you would be speaking of the matter of conclusive proof?"

"Yes. Despite everything we know, we have no evidence that would be admissible in court. No witnesses—in the normal manner—that Archambault and her associates committed the murders, and nothing directly incriminating from the scenes. A judge will not put on his black cap on the basis of a 'likely' footprint—Maisie Evans did not see Sir Richard's assailant, and asking questions at Broadmoor is not a crime, even if she lied about her name."

"Has Lebrun—"

"The good *inspecteur* agrees with our assessment as to the likely identity, but has no resources to spare. *Le comte* ails and has probably forgotten his misfortune. There are other names who fit such a face—Antoinette Sacre, for example, supposedly of Perpignan—again in the south—took a knife to a jeweller there and walked away with half his stock. If we delivered her to Paris for questioning, he would be most grateful, but otherwise . . . what do we have?. The best we might hope for, at the moment, is Lestrade warning Mlle not to get up to any 'funny business' in the future, do you see?"

Put like that, I realised that he was correct. And it was on such a depressing thought that I left Holmes to his ruminations.

Two days later, however, an early telegram came to my temporary quarters, one which changed my mood in a moment.

Come at once. Holmes.

Naturally, I made haste to Baker Street, where Holmes was waiting by the door, impatient, with a hansom ready.

"You are armed, Watson?" asked Holmes, once we were in the hansom and rattling towards Southwark.

I assented. My old revolver had been the first item I had reached for after receiving his summons. Almost as an afterthought, I had grabbed my medical bag as well.

"What has happened, Holmes?" I felt the excitement of possible action. I checked my half hunter, and found that it was only half past seven, the sky dull with threatening clouds.

"Madame Rostov has had visitors."

"Is she injured?"

"I believe not."

He explained that a surly, breathless East European boy of fourteen or fifteen had come to Baker Street, saying that *babushka* Bessovitch had sent him. He held a note which read:

"We are in play. Men have suffered. Awaiting your presence—bring the doctor. Rostov."

Urging the cabman to make haste, Holmes remained silent the rest of the journey.

Southwark was much the same as ever, or was it? Rain had come, but figures lingered on corners, in doorways, in the shadow of the few trees. Both men and women, strangely static. Holmes saw me taking a grip on my revolver as I dismounted the hansom, and he gave a tight smile.

"On our side, I believe, Watson. Or Mrs. Bessovitch's, at least. I made certain enquiries—it seems that our *babushka* has a degree of influence in the Polish, Latvian, and Russian communities."

I looked again and realised that we were being ignored—all faces were turned to the approaches, watching.

The front door was open.

Inside, Madame Rostov greeted us, her black hair more tangled than ever, her eyes seeming a colder grey than before.

"Before you begin with your gentlemanly concerns, Mrs. Bessovitch and I are unharmed. Your man, Bollins, was attacked whilst on watch. He will live."

"Good God! I should see to him."

"In a moment, doctor. I have another patient for you, in the front room."

She was curt, imperious, and I wondered at the imposture Catherine Weatherhead had created. Did it not only suit her work, but somehow protect her in times of stress?

The room in question had two occupants—Mrs. Bessovitch, holding an ancient, double-barrelled pistol, and a groaning man who lay on the settee, bleeding from a wound in his right thigh. Nowhere near a main artery, I saw at once, but I would not have been surprised if there was a pistol ball somewhere deep in there. I thought at first that he was contorted with pain, then realised that he had a deformity to the shoulder and upper back, a scoliosis, as described by Hippocrates himself.

"He needs a hospital," I said, probing the wound and eliciting deeper groans.

"Or I shoot again, aim better." Mrs. Bessovitch tapped the pistol with one finger.

Holmes glanced at her. "No need for that, Madame. Not yet, anyway."

The wounded man's eyes widened, either at Holmes's grim tone or from my ministrations. Not wanting to risk extraction of the ball under these conditions, I cleaned the wound as best I could, applied an iodine solution, and bound him up.

Madame Rostov, Holmes, and I retired to the kitchen, where a pot of strong coffee was waiting—and where she explained what had happened.

The disturbance came with the dawn, their first warning being a fracas outside the house. As the old lady armed herself, Madame Rostov cautiously opened the front door to find Bollins and the hunched man grappling.

"I pressed myself to the wall; Mrs. B came forward and fired that black powder curio of hers. And when the man fell, she took a copper bed-warmer from the wall and struck him across the back of his head, rendering him almost insensible."

"Astonishing," I muttered. "And astonishing that she hit the right man."

Mrs. Bessovitch's contribution at the point was more a growl than anything.

"After that, I helped Bollins upstairs—he is bruised and winded, but protests that it is nothing. The shot alerted our neighbours, and Mrs. Bessovitch has many friends. They are watching, now." Her lips formed a half-smile. "I believe our assailant had neither expected to encounter Bollins, nor that two women would be able to defend themselves."

"Foolish indeed," said Holmes.

"This man was at the Hungarian's shop when the murder took place."

"He has said as much?"

"He was there." Her eyes were on Holmes, challenging him, but he did not argue.

Instead, he announced that he would question the stranger in the front room, whilst, after a mouthful of black coffee, I and my bag went upstairs to tend to Bollins. As I had been told, he was winded—a chance blow to the belly, he said—but had suffered no permanent harm. Advising him to rest for a while, I returned to the others.

"Ah, Watson. This is Mr. Douglas Mallory. Mr. Mallory is no

common brute, but a man of some refinement, and much folly. He went to Oxford, d'you know?"

I was puzzled. "Why is he here?"

"Because he sought to impress. He is of the lowest grade in the Hermetic Order of the Golden Dawn. A lay-brother, in essence. He heard a certain Mlle Archambault discussing how we had visited this address, and hoped to discover more by cowing the ladies here, to ingratiate himself with his mistress."

"To ease her path," the young man retorted. "I am the Blade-bearer!"

"As I said," Holmes remarked, "a lay-brother, who fetches and carries. He imagines himself an esquire, though."

I had known heroic and romantic types in the army. Sadly, they were usually the first to rise, overly keen for battle, and the first to fall.

"Did he . . . ?"

"He was present at Becskei's shop and did nothing to stop them. That is crime enough."

"It is for the Greater Good!" Mallory protested. "When she has the full Blessing of Thoth, she will share it with all, guide us to wisdom—"

Holmes glared at him. "Your destination will be the cells, Mallory. I have sent word, and the police are on their way."

Madame Rostov, Holmes, and I adjourned to the kitchen.

"He is a fool, who worships the Frenchwoman, and will say nothing bad of her, nor expose her plans beyond this 'Blessing of Thoth' nonsense. I suppose that a night or two with our constabulary might persuade him of how low he is sunk, and loosen his tongue."

"He is not a murderer?" I asked.

"You have seen him, Watson. She had him carry that sword of hers to the places where murder was committed, but no more than that. At the moment he admits that to me, in shock, but I doubt he will say the same to the police, once his wits return. As it is, we can have him held on little more than common assault on a Southwark Street—and that only because Bollins blocked his way."

With a frustrated click of his tongue, Holmes sat down to wait for the constabulary to arrive . . .

We left Mrs. Bessovitch's not long after ten that evening. Bollins insisted that he would go back to his watch until dawn;

Mallory was despatched in a police van. The sergeant was told of nothing except the assault, to which Madame Rostov and Mrs. Bessovitch bore witness.

"I will inform Lestrade in the morning," Holmes murmured to me as the van drew away.

A hansom awaited the two of us.

I have many memories of returning to Holmes's rooms at Baker Street—rooms which I had often shared, of course. The exhausted trudge up those stairs after a fruitless expedition, and the light triumphant step after a case had been solved. Mrs. Hudson would be ready with a pot of tea and other sustenance for us as we discussed what had occurred. At other times, we would throw ourselves upon our respective beds, drained by events—or Holmes would collapse upon the sofa, deep in thought.

Never before had I found the old place in the state which awaited us that day. The inner door at the top of the stairs had been beaten down, splintered from its hinges, and inside there reigned a chaos far beyond Holmes's habitual untidiness and disregard for domestic propriety. My revolver came to my hand, but Holmes seemed unperturbed. He examined his Stradivarius, which had been tossed aside, and declared it unharmed; he replaced a handful of scattered shag in the old Persian slipper where it usually resided, and he smiled.

"Great Scott, Holmes, I see little about which to be amused."

He gave his usual dismissive wave of the hand.

"Disorder can be rectified, Watson," he said. "And now I do not have to engineer any convenient and very public absences from Baker Street—Archambault has done exactly what I wished."

"What you wished . . . ?"

"She has come in search of the Ace of Swords. I would hazard a guess that Mallory was encouraged in his foolishness, as a diversion. She must consider her bold venture to have been a great success."

He pointed to an overturned chair. Upon it lay a single card, not an ordinary playing card but one from the Tarot. It depicted a young man apparently on a journey, his bundle and stick over his shoulder, a prancing dog at his feet. Blood was spattered across the card's face.

"The Fool," said Holmes. "Not a Dadd work, clearly, but a touch of humour, mocking me, and a statement, for in Tarot games the Fool has many roles, including that of being either the lowest or the highest trump."

"The blood?"

"Her own, possibly, or that of one of her acolytes—a symbolic gesture. Why not, for she has won. She has the Ace, and thus the entire suit of Swords. Or . . . "

I knew that gleam, that quirk of his brow.

"You have somehow deceived her."

He snorted in amusement.

"The real Ace is in my breast pocket, Watson. What I left here, artlessly 'hidden' in my tobacco pouch, was a rather fine copy, which I had commissioned from that reformed counterfeiter Finny Watkins. He did, I must say, an excellent job. Naturally, I had him change several of the most minuscule details in the pattern on the reverse, but I am certain that his work will pass muster at first, even third, glance."

He tossed the card aside and set the chair upright, seating himself upon it as if it were a throne.

"It will buy us time, old chap, for I have indeed seized the initiative, as you proposed. Word will go out as to that hunched fellow, where he has been seen, who he knows; more pressure will be applied to certain members of the Golden Dawn. And . . . I have made an urgent request of Madame Rostov."

"That she stay out of this matter, lest worse befall her?"

"I doubt she would listen now. No, I have asked that she utilise whatever talents or contacts she has in one direction only—the identification of Archambault's lair, her retreat. I myself can find no trace of this elusive Frenchwoman being quartered in the usual places. And, Watson—" His raised hand silenced any retort I might be about to make. "I have promised Madame Rostov that I will not question her as to her methods or her sources. She has earned that of me."

I leaned against a disordered table, most of Holmes's scientific equipment already swept to the floor.

"Why did she leave the Fool, from the Tarot?"

"Fourteen cards in a suit, remember, Watson? But thirteen in a suit of playing cards. The Ace of Spades must have been used with Albert Smith's 'friend.' She had to improvise—or she enjoyed her joke."

"What if it is over, now?"

He peered at me and waited.

"The Frenchwoman has, as far as she knows, every Sword," I continued. "You said so yourself. What if she needs nothing else, if she is content and makes no more mischief? We might never hear of her again."

Holmes's response was blunt. "Mlle Archambault is a criminal, and—most likely—a murderer, or close accomplice. Four men are dead. We shall consider them to be our clients, and represent them in seeking justice. That is enough to warrant our pursuit of her."

I could not fault his statement. "And the proof . . . ?"

"A proper point. Finding the counterfeit Ace in her possession would be proof of burglary, and the man in police custody can provide evidence of her penchant for intimidation with violence. That, and other scraps gathered along the way, should satisfy Lestrade. She will not, at the very least, be able to remain in the shadows, or free of wider opprobrium. I doubt that the public eye will suit her. Let us find out tomorrow what our prisoner has to say."

"This Douglas Mallory is from Hampstead," said Lestrade. "Decent enough family, educated, but dropped out of his college before his finals. He claims that he gave up his studies to 'explore a more spiritual path,' and became an acolyte of Thoth Arisen," said Lestrade. "I've no idea what that means, but he's involved with these secret societies—not the Freemasons, thank God, or I'd have the chief constable on my back."

Holmes interlaced his long fingers. "I see. Has he indicated where Marie Archambault might be found?"

"He has." The inspector was obviously pleased with himself. "And to spare you the trouble, gentlemen, my men set out an hour ago, with orders to bring her—and anyone with her—in for questioning."

Holmes looked appalled.

"Lestrade, have you no sense of . . . no, it does not matter. I already know what your hasty, blundering action will achieve."

"What, Mr. Holmes?" An awkward, almost belligerent tone.

"Absolutely nothing."

And that afternoon we heard the news which Holmes had expected. A police raid on a secluded house near Seven Dials had unearthed a nest of unimportant clippers and purse-snatchers who said they knew nothing of Archambault, Thoth, or such matters.

Holmes went to see them in their cells, simply to satisfy himself—and possibly to make Lestrade's discomfort more intense.

"A more worthless bunch I never saw," he muttered when he returned, flinging his hat across the room. "The coins they clipped were clumsily done, and would have been flung back at them by any short-sighted grocer. They were totally ignorant of this case, naturally. Mallory must have heard of the address, or passed the den one day, and offered it up to waste police time. I saw Archambault's man again whilst there, and he is . . . 'much afeared,' as they say. The Frenchwoman has some hold over him."

"He believes in all this magic and Egyptian nonsense. If so . . . "

He turned on his heel, narrow eyed.

"Out with it, Watson."

"We have our own 'seeress,' do we not?"

"Ha!" His exclamation was not of derision, as I thought it might be, but of pleasure. "My dear fellow, once again, you prove your worth. Let us see—you must persuade Madame Rostov to perform for us."

"I must?"

He cleared his throat. "I believe that she finds you the more tolerable of the two of us."

Madame Rostov was willing. Not enthusiastic, I admit, but willing enough for some reason which I sensed she was not sharing with us. Some personal matter about this case bothered her, I was sure—but I did not enquire.

Lestrade, subdued after the Seven Dials episode, arranged for an interview room to be made available, and such was his awkwardness that he acquiesced to having a constable outside the door, not in with the prisoner—once I assured him that I would be in there should Mallory turn violent.

"But not Mr. Holmes?" he asked.

"I am to represent the agency," I said, feeling moderately pleased with myself. "I have Holmes's full confidence."

I hoped that was true, though I wondered if Holmes's absence was to avoid him expressing scepticism at whatever methods Madame Rostov might employ.

Mallory's bruises had darkened, but he had no more of them than when last we saw him. Handcuffs on his right wrist held him fast to a solid oak chair, which faced a plain, scratched table.

Without glancing at the cuffed man, she reached into her bag and brought forth what could only be a pack of Tarot cards, wrapped in pale silk. For his part, his entire attention was on my companion as she unwrapped the pack, ignoring me completely.

"Madame Rostov cares nothing for your Golden Dawn," she said, sounding more East European than usual. "She is mystery in self. Touch."

Mallory stared at the proffered cards.

"Touch!" she said again.

When he failed to reach out and put his free hand upon the cards, she nodded.

"Very well." With that, she leaned forward over the small table, a sudden movement, and struck him across the face with the pack. He gasped—in surprise, not pain, I thought.

"Da. Now they know you, as I do." She sat back as if nothing had happened, her deft fingers splitting and recombining the Tarot cards three, four times—after which, she took up the top dozen or so. "Now we see . . . "

She lay one card, face up, on the scratched wooden surface.

"High Priestess. She is reversed, and so she is conceited, having surface knowledge only."

Mallory scowled and spoke for the first time since we had entered the room.

"Trickery. You placed that there, somehow."

"Then you choose next."

He hesitated, then reached forward and drew from the remaining cards she held out to him. When he looked at it, he paled but placed it down.

"So. The Moon—also reversed. Inconstancy and deception. Your path is that of fools, of those who let themselves be deceived. One more, maybe?"

This time he almost snatched the card from her hand, slapping it on the table without looking at it.

"The Tower." Madame Rostov sighed, as if concerned.

"Upright—disasters and plans in ruin. Ah, how she has deceived and used you, Mr. Mallory. Is sad, da? And here you sit, chained. Prison and, yes, ruin is all that is left for you."

"S-s-she will —"

"Let you rot!" she snapped. "Rostov has seen it. 'The blade now, quickly' she say, as Becskei tremble, and she hold out her hand. 'Clean it,' she say, after he is dead. You remember? You tremble also, maybe worse; you wipe blade on black cloth, the blood is so very dark, and the books, so many books, seem to loom over you . . . "

"You were not there!" he shrieked, pulling at the handcuff, the rough chair to which he was shackled creaking. "You cannot know that!"

I stepped forward, but she waved me back.

"I am Rostov; I see this. You—you will see noose."

Such was the power of her performance, her "act," that I myself felt a chill at my neck, a dryness in my mouth.

I coughed. "If you tell the truth, Mr. Holmes will no doubt speak for you. His word has some weight."

Conscience did not allow me to state that Mallory would escape the hangman. After all, I had no idea if he had direct responsibility for any of the deaths.

He shuddered. "I . . . I cannot betray the secrets of Trismegistus, the inner mysteries of the Order."

"Is not necessary," said my companion, more gently. "But the woman must answer." She tapped one blunt fingernail on the High Priestess card. "You saw. Conceit, no trust, wisdom ignored. Is her."

And he began to speak . . .

At Baker Street, I recounted all that the prisoner had revealed. Holmes listened, making occasional comments, or insisting on clarification. Madame Rostov said little.

"It was a marvel, Holmes. Mallory became almost garrulous, in a manner which I do not think we or the police could have achieved. He is an accomplice, but as you suspected, not a killer. Marie Archambault allowed him to carry her ceremonial blade, but that is all. He believed in her, and in her tale that she had come to impart the wisdom of Thoth to the Order of the Golden Dawn, that she is a conduit for a 'Secret Master.' It's all rather nonsensical, but—"

"What is her ultimate intention?" he interrupted.

"Control, I'd say, though Mallory didn't state it directly. That Westcott chap is in a tricky situation. Mathers is in France, setting up his own 'temple.' Archambault is making a bid for power, perhaps to run the Order in London. It's the Grand Lodge, I suppose."

Holmes drew on his pipe for a few moments, so often a sign of deep contemplation.

"I wonder how much she herself believes in this Thoth nonsense?" he said eventually. "As we know, Richard Dadd seems to have truly thought, after Egypt, that Osiris had spoken to him—possessed him, even, at times. Yet this entire case may be one of simple ambition, to which poor Dadd never professed. We can assume that whoever runs the Order has access to their funds, and the ability to manage matters spiritual *and* temporal as he or she sees fit. An attractive situation, to those of a mind for that sort of thing."

"Plenty of politicians like that," I said, thinking of certain alderman and London officials I had met. "Without any mystic polish on the brass. People who manoeuvre to be in charge of committees, chairmen of companies, charitable foundations—all to let them pull the appropriate strings."

"Sadly true, Watson. Yet her obsession with Dadd's Tarot . . . I have to wonder if some part of Marie Archambault has been drawn in by tales of hermetic wisdom, of hidden knowledge."

"Authenticity," said Madame Rostov. "The link with both Osiris and Thoth—it is clear, surely, that such would be valued by the Golden Dawn."

Holmes smiled. "You consider her to be entirely a charlatan, Madame?"

"I consider her to be a determined manipulator. One performer can recognise another, Mr. Holmes. There should be a kernel of truth in every performance, enough to sway the less credulous in the audience. I *do* expect that she will utilise the cards as part of her repertoire to persuade other members of the Order that Marie Dorcas Archambault should be heard, even followed. Mallory indicated as much. As you know, the Swords represent intellect and wisdom, the domain of Thoth."

He bowed his head to her. "Indeed. We must always remember that against the true logic of the disciplined mind, we have to weigh the false logic of the criminal and deluded. So—according to Mallory, Archambault killed Soper, Becskei, and Cleves with her own hands. A ritual necessity, in her eyes. Did you tell him of her recent actions with regard to the Ace of Swords?"

"We did not."

"Good. We can presume that she cut herself with the *khopesh*, for similar reasons—hence the blood on the card she left. Or she cut whoever accompanied her — Jean Latour, the servant Mallory named, is the likely suspect. Not a member of the Order, merely her employee. Latour was at Becskei's. If Mallory is reliable, Latour may have been the one who put an end to Albert Smith. Lestrade may have that name in due course. I trust that you were discrete with the inspector, Watson?"

"I told him that, on the basis of what we had heard so far, we believed Archambault to be a mentally unstable murderess, and Mallory to be a besotted accomplice. He did press me, but I assured him that you would no doubt make sense of my 'muddled' notes and contact him with your conclusions."

"Excellent, excellent. Then our task remains to locate Archambault herself, as quickly as possible. Watson, read me again exactly what Mallory said."

I consulted my notebook.

"Although he agreed to talk of practical matters, and to write a statement as to Latour's guilt, and his own presence at Becskei's, he was still most hesitant to discuss Archambault directly. When Madame Rostov asked where we would find the Frenchwoman, where she was based, or quartered at this moment, he went silent."

Our new associate looked up. "When I reached for the Tarot once more, he only muttered: 'She is Maria Aegyptiaca, brought from ignorance to enlightenment, and worships in her own house.' But I have no idea what that means, Mr. Holmes."

"We shall see." He rose and went to one of the bookshelves. "It sounds very much like a reference to a saint or martyr. I have a hagiography somewhere here . . . yes." Taking down a dusty leather-bound volume, he wiped it on his smoking jacket and began to turn the pages. "Assuming he does not refer to *the* Mary, we have Mary Magdalene, of course, Mary of Clopas, and . . . ah! Maria Aegyptiaca—born in Egypt in the fifth century and subject to a revelation after a visit to Jerusalem, converting to Christianity. A desert hermit until her death."

"Never heard of her," I said.

"It appears that—as one might expect—she is more venerated in the East." He sat down again, cradling the book. "But her sainthood is recognised in the Anglican communion, so not as obscure as some. What does this tell us? As deserts are somewhat uncommon in England, and Archambault can hardly be in Jerusalem, then Mallory's allusion to 'her own house' must have been his attempt to help without helping. Another pipe, I think, and a little quiet."

We were dismissed, it seemed.

Her headaches have become more common, more intrusive, as if harsh fingers press and tighten at her temples. Seeking air to clear her head, she walks the city, but when she passes by Smithfield Market, the sensation intensifies. Butchers' apprentices sit and smoke at the market's edge, laughing, playing cards on a crate, ignoring passers-by. She pauses,

"Nice bit o' tongue for tonight, lady?" calls out a mutton-chopped older apprentice; the others snort or giggle. Her brilliant grey eyes fix on him, and he grows flush-cheeked, unable to look at her again. He fumbles, dropping some of his cards—where they fall, by his boots, lies a cleaver, worn but razor-honed. Its blade is as bloody as his apron.

She walks on.

Cards and blades. Cards and blades . . .

Part Four

Fourteen cards.

The entire suit of Swords, far more important in their way than the Major Arcana, with which any novice or fortune-teller can play and turn to their purpose, as Catherine did with Mallory.

Fourteen cards, painted by Osiris, inspired by Thoth. The Frenchwoman has them all now, and each holds a mystery, to be unlocked by the secrets within the Ace. They lie face down upon the altar, waiting to speak. Catherine can see them, feel them. Whatever the truth of it, they have been made into murder, tainted.

Why Archambault? Why does this woman walk through her mind? This is no Edwin Dry, the consummate assassin who danced within her visions before, eight years ago—this woman has purpose, yes, but nothing of his singular discipline.

This one is ambition, a common monster, where he was . . . unique. Unstoppable. Catherine cannot use Marie Dorcas Archambault, does not need Marie Dorcas Archambault—the woman serves no purpose except her own vain desires!

Dry-bladdered, empty-bowelled, Catherine perches on the water closet and shudders, close to weeping. Through misted eyes she watches Tarot cards being moved, arranged, recombined . . . the fingers which move them are inelegant, slender but calloused, a peasant's fingers. The Frenchwoman rose from poverty, and stole or stabbed, slashed her way to this place with no thought for the ruin which trailed behind her.

"I did not do it this way," Catherine tells herself. "I did not! The men who died back then, it was . . . justified. Necessary. No courts, where courts had failed. The justice of Mr. Holmes, but no, not the methods."

She tries to focus on the Tarot cards, the candle-lit place around them, but Archambault's face is before her, so close now. A faint scar across one eyebrow; a blemish by the mouth, half-hidden with powder; a nose which is not quite true. And between brow and nose, a fire.

Eyes. Dark coals alight, staring back at . . .
Catherine Weatherhead.
She is seen!

Douglas Mallory hanged himself in his cell, two nights after Madame Rostov and I visited him—an inattentive custody sergeant, who deemed the young man a decent sort at heart, and a lack of observation due to a brawl in the vicinity of the police station. I acted *in locum* for my friend Bland examined the body. I was satisfied. There was no sign or suspicion of foul play, of anyone else being involved.

When I reached Baker Street, I found that he and Madame

Rostov were in conference, various maps strewn on the floor. They looked up.

"It was certainly by his own hand, Holmes," I reported. "A sad business."

Madame Rostov crumpled a map in her fingers. "Another death. I lay this also at her feet."

My friend seemed less concerned about Mallory.

"Unfortunate, no doubt. But better news is at hand—I believe that I have identified Archambault's lair."

"Great Scott! How did you manage that?"

"Through logical deduction, naturally."

"I assume that you are to share your new-found knowledge, Mr. Holmes?" Madame Rostov's tone held a slightly acid edge; I may have been mistaken, but she seemed tense today, almost angry.

"Watson knows my methods. Observation, collation of known facts, and ratiocination. Marie Archambault is somewhere in London, with one servant and a small number of adherents. She must instruct them, and hold certain meetings, but does not wish the authorities to know her location or her business. Mallory gave her the fanciful name of Maria Aegyptiaca, and referred to her 'house,' no doubt a perverted reference to a house of worship."

At this point, he glanced at our companion, and coughed awkwardly.

"Madame Rostov offered certain . . . intelligence, concerning a vaulted ceiling, and an altar used for ceremonial purposes. The most reasonable combination of all we knew suggested that the Frenchwoman had established herself in some church or chapel in the capital. A congregation would hardly suit her need for secrecy, so the logical choice would be such a place which was no longer utilised for its original purpose—one which is derelict, deconsecrated, or abandoned."

"Are there many of those in the area?" I asked. I did not know if I was amused, appalled, or relieved to see Holmes taking on board information provided by Madame Rostov, who was, after all, a self-declared charlatan when it suited her. Did he still believe she had clandestine "inside" knowledge of this affair through human agency, or had he come to some plausibly scientific assessment of her gift?

"Many? Rather more than I had anticipated. However, I

enlisted the assistance of a retired clergyman I know, Thaddeus Perkins, who has an interest in these matters, and he gave me several suggestions." He pointed to a map by his knees. "Lo and behold, there stands in Hammersmith, in the tangle of streets behind Marlborough Wharf, a disused place of worship which went by the name of St. Mary-of-Egypt. You see? The house of Maria Aegyptiaca."

"A church?"

"A former Nonconformist chapel whose adherents, Perkins remembers, parted in acrimony some five or six years ago. He is a good sort, if forgetful, and had to confirm this from his archives—there was dispute over ownership of the property, which is why it came to mind—and it has lain fallow ever since."

Holmes recounted how he had visited the area at night, establishing that the chapel was intact, and whilst he had not seen Archambault, he did observe two men entering the building through a side-door. One of them was a fair match for Mallory's description of Latour, the Frenchwoman's servant!

Madame Rostov stood, and went to the window, gazing out onto the street.

"You will tell this to the police?" she asked.

"To let them blunder into the place and miss everything of importance? Or to find Archambault there and be outwitted? I think not, Madame. Watson and I have taken matters into our own hands before."

"I must be there," she said.

To my astonishment, Holmes said, "I expected as much."

"Then when do we go?"

He looked to me. "Given that it is only a matter of time before she realises I have duped her over the Ace of Swords, and that she is clearly willing to kill to achieve her ambitions, we shall not wait."

"Tonight?" I glanced at Madame Rostov, who nodded.

Holmes picked up his cane, swishing it in the air like a sword.

"Tomorrow morning, with the dawn. There are almost derelict houses in the area—houses which attract the impoverished, the drunken, and the forsaken. I have a temporary arrangement with one of the so-called landlords. It is from a room there that I observed the chapel over several hours."

"What of the Frenchwoman herself?"

"I have reason to believe she is in residence there. Last night, at nine, a furtive, heavily bundled figure came to visit the place. That visitor was none other than William Westcott—the very man who first named Archambault to me, if you remember, Watson. It seems he plays two games. And so, before we venture to Marlborough Wharf, you and I shall pay Mr. Westcott a visit. This afternoon he dines at a restaurant in Duke Street associated with the Theosophical Society. I anticipate that his digestion will suffer after I have spoken to him."

The man we sought was not seated in the more public dining area, but in a private room at the rear. Holmes gained admittance from the reluctant manager by sheer force of will, insisting that it was coroner's business and most urgent. Even before the manager was able to ask the guests' permission, my friend pushed past him.

A sparse table stood in the centre of the large, chandelier-lit room—with plates of what appeared to be nuts, fruit, and finely sliced vegetables. There was wine aplenty, however. Five men and two women stared at Holmes, and a somewhat corpulent, bearded man began to rise from his chair.

"How dare you—"

"Mr. Westcott, there is not time for umbrage or protestation. We must speak to you at once, sir, or Scotland Yard will be greatly disappointed."

The man paled and turned to the other guests. "A coroner's life is not his own," he said apologetically. "Please excuse me for a moment."

The manager, confused, showed us to a small side-room set with a card table and four chairs. Westcott blustered, complained.

"Mr. Holmes, I must—"

Once again Holmes cut him off.

"Mary-of-Egypt," he snapped. "You have spoken to Archambault, despite my warning."

Westcott's pale cheeks flushed.

"You do not understand the hold she has . . . "

"Then enlighten me. And yes, Dr. Watson here can hold his tongue if he chooses. That, or write most eloquently on your adventures for the journals."

Any remaining bluster fell away from the man as he babbled

what he knew. As the two surviving founders of the Golden Dawn, he and Mathers sought to instruct those who had joined the Order, and further its (to me) vague aims. But Westcott had to be cautious, given his position in society. Mathers and his wife in Paris were relatively impoverished but deep in their work.

Simply put, Marie Dorcas Archambault had influence with both neophytes and adepts, and access to money, having inveigled herself into the good books of one Annie Horniman, an eccentric-sounding woman of wealth who was Mathers's main funder. Archambault had decided to establish herself as part of a new triad controlling the whole Order, equal to these two men.

"You are against this? I was led to believe that the Golden Dawn is open to both men and women at every level," asked Holmes.

"I fear she would tear the Order apart. But Mathers remains conflicted on the matter, and I am pressured by the others to decide. Mr. Holmes, I have neither her charm nor her venom. I went to see her last night only to delay her, whilst I marshalled what support I could."

"Her claim to be a vessel of Thoth, to be in touch with 'Secret Masters'?"

"Cannot be disproven. She has Dadd's cards, imbued with the coded secrets of Hermepolis, Thoth's abode, and . . . well, ours is a fluid field, open to interpretation . . . "

Holmes's response was almost a snarl, an eruption of impatience. "Westcott, I care nothing for your mysteries. This woman has done murder and will answer for her crimes. Or you will, by association. What are her arrangements at St. Mary-of-Egypt? Why is she there?"

It was strange to see so large a man as Westcott made so small.

"She . . . she awaits my capitulation, or Mathers's vote in her favour. That place is a chapel to Thoth now, though not grand, and she conducts her business from there, with Latour, her flunky. I believe she may be quartered at the back of the chapel."

"She could surely afford a hotel, or to rent somewhere grander," I said.

"Her work is private. Two of three of the Order's neophytes attend her on occasion, sworn to secrecy."

"Neophytes such as Douglas Mallory?"

"I recall the name, yes. Not especially promising, but—"

"He is dead."

"Oh God."

"But which god, Westcott? Which god?" Holmes appeared disgusted with the man. "I am but days from establishing specific charges against this woman. You will not respond to any communication you receive from her, but will immediately inform me at Baker Street if any missive arrives. Furthermore, you will write to Mathers this day, and tell him that Marie Dorcas Archambault is wanted for questioning by Scotland Yard. Do you understand, sir?"

"I . . . yes. Yes, I understand."

Holmes drew a notebook and fountain pen.

"There is a pencilled message on the first page. You will duplicate it on the second page in ink, in your usual script, and sign it."

Westcott bent over the card table and did as instructed, giving the notebook back to my friend.

"Good," said Holmes. "I do hope we shall not have cause to cross paths again, Mr. Westcott, except in the course of your regular duties as coroner, naturally, where I feel you are on more solid ground."

And there we left him, flustered and shaking, to give whatever excuse he wished to his fellow diners in the other room.

"I thought we were taking action against Archambault tonight, Holmes?" I said as we sought a hansom on the street outside.

"We are."

"You do not trust Westcott?"

"He may do as I require—but if he panics and tells her of our visit to him, he is at least no wiser as to our specific intentions."

The tenement room co-opted by Holmes was cramped, its floorboards loose, and mould upon the walls. It did, however, give an unimpeded view across the street as the first shadows of dawn became noticeable. The sky was clear, a bright day coming . . .

St. Mary-of-Egypt Chapel, twenty or thirty yards from where we stood, was a plain, squarish building of old, smog-stained brick, one which passers-by might easily mistake for any one of a hundred missions or dissident chapels from this century or the last.

No board of services remained by the main door. If there had ever been a cross or a name on the outside, those too had gone. Its small rectangular windows were covered by peeling shutters, allowing no view of the interior.

"I wish you here for the questioning of Archambault, Madame Rostov—before she is given to the authorities. If we are physically obstructed, you must stay back."

"Mardy Cath knew how to fight," she murmured. "The backstreets of Keighley were not known for curtsey and 'beg your pardon.'"

Holmes pursed his lips. "If I had wished a Yorkshire pugilist at my side, Madame, I would have procured one. For today, I require your talents to remain in less physical realms. We must take this Jean Latour for questioning—Douglas Mallory's sworn statement still stands against him—and seek to confront his mistress."

"She can hardly be innocent," I said.

"What she says, precisely what she says and how she says it, may convict her. You two will be my witnesses. As for any minor members of the Golden Dawn who may be present, we shall see."

"Oh, I am here only for Archambault, Mr. Holmes." Said in such a tone that both I and Holmes stared at her, at which she turned her face away.

I knew my role and slipped into the cheap, slightly frayed jacket which Holmes had provided, passing him my revolver; a plain cap completed the look. I would have preferred to remain armed, but understood well enough that a common errand-runner, supposedly from William Westcott, would hardly have a well-oiled Army revolver to hand.

"I am ready, Holmes."

We crept down onto the street, closing on the chapel. As he and Madame Rostov moved into the shadows, I strode directly to the northern side entrance, the one which Holmes had seen them using. Tugging my cap down, I bent my knuckles to the door with appropriate energy and waited. It was not long before a dark-haired, unshaven man in his thirties, wearing some sort of white habit with a hood, opened the door.

"This is a private place," he said, his voice low. "No beggars or tradesmen."

My face took orders from me and assumed a flustered, almost panicky expression.

"But I bear a letter, sir—from Mr. Westcott. Most urgent, it is, he says, and requires a reply this very hour."

The man bit his lip. "Where have you come from?"

"Duke Street, your honour, with all haste."

This seemed to satisfy him. "Give it to me, then, and wait. Do not move from here."

"Yessir," I mumbled, passing over a folded note which Holmes had given me, that which Westcott had been made to copy out at the restaurant.

I stood in a short, plain corridor, hearing a singular chant from the right, silence from the left, and I judged that the right-hand end must open into the body of the chapel. Some minutes passed, the chant being interrupted or paused, and then continuing. The words being spoken were neither English nor French, of that I was sure.

The dark-haired man returned.

"You must come and speak to the mistress."

My alarmed look was not feigned. I was only supposed to occupy the doorway, to distract, until Holmes slid in.

"I don't know as if I should . . . "

His look made it clear that I had little choice, unless I chose to press the issue physically. Accordingly, I hung my head and accompanied him to the right, into a large open hall, lit by candles along either side. Some pews remained to remind me of the place's chapel origins, but most had been stacked in crude order by the sealed front entrance. A long table served as some sort of altar, bedecked with blue candles in large iron candlesticks, and statues which spoke of Egypt—*ushabtis*, if I recalled my visits to the British Museum with any accuracy. Between them, in the middle of the altar, lay the strange, curved sword, the *khopesh*—the blade we understood to have slain at least three men—on a square of black silk.

There were two women in the hall, though only one caught the eye. She stood behind the altar, tightly-waved dark hair tied back and rather more graceful white robes falling in folds to her feet. On her face was perched an elaborate domino mask, with a long slender beak or bill extending from between the eyeholes—meant to represent an ibis?—and its polished blue lacquer gleamed in the candlelight. She showed no sign of noticing my arrival, her eyes on the plain, unadorned beams of the ceiling.

At the side of the altar table, the other woman was garbed as the man who let me in, hooded, with the white habit secured by scarlet cord around the waist. She came over to the man, and they spoke—out of my hearing—apparently less than pleased at either my appearance or the missive I brought. These would be two of the Golden Dawn neophytes or acolytes mentioned by the coroner. As if losing an argument, the woman went up to the altar and whispered to the . . . priestess, I suppose I would have ranked her.

The blue domino regarded me.

"Take hold of him." The voice was accented, and yes, the accent was French. Surely, I stood in the presence of Marie Dorcas Archambault herself? "Thoth Thrice-Great has spoken to me, and we do not know him."

As the acolytes closed in on me, I heard a loud cough from the entrance corridor.

"I would leave Dr. Watson be, if I were you," said Holmes. "He is an excellent diversion, but a troublesome catch."

The man and woman hesitated; the masked figure smiled, scarlet lips drawn back.

"*M'sieur* Holmes! I did not realise that this shabby fellow was one of yours. My apologies—and such an honour. You have a mind which could be of great value to the Order—almost an embodiment of what Thoth seeks to teach us. But who is that in your shadow?"

Madame Rostov stepped into the hall, her hands thrust into the pockets of her heavy coat.

The ibis beak dipped in her direction. "*Une femme?* I'm afraid I do not know you, *mam'selle*."

"You should," said our companion, who seemed equally unsure. "Surely you have seen me before?"

What she meant by that I did not know.

Holmes rapped his cane on the scuffed wooden floor.

"There are charges levelled against Marie Dorcas Archambault—a series of deeds by her hand, or by her order. In short, the deaths of Gregory Soper, Josef Becskei, Sir Richard Cleves, and Albert Smith; an assault at this lady's house; and a burglary at my own chambers at Baker Street."

The smile left her face. "What are you saying? I know nothing of murder or any crimes."

Not only had her smile fled, I realised—her voice had taken on a cultured English accent.

Holmes tilted his head slightly, staring at her.

"In that case, I imagine you will be ignorant of Eliane Gueret, wanted by the Paris *judiciaire* for fraud, and of Antoinette Sacre, who knifed a wine merchant in Marseille four years ago."

"I . . . I've never heard of either, Mr. Holmes."

"You would not have, for I see that you are not Marie Archambault. May we have your name?"

"A moment, please."

She gestured to the female acolyte, who stepped up to the altar platform. The domino slipped askew, and a hushed, hurried conversation ensued. Holmes seemed at first to be waiting as calmly as he might for a train to arrive or a tobacconist to serve him—but then his nostrils flared, he sniffed the musty, incense-laden air, and . . .

"*Eau d'Lys-blanc*—Watson, that hooded woman is our quarry!"

His cane lifted to point at the female acolyte, and at this, the hall came alive.

By my side, the man cursed and turned towards the side-door, but as he tried to run, he was felled by a vicious kick to the shin from Madame Rostov, who drew out Mrs. Bessovitch's antique pistol and aimed it at his head.

Holmes started towards the altar; the supposed acolyte threw back her hood with one hand, taking up the *khopesh* with the other and pressing its wicked curve against the robed woman's throat. The ceremonial mask fell to the table, revealing the puzzled expression of a woman perhaps Madame Rostov's age, with lively eyes set in a strong face.

"Marie, what are you doing?"

"I do what is *nécessaire*," the Frenchwoman spat out. "You will be unharmed, if Mr. Holmes and his friends leave here. *Immédiatement!*"

"You know that I cannot, Mlle Archambault. I will call you that, though I suspect that we will never know your true name."

"Nor anything about me," she said. "I am like Thoth, self-begotten. And when I have left here, I will create myself again, if it must be so."

I took a surreptitious pace or two forward; the blade drew a bead of blood.

"I see you, *mon cher*, Dr. Watson. And as a medical man, you will be particularly aware of each delicate vessel that pulses beneath this fair skin."

I stopped, wishing that I had my revolver. Not that it would have been an easy shot.

Archambault laughed. "Let me introduce you to Miss Annie Hornimann, a great benefactress of the Hermetic Order of the Golden Dawn. It pleases me to indulge her, as I have today for our Greeting of the Sun. She has such a love of the stage, and has 'stood in' for me more than once at our ceremonies."

"I did not know—"

The blade pressed down, enough to silence Miss Hornimann.

"She is trying to tell you that she knew nothing of how I pursued Dadd's *cartes merveilleuses*, his mysteries—of what had to be done—only that I now had the full suit, and thus the secrets within. She tells the truth. But such changes we will bring, when I stand beside Westcott and Mathers—"

"That will not happen."

"Will it not? I am distraught at your words, Mr. Holmes." She smiled. "What evidence do you have that I have committed any crime? Where is your proof that I am any of these dreadful French felons you named?"

"The evidence merely awaits to be assembled. The police are already involved."

"But where are *les gendarmes*?" She stared around theatrically. "I see them not."

"I have come to hear your response to the charges. What you say may change the situation—marginally, at least."

"How so?" A scornful retort.

Holmes shrugged. "That is what I wish to determine. It is possible you are insane, afflicted much as Richard Dadd was at times. Such may be why you have such an obsession with his Tarot. And the asylum may be gentler than the prison—or the hangman's calloused hands. I see, however, no sign of a disordered mind thus far, only a criminal one. Madame Rostov?"

That lady kept her pistol steady on the fallen man.

"She has taken unnatural pleasure in her actions, but no. I would judge her to be mentally sound, and wicked—if that itself is not a disorder."

"Those eyes!" Archambault appeared to have come to some sudden realisation. "I have seen you!"

"As I have you. On fevered nights, I have watched you commit murder with that blade of yours; watched you scatter your cards of death, and take pleasure in doing so. Your deeds are burned within me."

"My dream. You were in my dream. Thoth Thrice-Great was warning me . . . "

Madame Rostov's laughter was short, hard.

"There is no Thoth, except in your imagined worlds, your self-imposed beliefs. Hard enough to believe there is a loving God, let alone a pantheon of powers forged from the pigments and stones of ancient ruins. The Tarot is a card game, made arcane by dilettantes—you may as well say that a man's fate can be read from the shove-ha'penny board in any public house."

Holmes and I stood, motionless, as the air became so charged between the two women that I half expected sparks to appear.

"But you, you have a gift," said Archambault, sounding slyer. "Where then does that come from, if not from the higher spirits?"

"I have a burden. And it comes from the flesh, from how I were made." The short, flat vowels of Yorkshire were beginning to re-emerge. "What I see is not to my liking. You are not to my liking, Marie Archambault. And if—"

It was then that the man at Madame Rostov's feet made his move, kicking out and trying to rise. The pistol fired, achingly loud in the bare chapel. Annie Hornimann twisted in Archambault's grip, the blade no longer at her throat, and dove under the table, scrabbling to get off the wooden platform—Archambault shrieked, swinging wildly, and fell . . .

My dramatic side urges me to write that the Frenchwoman accidentally impaled herself upon her own Egyptian blade, but as with much in life, nothing so artful occurred. She fell, in fact, upon one of the massive candlesticks, and the two- or three-inch iron spike—which stood proud to hold the candle in place—was driven into her breast by her own weight. She gasped, and dark blood frothed at her lips.

"Watson!" called out Holmes.

I looked around, dazed at the suddenness of it all. The man lay groaning, his arm shattered by a pistol ball and blood running down his robe. Archambault gripped the table with both hands, trying to rise to her feet.

"Archambault," Holmes insisted, to solve my dilemma.

But the spike had entered her body just below the breastbone, and gone in to its full length. From the amount of blood running down the candlestick, and of that same fluid pulsing from between her lips, I judged the internal damage to be severe—a rupture of the descending aorta seemed most likely. Withdrawal of the spike could result in immediate death.

"I'm not certain that she can be saved, Holmes," I said, my judgement hastened by the fact that the heavy drapes around the platform were smouldering, set off by still-lit candles which had toppled from their holders. "Not in circumstances such as this."

"Then first come assist me with this man, who should survive. I suspect him to be Latour, her servant. Lestrade will need his testimony, to add to that of Douglas Mallory."

I thought him a touch callous, but could not fault his logic. Latour—if it was him—was a simple case. No vital artery had been hit, but the bones of the lower arm were shattered; there was risk of shock and infection, and he might yet lose his arm below the elbow. Holmes used a pocketknife to cut a strip from the man's loose habit, and I applied a hasty tourniquet to Latour's arm, binding it to his side as best I could.

Madame Rostov was already guiding the complaining Miss Hornimann towards the exit, as more vigorous flames began to lick at peeling paint and dry beams. We had minutes yet, but it was certain that St. Mary-of-Egypt would be fully ablaze before any fire appliance could arrive.

I managed to get Latour to his feet; Holmes added his strength to mine.

"I must go back for Archambault," I said as we managed to get the wounded man into the open air. "Though I fear that moving her would kill her."

"No more than will the fire. Tend to your patient—I will see to the woman."

I led Latour, who groaned but made no other protest, to where Madame Rostov and Miss Hornimann stood.

"I did not know!" the false priestess was protesting to our companion. "I swear it." She plucked at her begrimed white robes. "She said she spoke with intelligence from the Secret Master, that there were games to be played, actions which were needed for renewal of the Order, but this . . . "

"The police will require you," I snapped.

"Let them have me." She looked directly at me, jaw firm. "I have been deceived, Dr. Watson, even used. I am no murderess, nor thief."

I hesitated, not because I was interested at that moment in what she had to say, but because if I went back to assist Holmes, I left Madame Rostov in the company of two strangers, one of whom at least was a villain. I looked to her.

"Go," she said.

If there had been recent rain, or if the morning air had been damp, it might have been different. Dry and clear. The chapel burned with a vengeance, removing itself from Hammersmith in a tower of sparks and billowing smoke. I thrust myself through the side-door and found Holmes already heading towards me, arm over his mouth and nose. He had the *khopesh* in its silk wrappings under one arm.

"She is not there!" he said as he threw the blade to the ground at Madame Rostov's feet. "It may be vital evidence," he said to her, and then: "Follow me, Watson."

"She is not there"—how could that be?

Holmes ran for the other side of the building, ducking as flames jetted from a ruined window, and I was at his heels.

"I thought . . . " I gasped, "the other side entrance . . . was locked?"

"It was."

And yet we saw, as we turned the corner, that it stood open, a heavy iron candlestick cast on its side in the doorway. She herself must have torn it from her breast.

Holmes scanned the rough earth around us.

"A woman's boots, dragging—and a trail of blood. No other fresh prints. She is alone."

"Astonishing that she can stand," I said, casting around into the grey morning.

Around us, mean dwellings and warehouses, a hundred blank walls and closed doors; beyond them, the Thames. A child's face, pressed to a grimy window, showed little interest in us.

"She heads for the river." Holmes darted forward like a young bloodhound, reading the earth as we went. "She paused . . . Watson, that bundle by the corner—she struggled from her coarse habit . . . it must have been impeding her."

I had not been wrong about her wound, I knew. No normal

woman could have done these things, and I wondered at the sheer willpower which drove her.

On we went, down an alley between two commercial buildings—a fresh, bloody handprint on a weathered wall, the deeper imprint print of two boots where she must have paused. We followed, turned, nearing the river and Marlborough Wharf . . .

"There, Holmes!"

The pink-tinged light of dawn betrayed a solitary figure by a workman's shed, only yards from the sluggish waters of the Thames; a coal-barge was heading upriver, the bargeman and his boy staring in our direction. They must have been wondering at two men closing in on a lone woman, for the bargeman yelled something which was swept away with wind and tide.

Holmes slowed.

"Archambault," he called out, a clear voice. "I have the doctor with me."

She turned towards us, and I saw that she had something clutched in her right hand, pressing it to her wound.

"The flesh may weaken, *M'sieur*." Her voice was hoarse, weaker than before. "Yet the spirit endures. If this body fails, Thoth will guide mine to new wonders."

"He will not!"

A sudden voice from behind me made me start and wheel round. It was Madame Rostov.

"Thoth is not here," she said. "Nor does he dwell in what you hold."

"I am his Blade." The Frenchwoman spat, gripping her burden the more tightly. "I have the Swords which hold His wisdom."

And I realised that what she held in trembling fingers was the suit of Tarot cards which had cost so many lives. I looked to Holmes, opened my mouth to speak, but he stood impassive, leaning on his cane with his attention clearly on the two women.

"How do you think we knew you, what you had done?" asked Madame Rostov. "Through divine enlightenment, or the hoary voices of 'Secret Masters' upon the Aether?"

"With trickery, small betrayals." Archambault sneered at her. "Fragments wormed from the weak and easily cowed. I am not them. And I have all within my grasp."

Our companion stood unmoved, unimpressed.

"You deceive yourself, Marie—as you have always done, I

suspect. You were betrayed by my sight, and by Sherlock Holmes's intellect. All that you will grasp is grave-dirt and the worm."

If I had sometimes chided Holmes for his coldness, I shivered at our companion's tone, by the ice in her eyes and on her tongue.

The Frenchwoman spat again—not, I thought, from disdain this time, but to clear her throat of bloody phlegm. "You—you should have been my aide, not that dilettante Hornimann. And I still have Richard Dadd's cards, still to reveal their secrets."

"Because the Ace of Swords is the key."

"I see you understand."

"Only your folly and your failure, Marie." Madame Rostov seemed oddly sad. She slid her hand under her coat and brought out a single Tarot card. "For I have the true Ace in my hands, given to me by Mr. Sherlock Holmes after your poor Mallory tried to enter my home. If this card will unlock hidden truths, it will not do so for you—yours is a counterfeit, artfully altered, a nonsense which would have taught you nothing."

"I do not . . . "

"Look at me."

Their gazes met, grey eyes and brown; the moment seemed eternal, but Archambault was the first to look away, turning to Holmes.

"*C'est vrai?*"

"It is true. I would not lie, *mam'selle*," said the detective. "Not in this weighty matter."

She stared down at her clutching hand, and—to my astonishment—threw the Tarot cards to the wind, with what must have been the last of remaining strength. Her hair was loose, wild, and her bloody lips were smiling.

"To my Secret Master, then!" she cried out, and before we could move, she cast herself into the river, a short plummet from the cobbled wharf-side and into the Father of London.

Holmes and I rushed forward, but there was nothing to be seen or to be done—the Thames had opened its muddy weed-choked jaws and swallowed her, entire.

"Could she be alive?" he asked.

I did not answer, but gazed upon the waters, wondering if at any moment, a bedraggled head might arise above the surface.

It did not.

"The trial would have been . . . a complicated affair," said

Holmes. "Westcott and Mathers will be relieved; Lestrade will be annoyed, but will accept what we give him."

"Hornimann?"

"Most likely a dupe, as she herself protested. There is little with which to charge her, unless play-acting and being deceived are crimes within the statute book. Obstruction, perhaps, but we are not police officers about their public duties."

"No, Holmes, what I meant was, where is she? I left her and Latour outside the chapel—I thought that Madame Ros—"

"Miss Hornimann awaits our return, a wary constable at her side." Our companion was down on one knee on the cobbled lane, picking up abandoned Tarot cards. "He came running to investigate the fire, and I used your name freely, Mr. Holmes, before I followed you."

Holmes frowned. "You did not know where we had gone."

"I did not need to. My mind saw the river, and her desperation. It was enough. Doctor, will you take these for a moment, please."

And she thrust into my hand several Tarot cards. Before I could protest, she kneeled to retrieve more of the cards, ones which lay nearer the water. Those I held were slick with Marie Archambault's blood—tainted, so it felt.

"These damnable things . . . " I found my handkerchief and wrapped them within, trying to wipe my fingers clean, and failing. "I never want to see them again."

"I have them now," said Madame Rostov, standing up and taking the cards back from me. She had the entire suit in her left hand, the true Ace of Swords upturned on top. "Upright, unequivocal in its meaning. Truth and justice; the virtues of the mind, applied with wisdom. Or so others might say. A memento for you, Mr. Holmes?"

She held them out in front of her; Holmes drew in a long, deep breath.

"A bloody dawn, hardly a golden one," he said. "I suggest they stay in your keeping, Catherine Weatherhead. I do not think they could be in safer hands, nor—without their destruction—less likely to be misused again."

"You do not fear their 'secrets'?"

"Richard Dadd was ill, a troubled man. No doubt that is reflected in his creations, and I suspect that in the intricate details, in the finest lines of his brush or pen, there would be found only chaos and confusion, not orderly intelligence. I do not need Rosicrucians or Hermetics to persuade me of any other conclusion."

"An apt judgement," she said. "In its way."

The Swords slid inside her coat, lost from sight. What became of them afterwards, I do not know. Perhaps they lie idle inside an old copper mug on one of Mrs. Bessovitch's shelves, or have been thrust, forgotten, under an old mattress. The matter was never mentioned again.

On Marlborough Wharf, I doffed my cap to Madame Rostov.

"Madame, you have been invaluable."

"I have been what I am, Doctor Watson. But thank you."

And there we parted, Holmes and I to find the constable and his charges, our companion presumably to return to Southwark.

"A fine woman," said Holmes, his aquiline features betraying no emotion as we walked. "Perceptive and most able. Nevertheless, her methods are . . . best not dwelt upon."

Smoke drifted in our direction—St. Mary-of-Egypt was still burning—and I heard the distant clang of a fire bell.

"Though Madame Rostov's visions still puzzle me," I said—knowing that I should not have done. "Surely one who had been born with some sense of others' thoughts, a 'telepathy,' not yet properly investigated or defined, which let them into others' minds . . . "

"What of it?"

"Well, she did not report the Frenchwoman's inner thoughts, did not claim to know them in that way. Instead, she described Archambault's murderous tableaux as if from outside, an observer in a place where she could not rationally be. Dashed odd, that."

Holmes traced the tip of his cane through a congealing pool of blood on the cobbles and was silent for a moment. Seeing his dark expression, I gave an exaggerated laugh, as if freeing myself of what I had raised.

"But what does it matter, eh? You and I are men of science, of that which can be measured and defined. Great Scott, we have more than enough wickedness to deal with in this mundane world, without wasting time on idle conjecture!"

A thin smile acknowledged my clumsy attempt to change course.

"For my part, Watson, I believe . . . "

I waited, wondering what his response might be.

"I believe," he continued, "that all this smoke makes me crave a plate of buttered, well-scorched toast. And a bracing cup of Darjeeling from the 'mystic' East. I would rather not face poor Lestrade on an empty stomach."

"A capital idea, Holmes," I said. "A capital idea."

The mournful hoot of a steam-tug sounded upriver. Hammersmith Bridge was alive with early traffic. London was awake, hungry—and so, strangely after what had just occurred, was I.

For those curious about the *sequelae* to such affairs—as readers of my accounts so often are—Georges Latour was not French, but a Kentish sailor and card sharper, who had fallen into Archambault's company in Dover port. He may not have struck the blows which killed Soper, Becskei, or Cleves, but his seaman's knots were the ones which bound them. In the end, he was hanged for the murder of Albert Smith, for Holmes soon found evidence enough to connect him to that brutal act, upon which revelation he confessed.

William Westcott resigned from the Golden Dawn, encouraged by a polite but terse communication from the Lord Chief Justice. I know this because I saw the very pointed note which Holmes despatched to Lord Russell of Killowen, the occupant of that lofty post at the time.

Of Miss Annie Hornimann, I heard only that she assisted the police without argument, and thereafter maintained a lower profile in the circles of the mystic and the arcane, directing more of her energies to supporting theatrical ventures.

I will not commit this story to the pages of *The Strand*, for reasons which I feel are quite obvious. And, yes, it may be some time before I play cards again . . .

Catherine no longer starts with alarm in bed at night; she does not wake to find her shift drawn tight to her with sweat. No scene of threat or bloody murder has come to enter her mind unbidden. Not since St. Mary-of-Egypt and Hammersmith.

But if she dreams too deep, too long, she has other fears. She fears that she will be drowned, enfathomed, staring up through tangled weed and silted current. In the grip of shifting waters, she tries to breathe; her bloated fingers reach vainly for the light, as her treasonous skin, ever more grey and mottled, peels away with each new tide.

Above her lies a world of air and life, of blood, semen, and ordure, so far from her grasp . . .

Yet the spirit endures.

The Adventure of the Tarot Card Prophecies

Angela Yuriko Smith

Upon my recent return to our shared lodgings at 221B Baker Street from an ambulatory sojourn, I harbored the notion that I might coax my esteemed companion from the confines of our quarters to partake in the invigorating air of the morning. The city, having been thoroughly drenched by a recent downpour, now appeared washed anew, and the day's promise seemed to beckon for participation.

Holmes, as usual, was ensconced in the daily news.

"Watson, an odd assortment of people have been vanishing from the streets of London with no witnesses, evidence, or seeming connection."

A perfect opportunity, I thought to myself, to entice Holmes out of the flat and into the fresh air under the pretense of investigating.

However, scarcely had I an opportunity to propose my plan, when an insistent jangle of the doorbell rendered the matter moot, and within moments, our solitude was interrupted.

A young lady of some distinction was ushered into our sitting room, introduced to us as Miss Pamela. Her bearing was one of self-assured poise, yet beneath this, her agitated state was discernible. An attractive woman, she was adorned in a manner that suggested a taste for the dramatic, a touch of the exotic, and possibly an affiliation with the theater. She was garbed in a striking dress of claret velvet, embellished with silver cord, and sported a prominent toque of the same vibrant hue, decorated with silver beads and a pin bearing the Egyptian Eye of Horus. Encircling her neck was a peculiar amulet, a sapphire blue glass bauble shaped like an eye. Her countenance was a study of delicate features, set against a dusky complexion. Her gaze was alert, intelligent and possessed of a certain enigma, yet bore no trace of hostility.

Throughout my travels, which encompass several nations and three continents, seldom have I encountered a woman whose visage so strongly suggested a combination of astuteness and benevolence. Despite her self-assured demeanor, I could not help but observe a moment's hesitation as she accepted the chair Holmes had proffered, her hand faintly trembling and a subtle air of defiance about her.

"I am grateful for your time, Mr. Holmes," she began, "I sought your aid as the tales of your extraordinary deductive prowess have not escaped my notice."

"Ah, word travels," he said pensively. "Indeed, not every consulting detective is privileged with a constant witness at his continual disposal. However, I must refute any attribution of my deductions to any form of sorcery. My methods are firmly grounded in the sciences and astute observation."

"Regardless of the source of your abilities, they appear nothing short of miraculous to me. This happens to align with my own area of expertise and source of livelihood. However, if you disclaim any supernatural inclinations, I am willing to accept that, provided you can assist me. I am hard-pressed to conceive of a more baffling predicament than the one I currently find myself in."

Holmes rubbed his hands together with a sense of anticipation, his eyes gleaming with the promise of an intellectual challenge. His hawk-like features sharpened into a visage of keen focus as he leaned forward in his chair. "I entreat you to acquaint me with the particulars of your predicament," he urged in an energetic tone.

"Permit me to summarize," she resumed, "the salient details are thus: I am a professional medium, earning my livelihood through communication with the spirits, prognostication, the crafting of charms, and the vending of esoteric artifacts of notable potency. Of late, I have come into possession of a series of paintings by the deranged artist and murderer Richard Dadd. His insanity fuels his brilliance, and his artwork channels realms beyond our mortal ken, serving both as conduits for active sorcery and divination. I have discreetly commissioned Dadd to produce a series of paintings for my own purposes: to illustrate a Tarot deck of my own design, a deck of peculiar significance. The deck has been completed and all the prints returned to me by the engraver. I had them secured without fear for their safety until I performed a reading for myself last night, and all the cards drawn belonged to the Suit of Swords. Upon drawing the Ten of Swords, I felt a sense of impending peril. My card reading indicated a betrayal, hinting that the culprit may be an acquaintance. I initially intended to identify the perpetrator using my own methods, but subsequent draws revealed nothing more than warnings of loss and betrayal. I took every precaution to secure all entry points to my residence and fortified my charms. Yet, at dawn, I awoke to find the cupboard where I had stored Dadd's paintings ajar and devoid of its contents. I hastened to dress myself and set out directly for here—" Here she faltered, clutching the amulet around her neck, her words stifled by a sob.

"You ascertained that the paintings were in the cabinet before you retired, yet they were absent upon your awakening?" inquired Holmes, flipping open a leather-bound notebook.

"Indeed, I distinctly recall securing it after my examination."

"And the entrances to your abode? Were any found to be compromised when you arose?"

"Not to my recollection, but I assure you I verified each one before my departure."

"Who else was privy to the fact that you kept the paintings at your private residence?"

"I reside above my establishment, so it stands to reason that one might deduce the paintings' location. However, the engraver personally delivered them to me the day prior."

"Was he accompanied? Was there any other item of value missing that you took note of?" pursued Holmes.

"No, and he was only accompanied by his young apprentice, a lad who can't be more than eleven summers old. I find it highly unlikely that either he or the printer would purloin the paintings. The printer, in fact, was quite intrigued by the project of printing this Tarot deck, having a keen interest in the occult himself. He offered me his services at a rather favorable rate. The paintings have been in his care for the past half-year; if he had designs on them, he could have feigned their theft during that time.

In terms of their monetary value, the paintings are of moderate worth. Their creator is a patient at Broadmoor Hospital. He is a remarkably gifted individual and, in my estimation, a genius whose recognition will only grow with time. The only other item missing is one of the earliest printed decks. The printer brought two samples when he delivered the paintings so I could assess the quality of his craftsmanship. This is the remaining deck. As you can see for yourselves, the work is of impeccable quality." As she spoke, she untied a paper parcel and presented us with an oversized deck of cards, their reverse adorned with intricate runes instead of the more traditional pattern of playing cards. Holmes received the deck from her.

"Your account is most intriguing," declared Sherlock Holmes, examining the strange cards one by one. "How did you ascertain so quickly that one deck was purloined?"

"After the unsettling reading last night, I left the cards strewn across the table. I was too discomposed to perform my usual rituals to cleanse the cards, so I let them be. It was then that I made certain all the doors and windows were secured and confirmed the safety of Dadd's paintings. This morning, however, I found my table pristine. Whoever made off with the paintings also swept clean the deck from my table and absconded with the entire set."

"Upon my word, this is indeed a tantalizing enigma," Holmes remarked. "What is your intended course of action, Miss Pamela?"

"That is precisely what I hoped you might advise me on."

"We may need a thorough inspection of your dwelling and your place of business, given their close proximity. If you have no objection, Dr. Watson and I would like to inspect the premises, if it becomes necessary. He and I have collaborated on numerous occasions and I consider him to be of the highest caliber."

"Would it impose upon you to accompany us?" she queried, a flicker of uncharacteristic timidity in her eyes. "If it becomes necessary?"

"I would consider it an honor and a pleasure," I replied promptly, "if I may be of assistance in any way."

"I am deeply grateful to you both," she responded. "Shall we depart together forthwith, or would you prefer to rendezvous with me there at a later time? I can provide the address."

"Provide us with the address and we shall follow if needed," Holmes responded. "There is, however, one additional matter. Might I retain the remaining deck of cards for a more detailed examination? I assure you they will be returned."

"Yes, of course," she replied. "Your insight is most appreciated."

"You have my gratitude," he said, accepting the cards from her. "Let us examine these, then." He spread the pasteboard rectangles across the table, casting quick, darting glances from one to another. He flipped and rearranged them, creating different configurations. "The artwork of this artist is indeed distinctive," he remarked, "but there can be no doubt as to the quality of both the art and the printing. I shall commence my investigation here and then follow where it leads."

"I am indebted to you both for your assistance."

"I anticipated such a response. Be safe on your return. It's only half past eight. Good day to you."

"Good day," responded our visitor, and with an optimistic glance cast between the two of us, she hastened down the staircase and through the front door. Approaching the window, I observed her disappear down the street until her claret toque and silver beads were swallowed up by the more modestly attired crowd.

"What is your opinion of her purported divination abilities?" I queried, turning to Holmes.

He flashed an indulgent smile. "It is crucial," he said, "not to allow your judgment to be swayed by flights of fancy. Whether or not she possesses the ability to predict the future through some spiritual connection is immaterial in this instance. Keep your focus on the facts at hand, Watson. Her metaphysical qualities bear no relevance to the situation which involves, let us remember, the theft of paintings, and nothing more."

"But in this particular case—"

"One must never allow for exceptions. An exception undermines the rule. Have you ever delved into the realm of the supernatural? The majority of it is naught but misdirection and chicanery. But I won't condemn a person for earning a living through their intellect, especially since there are many who lack their own and are thus compelled to pay for others to think on their behalf. Whether or not there is a communion with spirits is immaterial to me. She claims to hear the voices of spirits. If she professed to hear cats speaking, or a carriage horse, it would not alter my work by a jot."

"Yet, it does seem she may have foreseen her own burglary," I countered. "The paintings disappeared overnight from a secured cabinet while the doors and windows remained locked."

Holmes shook his head. "I do not predict the need to seek an opportunity to investigate Miss Pamela's living quarters and place of business at this point. In fact, it may be unwise to do so. We must not draw attention to ourselves, nor draw any conclusions," he said.

"We do not plan to investigate her premises ourselves? What do you plan to do instead?" I queried, both incredulous and disappointed.

"Smoke," he replied. "There is a freshness to the air that I find myself compelled to sully, and I beg you not to engage me in conversation until it is time for us to depart." He curled up in his chair, his eyes closed, his hawk-like nose acting as a shelter for his black clay pipe. He was so quiet that I began to believe he had drifted off to sleep, and was contemplating joining him, when suddenly he leapt up, his eyes bright and alert, and set his pipe on the mantelpiece.

"I believe it is time for us to be on our way," he said. "Don your hat and let us proceed. I plan to traverse the City first, and we can have some lunch on the way. I would also like to pay a visit to the printer, who may be able to provide us with some useful insights. I am confident that he will prove more beneficial to our investigation than any spirits. They have never been of assistance to me in the past, and I do not anticipate that they will be inclined to aid me today."

"But how do you know which printer to visit?" I inquired, genuinely puzzled. "I don't recall Miss Pamela providing a name or an address."

"My dear Watson, the printer's mark is hidden within the design on the backs of the cards. In small print, just here, you can discern the name of his shop. There, do you see?"

He held up one of the tarot cards, tapping his long, pale finger along the bottom edge. I leaned in for a closer look, and indeed, I could make out a name. Brackenbury Prints & Co.

"Holmes, to even notice, let alone read—"

"Yes, Watson. With keen observation, the world can keep no secrets from us. Neither this one, nor the next. Let us be off!" He was already halfway down the stairs, coat snatched from its hook, and I was in danger of being left behind. I hastily followed, with no further delay.

We journeyed via the Underground to South Kensington, and a brief amble brought us to Holland Park, where Brackenbury Prints & Co. was situated. It was an unpretentious establishment, devoid of any outward signs of gentility, yet one could perceive a tangible aura of diligent craftsmanship and expertise. The signage was weather-beaten and exhibited a certain shabbiness, but the gold lettering on the faded wood and the door was freshly daubed and sharp in its clarity. The door itself, upon our entry, gave such a plaintive groan that it became clear why no additional bell was required to herald the arrival of patrons.

A young lad appeared behind a well-worn, ink-stained counter.

The shop, barring the ink blots, was maintained with an immaculate attention to detail that could have rivaled Mrs. Hudson's own housekeeping standards, assuming she could overlook the stained wood.

"Can I be of service, gentlemen?" the boy inquired, and I immediately surmised that he was the apprentice to the printer, presumably Mr. Brackenbury.

Holmes, initially silent, scrutinized the lad meticulously, his gaze darting around the room before returning to the boy. After a moment, he finally addressed him.

"I have a matter to discuss with the proprietor of this esteemed establishment," said Holmes, "in relation to the printing of these." He retrieved the small, paper-bound parcel from his coat pocket and presented it to the boy. The child recoiled as soon as his eyes alighted upon the stack of cards, his expression one of palpable unease.

"Yes, sir. I'll fetch Mr. Brackenbury for you posthaste." The lad made to turn, but Holmes restrained him, extending the cards towards him and observing how the boy recoiled in their presence.

"You appear to harbor a certain aversion to tarot, young man. Is it the suggestion of mysticism or the artistic representation that perturbs you?" Holmes questioned.

The boy shook his head vehemently. "I find none of it to my liking," he said, retreating slightly. "Neither the spirits, the art, nor the sorceress who brought them to us." He turned as if to dart away, but a tall, gaunt gentleman had entered the chamber.

"Such is no way to speak of a valued customer," the man admonished, "and it is unspeakably rude in the presence of potential, esteemed patrons. To the back with you to clean the ink from the plates." He dismissed the boy with a wave of his hand, and the lad complied, exuding the relief of one liberated from the gallows on his death day.

"How may I assist you, gentlemen? And please accept my apologies for the boy's unacceptable conduct." His gaze fell upon the deck of cards in Holmes' hand.

"Curious," Mr. Brackenbury remarked. "Are you acquainted with Miss Pamela? Perhaps you are a client of hers? You don't appear to be the sort, but I refrain from judging a book by its cover in my profession. I am somewhat taken aback that she would relinquish a set. I provided her with only two for proofing, and she insisted that she required them both urgently. Normally, I furnish only a single set for client approval, but she possesses a certain persuasive charm, as I'm sure you gentlemen have observed."

"I have made no such observation," Holmes countered. "How did you come to know Miss Pamela? Was there an introduction, or did she discover you through other means?"

Mr. Brackenbury appeared to flush slightly, an unusual occurrence for a man of his pallid and lean countenance. Some might consider him handsome in a scholarly manner, more suited to the quietude of a library than the rigors of the outdoors. His attire was uncomplicated and practical—sturdy breeches and a plain China blue shirt with rolled-up sleeves, marked by ink stains. His hair was dark, thin, and straight.

"She was first mentioned to me by a mutual acquaintance, a wealthy patron. Miss Morgana, as she is named, is deeply fascinated by the esoteric occult and frequently employs me for projects such as this. She told me Miss Pamela had expressed an interest in commissioning a tarot deck. Miss Pamela simply walked into my shop one day and inquired if I could assist her with a project of a unique nature—" Mr. Brackenbury halted mid-sentence as he noticed Holmes' penetrating gaze fixed upon him, his eyes narrowed over his aquiline nose. He resembled a hawk swooping down upon its unsuspecting quarry.

"Is . . . something the matter?" Mr. Brackenbury seemed disconcerted by Holmes' intense scrutiny.

Holmes began rifling through the cards in his hand, evidently searching for a specific one. "Tell me, Mr. Brackenbury, did you serve as a model for any of these cards?" Holmes finally found what he was looking for. "Aha! This one, for instance?"

I glanced at the card Holmes brandished. It portrayed a man suspended from a tree by a single ankle. The man's attire was of a medieval flavor, featuring red stockings and a blue, peasant-style shirt. With his hands bound behind his back and one leg folded behind the other in his suspended state, it appeared to be a decidedly uncomfortable position, yet the man's expression was one of tranquility. He even sported a halo. At the top of the card, the Roman numerals XII were inscribed in bold type, and at the bottom, it simply read XII THE HANGED MAN.

"By Jove! I must say, it does bear a striking resemblance to you," I blurted out.

Mr. Brackenbury's blush deepened at my observation.

"I cannot deny that I've had similar thoughts, and I suspect that might be why Miss Pamela was so eager to commission my services. She offered to triple my usual rate if I could have the decks ready by the 19th of March, though usually those of her profession are not as flush with earnings as might be claimed. I suspected Miss Morgana was behind the actual funding. She did indeed compare this particular painting to me, lauding my appearance. She is quite a forthright woman, that one. No disrespect intended. I was rather flattered. She seemed quite pleased that I resembled the man in the painting."

"Do you know who the man in the painting is meant to represent?" Holmes inquired.

Mr. Brackenbury shook his head. "I'm afraid not. She did mention a name, but as it was unfamiliar to me, it didn't stick. I believe it was something akin to Gladd or Dadd, but I can't be certain."

"Could the name have been of one Richard Dadd?" Mr. Brackenbury gave Holmes a puzzled look, so Holmes continued on to enlighten him.

"Currently installed at Broadmoor Hospital after being committed as criminally insane for murdering his father and attacking an innocent man with a razor en route to Paris in a misguided attempt to escape. He was first committed to the criminal department of Bethlem Royal Hospital, also known as Bedlam. He became mad in the company of one Sir Thomas Phillips, the former mayor of Newport, who entreated Dadd to accompany him on an expedition through Europe that ended in Egypt. It was there that Dadd became afflicted, insisting that he was under the influence of the Egyptian god Osiris. He is a painter of great skill. They allow him to continue his art as therapy, fortunately, as he is quite talented. Was this the Dadd that Miss Pamela referred to?"

Mr. Brackenbury seemed taken aback. "Perhaps, I am not positive. You know quite a lot about this seemingly obscure artist."

"I enjoy his work," Holmes answered. "I find it evocative of intense observation, perhaps even beyond what can be observed by those inflicted with sanity." Holmes slid XII THE HANGED MAN back into the deck and then paused, once more scrutinizing the cards with great intensity.

"Even more intriguing," Holmes remarked. He held up another card for our inspection. The man depicted had piercing eyes, peering out from the card above a prominent, beak-like nose. His thin lips were set in a pale face. Rather than feet, he perched upon talons. He was nude, save for the dense fur that covered his lower body. Horns sprouted from his head, and an inverted star adorned his forehead. Bat-like wings unfurled from his back. In one hand, he brandished a flaming torch, while the other was raised towards the heavens in a peculiar gesture. A man and a woman, both unclothed, were chained beneath him. At the top of the card, the Roman numerals XV were printed in bold type, while at the bottom, it simply read XV THE DEVIL.

"Rather risqué, indeed," I commented.

Mr. Brackenbury furrowed his brow, squinting at the card in Holmes's hand. "If I may be so bold, sir, what about it has caught your interest?"

Holmes turned to him, his hawk-like gaze intense. "It seems Miss Pamela has developed a peculiar fascination with my visage, as well. Yet, the symbols and images within these cards suggest a narrative far more disquieting."

"Do you imply these cards reflect some darker intentions of Miss Pamela?" I asked, my interest piqued.

"Possibly, though she seems perhaps more of a pawn in this game," responded Holmes, a knowing smirk playing on his lips. "But to ascertain that with any certainty, perhaps we should pay Miss Morgana a visit first and hear what she has to say for herself."

Mr. Brackenbury's expression turned grave. "I must caution you, gentlemen, Miss Morgana is not a woman to be trifled with."

"Perhaps," I began, but my words trailed off as a jolt of comprehension hit me. "By Jove, Holmes! That's you!"

"Indeed, it would seem so," Holmes replied calmly. He slid the card back into the deck and rewrapped the package. "Most intriguing."

Mr. Brackenbury's countenance grew serious. "I must caution you again, gentlemen, Miss Morgana has certain powers. I am not normally a superstitious man but there are things in this world which are unexplainable. She is one of them. I would advocate for prudence."

"We shall heed your advice," Holmes replied, rising from his seat. "Your help has been invaluable, Mr. Brackenbury. We are grateful."

As we exited the shop, an unsettling sensation crept over me. The cards we had just scrutinized were unnerving, to put it mildly. The fact that Miss Morgana had shown such a pointed interest in both Holmes and Mr. Brackenbury was disquieting.

"Do you believe her to be a threat?" I asked Holmes as we traversed the bustling London streets.

"It's premature to draw any conclusions," he replied, his eyes diligently studying the surrounding throng. "Nevertheless, we must remain vigilant. I'm afraid we will not be inspecting Miss Pamala's abode, Watson. There are more pressing matters."

We reached Miss Morgana's residence just as dusk was descending. The estate was expansive, encased within a towering stone wall.

As we neared the majestic entrance, the gates creaked open, granting us access. A single, silent butler met us at the door, as if we were expected, and granted us admittance. The mansion was dimly illuminated, with sparse torchlight casting eerie shadows along the walls. We wound our way through the labyrinthine corridors, flanked by ornate vases and paintings depicting grotesque creatures. The air was laden with the heady aroma of incense, and the distant murmur of chanting echoed from the depths of the mansion.

At last, we entered the grand hall. Miss Morgana was ensconced on a throne-like chair, garbed in a billowing black gown, a silver tiara nestled in her raven tresses. Her gaze, affixed on us, shimmered with an uncanny intensity.

"Pray, enter gentlemen," she beckoned, her voice dripping with a certain saccharine charm. "To what do I owe the pleasure of this visit?"

Holmes, with his customary composure, held the gaze of Miss Morgana as he advanced a step. "We wish to gain insight into the provenance of a tarot deck I believe you commissioned with Miss Pamela as your envoy," he spoke, the words deliberate and even.

A hint of a mischievous smile danced on Miss Morgana's lips. "My tarot cards? Do they pique your interest, then?"

"They provoke concern," I interjected, no longer able to maintain my silence in the face of disquietude.

"Concern?" The smile of Miss Morgana broadened. "Indeed, isn't that the crux of their allure? The cards are intended to expose the murkier facets of our being, the elements unuttered in genteel society."

"But what of the figure in the Hanged Man card? The image resembles your long-time printer, Mr. Brackenbury," queried Holmes, his voice dropping an octave. "And what of the figure in XV, the Devil?"

A flicker of amusement crossed Miss Morgana's eyes. "Ah, Mr. Brackenbury. He is a cherished associate of mine. As for the Devil, he personifies the shadowy impulses harbored within all of us. Those aspects we strive to restrain, yet often find ourselves unable to."

"Indeed," replied Holmes, his countenance betraying no emotion.

Suddenly rising from her seat of authority, Miss Morgana advanced towards us, her movements embodying a captivating blend of elegance and menace. "However, I presume you did not journey here merely to debate my choice of divination tools?"

A wordless exchange passed between Holmes and me. My mood was thrown off balance by her abrupt shift in mannerism. In this dark hall it was easier to believe in the occult. Undeterred, Holmes stepped forward, fixing Miss Morgana under his penetrating scrutiny. "We are investigating a curious burglary in the vicinity. Have you heard anything pertaining to such?"

A shadow flitted across Miss Morgana's face. "Rumors have reached me, certainly. But I assure you, I am not implicated."

A single eyebrow arched upward on Holmes' forehead. "However, your fascination with the more somber facets of human nature and the occult could suggest otherwise."

An amused chuckle escaped from Miss Morgana, its melodious resonance sending an involuntary shudder down my spine. "Oh, Mr. Holmes, so eager to leap to assumptions. While I may harbor an interest in the macabre, it hardly implicates me as a burglar."

Unperturbed, Holmes responded, "Nevertheless, your insight on the matter would be of considerable aid."

Miss Morgana reclined leisurely in her seat, her eyes sparking with mischief. "I might have chanced upon some information," she murmured, her tone provocative. "But what is my incentive to assist you?"

Holmes inched closer to Miss Morgana, his visage as unfathomable as ever. "The gratification of facilitating justice," he offered, his voice barely louder than a hushed murmur.

Miss Morgana's gaze narrowed, and for an instant, I

anticipated a denial. However, she exhaled a sigh of resignation and leaned in. "Very well," she conceded. "I've listened in on hushed murmurings about a covert assembly operating within London's shadowy underbelly. They dub themselves The Order of the Black Hand, and they are believed to be orchestrating many crimes connected to the occult, going so far as to even kidnapping innocents."

Holmes contemplated her words with a nod. "Do you have any notion of where they might be located?"

Miss Morgana responded with a shake of her head. "Regrettably, no. Their operations are shrouded in secrecy, making them elusive. However, I am aware of their keen interest in the arcane. If I discover anything I think will be of value to you, I will be sure to alert you."

"Your cooperation is appreciated," Holmes acknowledged, turning to make his exit. "Should we require further clarification, we may seek your counsel once more."

With that, we took our leave.

As we tread the cobblestone streets under the cloak of darkness, an involuntary shiver traced my spine. The existence of a secret society operating clandestinely, responsible for the mysterious abductions of unsuspecting citizens, was a ghastly thought. A sidelong glance at Holmes revealed him engrossed in deep contemplation, his cerebral gears undoubtedly whirring with hypotheses and possibilities.

Upon our return to our quarters, Holmes immediately plunged into his investigative mode, sifting through dossiers and maps, hunting for any clues that could lead us to The Order of the Black Hand.

The night dwindled into an indistinct whirl of deduction, but as the dawn broke, Holmes emerged from his brown study, his face etched with resolve.

"We must pay a visit to the local purveyors of occult paraphernalia and discern if any of them have knowledge of The Order," he intoned, his voice hushed yet serious.

United in purpose, we ventured once more into the maze of London streets, directing our course towards the less reputable districts known to harbor occult establishments.

As we neared a particular shop, a wave of trepidation washed over me. Its windows were shrouded in black, and bizarre glyphs were daubed onto the door. Holmes, however, exhibited no signs of perturbation. He pressed the door open and motioned for me to follow.

The interior of the shop was dim, the only illumination provided by a smattering of candles flickering ominously in every nook and cranny. The shelves were burdened with peculiar trinkets and tomes bearing titles that sent a chill through my veins.

Behind the counter sat a woman, her hair disheveled and cascading long, engrossed in a book, her expression one of intense focus. As we advanced, she looked up, her eyes registering evident surprise.

"Mr. Holmes," she rasped, her voice low and gravelly. "To what do I owe the pleasure of this visit to my humble establishment?"

"Good day, my dear Hettie. We seek knowledge concerning The Order of the Black Hand," Holmes stated, his voice unwavering. "I believe you might be able to assist us."

The woman's countenance darkened. "The Order?" she hissed. "I hold no knowledge of their affairs."

"Are you certain, old friend?" he probed, his gaze unwavering.

She averted her eyes, allowing them to wander towards the shelves behind her. "I might have chanced upon some whispers," she conceded, her voice barely audible. "And you are no friend."

Holmes leaned in, his eyes aglow with intrigue. "What have you discerned?"

She emitted a sigh. "Rumors abound that The Order intends to conduct a rite, a rite that will summon formidable power."

"What nature of power?" I interjected, my curiosity finally getting the better of me.

She offered a nonchalant shrug. "None can claim with certainty. However, whispers suggest it will bequeath them with tremendous sway and dominance over the city."

Holmes absorbed her words with a thoughtful nod. "Do you know the location of this proposed rite?"

Hettie wavered, her eyes reflecting a flicker of apprehension. "There are murmurs suggesting it is scheduled for tonight, in a disused warehouse on the city's fringe but I have no further details as to the exact location."

"Your assistance is appreciated," acknowledged Holmes, pivoting to depart.

"Mr. Holmes," said Hettie. She chewed her lip before

continuing. "Beware of those that bear the mark of an eye lined with snakes. It is a bastardized version of the Eye of Horus, a symbol of protection modified to be a sigil of poison."

Holmes considered her words, nodding before he tipped his hat. "Always good to see you again, thank you." Hettie scowled and turned her back on us.

Upon returning to our rooms, we found a small card had been delivered to Holmes in our absence. The paper was midnight blue and flecked with fibers of silver. The edges of the card bled darker, almost black at the edge. The message itself was also written in a metallic ink that resembled engraving upon the heavy cardstock. Holmes felt the weight of the envelope and sniffed it before cutting it open with a blade.

"Miss Morgana," he said simply as he read. Then he tossed the card carelessly to the side table. "It seems we have conveniently been given the address to the warehouse where apparent dark deeds are to occur."

"That is too convenient, Holmes," I exclaimed. "Perhaps this is not from the kindness of Miss Morgana that we have this information. Perhaps this is to entice us closer, to our own detriment."

"I wonder as well, Watson, but we must not shy away in fear. The path to knowing is fraught with dangers, some real, some imagined. We will only know the truth when we find it."

As the shroud of night descended, we gravitated towards the warehouse with apprehensive energy. The structure stood desolate and dilapidated, punctuated by shattered windows and rusted metal doors. It was for all intents and purposes abandoned, but as we drew near, the faint strains of incantations and the soft flicker of candlelight seeping from within became discernible.

Inhaling deeply, Holmes quietly opened a side door, and we ventured inside. We walked down a short corridor toward flickering firelight and looked around a corner from behind a stack of wooden crates. The tableau that awaited us sent chills coursing through my veins.

At the room's heart, a congregation of robed individuals encircled an expansive, elaborate sigil. At the center of the sigil lay Mr. Brackenbury, seemingly inanimate, his limbs sprawled out at unnerving angles to mimic The Hanged Man card which depicted him. I discerned the rhythm of his breath in the slight rise and fall of his chest, but aside from this, he seemed ensnared in a profound slumber.

The incantations amplified, and I could perceive the room's energy contorting. I instinctively sensed the power and peril pulsating from their undertaking.

Holmes advanced, his gaze resolute and steely. He stepped forward abruptly into the light and in full view. "Cease this at once," he commanded, his voice echoing with authority.

The congregation turned in our direction, their countenances concealed by the shadows cast by their hoods.

"You've arrived too late, Mr. Holmes," one of them intoned, his voice a threatening murmur. "The ritual has already commenced. The first sacrifice has begun. The antichrist will become entombed in flesh."

Without a moment's hesitation, Holmes retorted, "I shan't permit this to continue." His hand shifted towards his pocket.

Before Holmes could retrieve his weapon, the robed figures set in motion, their hands emerging with hidden weapons of all sorts. Suddenly, the room was plunged into pandemonium. The din of fist and metal clashing against adversaries filled my ears as Holmes and I engaged in a skirmish with the enigmatic assailants. A lantern was knocked over and flames spread across the dry rotted floor. Despite their numerical advantage, after a brief scuffle, the robed figures fled when confronted by the flames. I felt the room's heat quickly becoming unbearable.

Holmes swung towards me, his countenance grave. "We must remove Mr. Brackenbury," he stated, urgency underpinning his voice.

Together, we navigated towards the center of a large sigil painted on the floor, where at the center Mr. Brackenbury lay inert. Drawing closer, I noted his breathing accelerating, as though he were ensnared in the throes of a nightmare. His wrists and ankles were tied, with another rope across his chest.

Kneeling beside him, Holmes scrutinized the ropes hooked into the floor. "He may be drugged," he declared.

I cast about in desperation, seeking something utilitarian. Then my gaze fell upon it - a rusted sliver of metal, discarded in the room's corner.

Seizing it, I dashed to the sigil and began to carve away at the thick rope, my pulse racing with terror and adrenaline.

As I persisted in my task, I could sense the room's temperature increasing, as if the fire were ready to consume the entire district.

At last, having cut the final cord, Mr. Brackenbury's form spasmed as though liberated from a potent enchantment.

The three of us made our way out of the rising inferno, heat rippling as the building began to collapse, and out into the cool street. Together, we staggered to a safe distance, a small shack still within view. Disused, poorly repaired but apparently still of some use. A small boy's washed jacket hung over the sill in the window to dry. Somewhere in the city, mechanical sirens began to wail.

Surveying his surroundings, Mr. Brackenbury took in the aftermath of our skirmish. He rose to a sitting position, his eyes vacant and bewildered. "Where am I?" he enquired, his voice raspy. "Mr. Holmes? Dr. Watson?"

Holmes lent him support to rise, his countenance softened. "You were the victim in a perilous ritual," he elucidated, his tone soothing. "You are safe now."

"We are here to obstruct The Order of the Black Hand," I stated, my voice resolute.

Mr. Brackenbury's eyes widened in shock. "The Order? I have heard rumors. Were they the ones responsible for my predicament?"

Holmes nodded in affirmation. "Indeed. However, we managed to intervene before it was too late."

Mr. Brackenbury expelled a quavering breath. "Thank you," he murmured, his voice a mere wisp of sound. "How did you find me?"

"We were given the address by Miss Morgana," answered Holmes. "It seems she needed a devil to rescue her hanged man."

"But how would Miss Morgana know I was here?" asked Mr. Brackenbury. He was overtaken by a coughing fit. I put his arm around Mr. Brackenbury's shoulders, supporting him as he struggled to recover.

"How indeed, Mr. Brackenbury?" Holmes replied. "That is indeed the question."

Once the authorities came, we released Mr. Brackenbury to them, and called a carriage. Once safely inside, Holmes produced a small pocket-sized diary with a packet of papers shoved carelessly between the pages. He began unfolding them with interest.

"What have you there, Holmes?"

Holmes neglected to reply for a moment as he read.

"Conveniently enough, the location of the second ritual planned by The Order, Watson. I borrowed it from Mr. Brackenbury's pockets while I consoled him."

"This is convenient indeed, Holmes. I smell a trap. But how would they know we would rescue Mr. Brackenbury, let alone borrow his diary?"

"Regarding the diary, the pages are empty. This book has never seen ink. The purpose of it would seem nothing more than to hold this packet of papers. As for how they would know we might be here? How were we alerted to this location, Watson?"

The idea struck me like a bolt. "Miss Morgana practically sent us an engraved invitation!" I exclaimed.

Holmes turned to look at the window thoughtfully. "Engraved, indeed. Watson, are you carrying your service revolver?"

I assured him I was, and Holmes directed the carriage to abandon us before a derelict mansion on the city's fringe.

Aged and in a state of disrepair, its walls were ensnared by climbing vines and windows besieged by ivy. We trod warily through the untamed garden, our footfalls cushioned by the plush carpet of grass beneath.

Upon reaching the main entrance, we could discern the murmur of subdued voices emanating from within. Holmes signaled me to hold my position as he pulled out his revolver and pushed open the badly warped door. It was his Webley RIC, the one he always carried but I seldom saw him brandish. If nothing else, this reasserted to me the dire situation we currently found ourselves in.

The voices echoed down the hall. Wallpaper peeled off the stained walls as if the house was blistering from the inside. The light illuminated our path enough to step carefully around the rubbish strewn at random. The voices murmured in unison, chantlike, in a singsong rhythm whose words were indiscernible. We stood just outside the ballroom, the source of the voices and light, and looked cautiously in.

It was an astonishing spectacle. The room was teeming with a dozen shrouded figures congregating around a sizable wooden table, empty. One of the figures held an ancient tome, its parchment adorned with esoteric symbols and chants. Behind us, in the dark, we heard the distinctive click of a revolver's hammer being made ready to fire. Holmes dropped his gun just inside the room and another robed figure emerged from the dark hall to usher us forward.

The robed figure at the head of the table intoned, his voice smooth as oil, "Anticipation has ever been our companion, Mr. Holmes."

Undeterred, Holmes shot back, "The Order's intentions, I demand you lay them bare."

A collective, ominous chuckle rose from the figures. "Your presumption amuses us. The wheels of the ritual are already in motion. The power we invoke shall surpass your wildest understanding and you will have the best view."

Unyielding, Holmes declared, "Innocents shall not pay the price for your lust for power. Your dark plans will be thwarted."

The robed figure laughed. "You, Mr. Holmes, are hardly innocent. Why, your refusal to believe in the arcane makes you the devil, one who would deny magic over the fallible intellect of man. How has your intellect served you this day? It has caused you to walk blindly, a lamb to slaughter, into our clutches. We wanted you, we requested you and here you are."

The individual behind us nudged us forward and the robed figures approached with the intention of securing our imprisonment. Without warning I ducked and spun, driving my elbow into our armed escort's stomach. I continued to spin, following my elbow with a solid fist to his chin.

Holmes did not waste the opportunity. He flung himself forward, hosting up the remnants of a chair to swing at the closest attackers before diving to the floor to retrieve his discarded pistol. He fired once, and I heard the bullet hiss past my ear, twice and then three times as the robed figures dispersed. Within moments, the room was empty and the sound of horses clattered into the distance.

A gust of wind blew in through a broken window, setting the pages of the discarded arcane book aflutter. Holmes retrieved it, rapidly flipping through the aged parchment, his gaze devouring the inscribed text.

"Indeed, a summoning spell," Holmes affirmed, his tone gravely serious. "Their misguided aim was to call forth a demon to execute their will." He glanced around the room. "Apparently, they had all they needed except the one who was to be sacrificed."

My heart plummeted as I pondered the catastrophic outcomes had we not been able to disrupt them. "That was meant to be you," I declared. "You are The Devil. Mr. Brackenbury was the Hanged Man. Will they stop at no evil to accomplish their deadly folly?"

"I think not, Watson. I am in debt to you for your quick thinking, but we must not rest. I fear they may be planning something far worse, for a far more innocent victim."

In silent accord, Holmes and I emerged once again into the enveloping darkness of the night. As we sought the safety of our carriage, cunningly concealed at a prudent distance, three figures erupted with alarming suddenness from a copse of nearby shrubs. Taken unawares, Holmes and I found ourselves abruptly sprawled upon the cool earth as a band of ruffians descended upon us. Then, as abruptly as they materialized, they vanished into the night's embrace.

"Holmes!" I called out, my voice echoing in the empty path as I rose to my feet, looking around for any sign of our assailants. "Are you alright?"

Holmes rose to his feet, dusting off his coat. "I'm fine, Watson," he said, his voice steady. "Their goal was easily achieved. They've taken the book."

"We must stop them, Holmes," I said, feeling a surge of determination. "We can't let them continue this madness."

We conducted a thorough search of the vicinity, but our efforts yielded no further threats nor any sign of the book. Exhausted from the recent events, we finally made our way to our shared lodgings.

Upon the morrow, we were greeted by an unexpected parcel stationed on our doorstep. It was a diminutive wooden box, its surface adorned with cryptic symbols and patterns. Upon opening the box, we discovered a note, its text penned in an indecipherable language and another tarot card of the same style as the other two. On it, a man lay on his stomach, a series of blades protruding from his back. Past him, a desolate wasteland devoid of plant or beast. Featureless landscape, the mood of the entire illustration spoke of desolation, loss and pain. The card was named TEN OF SWORDS.

Holmes scrutinized the note meticulously, a crease of deep thought marking his brow. "This text is composed in a language that precedes even the Sumerians," he declared, his voice hushed. "Our sender appears to be deeply entrenched in the realm of the occult. The card speaks for itself."

"What is its meaning?" I queried.

Holmes paused, carefully translating the ominous note. "It appears we've incurred the wrath of our unknown sender. They assert that we have meddled with affairs beyond our understanding and vow vengeance. They assure us we will rue the consequences of our intervention. The Ten of Swords."

A chill ran through me as Holmes relayed the words. "What is to be our course of action?" I asked, my voice betraying a hint of fear.

Holmes met my gaze. "We shall proceed as we always have—opposing malevolent forces and safeguarding the innocent. We shan't be deterred from our cause by these menacing proclamations."

Remembering Mr. Brackenbury and even Holmes' own recent near miss, I nodded in agreement. This was not merely a threat; it was an ultimatum we could ill afford to ignore.

"We must begin by identifying the sender," I asserted, my resolve firm.

Holmes signaled his agreement. "Precisely. An investigation into any recent occult activities in the vicinity might be fruitful."

That morning, we immersed ourselves in exhaustive research, perusing ancient texts and news articles, seeking any lead that might hint at the identity of our mysterious adversaries. Holmes enlisted his network of informants, who scoured the city for any evidence of occult behavior.

Finally, we received a promising lead that guided us to an antiquities shop situated on the outskirts of the city. The establishment was laden with peculiar artifacts, each imbued with a palpable aura of mysticism.

As we neared the counter, we were greeted by a wizened man. His piercing azure eyes seemed to probe our very souls. "How might I assist you, gentlemen?" he asked, his voice a soothing whisper in the cacophony of the city.

"Pray, sir," began Holmes, his sharp eyes sweeping the shop, "we are in search of knowledge regarding a particular package. We hope to identify the sender by it."

The old man arched an eyebrow, evidently intrigued. "May I ask as to the nature of this package?"

"A diminutive wooden chest it was," I responded, maintaining my composure. "Within was a cryptic note penned in an archaic tongue." I took it from my pocket and set it in front of him.

"I see," the elderly shopkeeper responded slowly. "It is not often that I entertain customers with such an interest in ancient languages and relics. Perhaps I may have items of protection you are in need of."

"We aren't here to procure anything," stated Holmes resolutely. "We only seek answers."

A ripple of amusement traveled over the old man's countenance. "Why, of course. I am always amenable to assisting those who share a fascination for the esoteric."

He guided us to an adjoining room crammed with dusty books and curious artifacts. In the process of presenting us an old book brimming with peculiar symbols, we spied a particular mark on his wrist—the modified Eye of Horus—a mark bearing an uncanny resemblance to that of The Order. "Pardon my forwardness," I interjected, lowering my voice, "But you bear the insignia of The Order, do you not?"

His expression twisted in indignation. "You presume to level such an accusation at me?"

The mark was too distinct to be a coincidence. An Egyptian-styled eye with snakes edging it and coiling beneath. Holmes closed in, his gaze locked unblinkingly onto the man. "We know of The Order's malevolent designs," he said, his voice laden with threat. "We will not stand by while innocents are targeted. Confess what you know about this organization, or we will have to resort to more stringent measures."

With a wavering gaze that flickered between us, the man finally acquiesced. "Very well. I shall recount all I know. But brace yourselves."

We held our breaths as he began to disclose the harrowing secrets of The Order—their macabre rites, sacrifices, and their lust for power and dominion. He spoke of puppeteers in the dark, their manipulation of people, and a reach far beyond what we had ever encountered.

A chill descended upon me as we digested his revelations. This was more than any threat we had previously faced. The Order wasn't merely a sinister cult—they were a formidable entity, wielding control and resources that threatened to cast a shadow far and wide.

Finally, the old man broke down in tears. He confessed to being an unwilling assistant to the order but when they had resorted to kidnappings he had withdrawn. If he alerted the authorities, he felt he was sure to be murdered. If he cooperated, they assured him he would be free to live on. Despite his misgivings, he had acquiesced, feeling as though he had little choice but the situation haunted him.

In the seclusion of this back room, Holmes mulled over the information the old man provided. His countenance bore a stern resolve. "We must find the puppet masters," he declared, his tone unwavering. "The Order must be brought to its knees."

"I concur," I replied, a surge of determination quickening my pulse. "Yet, how do we locate them? They could be concealed anywhere, orchestrating their malevolent agenda from obscurity."

Holmes paced, his brow furrowed in contemplation. Abruptly, he halted and turned towards me. "We must turn their machinations against them. We infiltrate The Order."

My eyes widened in surprise. "Infiltrate? How? They would hardly entertain the notion of an outsider joining their ranks."

Holmes' lips twitched in a sardonic smile. "That, Watson, is where your charm comes in. You possess an innate ability to ingratiate yourself with people. You could present yourself as an interested guest."

Trepidation coupled with a peculiar sense of exhilaration seized me. This was a precarious gambit, riddled with numerous potential pitfalls. Yet, I had to concede Holmes' logic—it was the only way.

"I agree to your proposal," I responded, my tone resolute. "Yet we must tread lightly. They cannot discern our true identities."

His eyes alight with anticipation, Holmes nodded in approval. "Indeed. We shall commence preparations tomorrow. We need to concoct a plausible alias for you, and we must unearth The Order's base."

Our gaze fell on the elderly shopkeeper who had served as our informant.

"His assistance will prove crucial," Holmes continued, his piercing gaze fixed on the old man. "His knowledge of The Order extends beyond what he initially admitted. With his expertise, we stand a chance at unearthing more about their intentions."

The elderly man looked apprehensive. "I shall assist in any way possible," he conceded, a resigned undertone in his voice.

"Very well," Holmes replied, an eager glint in his eyes. "We set our plan in motion tomorrow. The Order won't anticipate our assault."

The Adventure of the Tarot Card Prophecies

Though I was willing to risk it all, the prospect of infiltrating The Order was chilling. The following day, Holmes and I, with the old shopkeeper's assistance, fashioned an untraceable identity for me. To our fortune, the shopkeeper managed to procure an invitation to an upcoming ritual of The Order that was to take place the next evening in the guise of a large masquerade.

The venue for this gathering was a large, secluded mansion on the outskirts of London, flanked by an expansive, gloomy garden and patrolled by armed men. Costumed partygoers were already scattered across the grounds, and we could see light shining from every window. One false move and I feared we may meet an untimely end.

A masked doorman took our invitations, scrutinized the signature closely, peered at us hidden by our own masks and then granted us admittance. This hardly seemed a triumph to me as we had been unexpectedly expected at the last Order gathering.

Swallowing my apprehension, I followed Holmes into the mansion. The scent of incense was overpowering, the monotonous drone of ominous chanting hung in the air, and our footfalls echoed hauntingly against the stone walls. At length, we entered a vast room teeming with fancily dressed figures, their identities also concealed by masks and intricate costuming. An ornate box, identical to the one sent to us, lay on a pedestal in the room's center.

"We must get a closer look at that box," Holmes murmured next to me. "We need to examine its contents."

Summoning my courage, I nodded and we began navigating through the throng of people. Just as we neared the pedestal, a voice behind me caught my attention.

"You don't belong here. Who are you?" The voice belonged to a figure cloaked in red, his face hidden behind a mask resembling a stallion.

Feigning calm, I replied as instructed by the old man in the shop, "I am a novice, extended an invitation by one of your own."

The figure eyed me warily, but before he could respond, a commanding voice resonated through the room, demanding silence. An announcement of merit was about to commence.

A towering figure adorned in a black robe, and masked with an unnerving skull-like facade, commanded the attention of everyone.

"We have gathered tonight to discern the identity of our reborn savior, the one who will lead us from the dark and into a brighter new world free of sin. The candidates have been vetted and properly prepared."

He then motioned towards the box on the pedestal.

Two members, hooded and masked, approached and stood on either side of the box.

"The Devil has been named and being dealt with. The Hanged Man lives still, but will be returned. Now we ascertain the identity of our savior. Which of the three candidates will it be? Lord of Darkness, Angel of Light, Bringer of Peace we ask you to reveal your corporal desires." He raised his arms toward the ceiling, as if entreating the plasterwork cherubs overhead to answer him.

In response, one of the men flanking the box picked it up, approached the leader and knelt before him with the box raised. The other man also approached the leader. He opened the box and then knelt as well. They stayed bowed while the leader stepped forward, reached into the box and removed the contents. It was another tarot card, and from our vantage point, it appeared to be from the same deck. He held it aloft.

"It is The Moon," he cried out. From around the room came exclamations of joy from the attendees. "The Moon! Fair of hair, bright of eye, golden halo, this sweet child is nigh!"

The revelers surrounding us were overcome with joy. Embracing as they held their goblets of wine skyward in so many toasts. More than one cheek glittered with real tears beneath the gaudy costumes. The leader clapped his hands and the celebrating throng fell silent.

"And who shall give their blood that this holy event may transpire?"

Again, the leader reached into the box and removed something to hold aloft. It was another tarot card that appeared to be from the same deck.

"It is The Empress, the mother, an appropriate sacrifice. What mother would not give her life for her child? The mother's blood will build the bridge between worlds, that our Savior may travel upon the bond to cross the veil and become flesh. Tonight we celebrate, tonight the world begins anew with us as the Chosen Ones."

Again, the revelers were overcome with joy. A man in a wig of lace with the visage of a fanged beast obscuring his features clapped Holmes on the back heartily. Tears of happiness coursed down his cheeks, at odds with his celebratory tone.

"Isn't it wonderful! We have waited so long . . . the future is here."

Shaken by the revelation of a potential double murder, that of a mother and child, Holmes waved the man away distractedly.

"Not now sir, I need a moment to think on this."

It suddenly occurred to me how odd we must look, the horror on our faces barely obscured by the masquerade masks. While the entire room was dancing with festive laughter, only Holmes and I stood still in shock. Our dismay was so great it emanated from us as a cloud that tainted and silenced those around us.

Recognition dawned in the man's eyes.

"Say, good sir, may I be so bold as to request your name?"

"Wofford," muttered Holmes. He began to push past the man toward the door. "Wofford Curmuddington. Excuse me, it must be the wine." Holmes motioned for me to follow, which of course I did.

I was aware of the celebratory mood calming, the room growing quiet.

"But sir," our unwelcome companion declared loudly. "You say the wine has made you ill, but you have not touched a drop since you arrived, nor do you participate in the joyous moment at hand."

Holmes stopped, and turned slowly to face both the man and myself who was just a step behind Holmes. Our eyes met and he said, too low for much of the room, "Watson, we must run."

To the man, and the room he declared in a louder voice.

"Indeed, I have not partaken in the frivolities of this most celebratory of occasions because, to the fault of my own character, in my haste I began somewhat earlier than the rest, so eager was I to commemorate this day. Alas, my poor stomach can take no more celebrating."

He turned and continued to the door, his hand clutching his waists to demonstrate his discomfort. The man called out again, stopping Holmes in his tracks.

"But sir, if you are truly one of us, you should have been fasting in preparation all this week."

Holmes gave no response save to turn back, and lock eyes with me. Understanding passed between us. Without hesitation, he darted to the door with me close at his heels.

Before we could clear the door, pandemonium erupted at the entrance. A woman screamed and fainted. Homes and I lost no time in leaping past, pounding down the hall and out the front door onto the lawn. I discarded my mask to relieve myself from hampered vision and breath. Holmes did the same, discarding his on the expansive porch as we leapt free.

Costume-clad partygoers exploded after us as the men patrolling the yard became aware of the commotion. Running around the side of the house we surprised a man and woman with their masks off as they embraced. Without hesitation, Holmes snatched one of the masks dangling carelessly from their fingers and I, taking my cue, snatched the other. Holmes vaulted through an open window and I followed suit.

As I tumbled on the floor, Holmes righted me immediately. His mask already in place, I nearly mistook him as one of the partygoers, his demeanor was so calm and collected. He pulled the mask from my grip, affixed it to my face and shouted loudly behind me.

"That way," he yelled, pointing back to the rear of the house. A group of men ran to the windows, acknowledged his indicated direction and ran on. The lovers we had disrupted had vanished, as happy to remain anonymous as ourselves. As soon as the men had hurried on, Holmes tugged me again to the front door.

"We must make haste or I fear we may not leave this place unscathed," he said low.

Together we ran back out through the front, this time with halting steps as if we too were seeking the imposters. Holmes retrieved a discarded bowler made of crisp red felt and placed it on my head. A few steps later he rescued a lightly trampled hat that a sea captain might wear and placed it upon his own head. It was in this manner that we made our way back to our waiting carriage.

Exhausted as we were, we knew there was not a moment to rest with both a mother and child at risk. A brief meal of cold meat and cheese refreshed us enough to continue. As the evening wore on, we delved into our research, pouring over old texts, tracing back the roots of The Order and trying to find any leads on the larger organization they were supposedly part of. Despite our fatigue, our minds were alight with curiosity and determination.

Suddenly, Holmes leaned back in his chair, his face lighting up with an expression of realization. "Watson, I think I've found something," he said, excitement seeping into his voice.

He held up an ancient manuscript, its pages yellowed and brittle with age. As he pointed towards a specific line, I saw his hand shake slightly – an unusual display of emotion from the usually unflappable detective.

"Holmes?" I asked, moving closer to inspect the page. "What is it?"

He traced his finger along the line of text, his brow furrowed. "It seems our hunt may be more dangerous than we initially thought. If this text is to be believed, we aren't just dealing with a secret society, but a cult of sorts. They believe in a prophecy, one that involves . . . " He trailed off, lost in thought.

A prophecy? This sounded more ominous than ever. I could feel the weight of our mission bearing down on us.

"Most urgently, we must alert the police," Holmes declared. "This foul business is beyond our abilities or even authority."

Without hesitation we ran back down to the street, hailing a cab destined for the precinct of the local constabulary. Barging past the weary constable at the front desk, we insisted upon seeing the inspector on duty. The gravity of our expressions seemed to convince the officer, and we were swiftly ushered into the presence of the chief inspector.

"I am afraid we find ourselves amidst a most heinous plot," Holmes began without preamble, "one that involves ritual sacrifice under this very night's full moon and I have determined the location of this impending crime."

The inspector listened with rapt attention as we relayed our findings, the color draining from his face as the gravity of the situation dawned on him.

"We shall require backup," he declared, his voice echoing throughout the small office. "I shall summon the force at once, but it will take us some time to gather a retinue of constables. Make haste to the location and watch in case they relocate, but do not engage on your own."

Holmes made a noncommittal answer and moved to the door in haste.

"I mean it, Holmes," the constable reiterated. "It will be too dangerous for the two of you, as competent as you are."

"Agreed," said Holmes as he exited, but I felt a lack of conviction in his reply.

Returning to the scene, we marched on the secluded manor, the eerie chorus of the ritual reaching our ears from behind the place. As we approached, we came across a large, glass greenhouse at the rear. Inside, we could see glimpses of robed figures from between the tropical foliage of the greenhouse interior.

The innards of the edifice were dimly illuminated, yet the faint resonance of chanting trickled into our ears from the murky depths. We sought out the source of the noise, creeping through the shadows as the cryptic litany grew louder and more fervent.

As we approached, we could see a scene unfolding through the glass. Through a clearing in the shrubbery, the sight before us set my blood to freeze in my veins. The greenhouse was filled with people, as many as we had seen at the masquerade earlier. Quite a few seemed to have moved directly from the party to this new location, still garbed in their ostentatious glitter.

There, at the epicenter of the crowd amid a ring of robed figures, was a small girl, prone upon a stone altar. The child's eyelids were shut tight and her little chest rose and fell in rapid succession, as though afflicted with great distress.

The robed assembly was deep in a chant, their tongues weaving an alien language that rose in pitch and intensity with every passing moment.

"We are compelled to put a stop to this, Holmes," I urged him in a whisper.

He nodded solemnly, a grim cast shadowing his features. "I shall provide a distraction. You are to secure the child and make haste from this place."

Before I could voice my protest, Holmes boldly strode into the greenhouse in full view, attracting the robed assembly's attention.

"What in blazes is this spectacle?" he roared, his voice booming with the confidence of authority. "Release the child forthwith and yield to the constabulary!"

The robed figures wheeled around to confront him, their eyes aflame with wrath.

"Do you dare interfere in our sacred ritual?" one of them hissed venomously. "You shall suffer for your audacity!"

The Adventure of the Tarot Card Prophecies

As the robed figures closed in on Holmes, I sprinted around the greenhouse, through the opposite door and towards the altar, my heart pounding a wild tattoo in my chest. The child seemed so fragile and diminutive, compelling me to swift action. I gathered her in my arms and spun on my heel to make my exit, but a hand sprung forth from the gloom and seized my shoulder. I whipped around to confront my assailant, poised to retaliate if need be.

To my surprise, it was Miss Morgana, her visage enigmatic.

"I am at a loss as to your intentions," she said, her voice barely above a murmur. "But I assure you, you're committing a severe blunder. The child is destined to be a sacrifice - the solitary means of averting an apocalypse."

I gazed at her in stupefied horror, scarcely believing her words. She must be weaving a web of lies, or mad, or perchance both.

"You cannot possibly mean that," I stammered, my voice wavering. "You can't genuinely conceive that the slaughter of a child could be a solution."

The stern expression on Miss Morgana's face softened, if only momentarily.

"I comprehend that this may appear inhumane to you," she asserted. "However, occasionally, sacrifices must be proffered for the greater good. I assure you, this child's demise will safeguard a multitude of lives in the future."

I shook my head, baffled by her reasoning.

"You are utterly deranged," I retorted. "We must put an end to this madness at once."

The corners of Miss Morgana's eyes tightened as she drew nearer.

"I shan't permit your meddling," she warned, her voice resonating with an eerie chill. "Should you endeavor to thwart us, you shall live to rue this day."

Before I could issue a response, an uproar emanated from the assembly of robed figures. I swiveled to behold Holmes, his fists a blur as he engaged a multitude of attackers in combat. I was starkly aware that swift action was required lest we succumb to overwhelming numbers.

Inhaling deeply, I summoned every ounce of fortitude within me and pushed her to one side as firmly as I dared, considering she was still a woman. She staggered backward, almost falling.

"You shan't stand in our way," she spat out venomously, before spinning on her heel and disappearing into the darkness.

I couldn't afford to spare any concern for her. Sprinting towards Holmes, I clutched the child protectively to my chest. Holmes had fended off the majority of the robed figures, but a few still remained.

"Holmes!" I shouted. "We must leave this place!"

United, we battled our way past the remaining assailants, making a dash for the exit. The sound of thunderous footfalls echoed behind us, but I dared not risk a glance backward.

Finally, we managed to lose our attackers and could rest. We fell onto the ground, gulping in lungfuls of air as we gazed skyward at the luminous orb of the full moon casting its light upon us.

"Is the child unharmed?" queried Holmes, his voice raspy.

I glanced down at the infant in my embrace. The little one's eyes were shut, seemingly asleep. I laid a hand against her chest. Her heart was still beating, albeit faintly and irregularly.

Clasping her closely, I labored to my feet as Holmes mirrored my actions. We commenced a dash across the vacant expanse before us, our carriage patiently awaiting us on the far side.

Suddenly, the drumming of approaching footfalls amplified. I turned to perceive the figures sprinting across the expanse of a meadow towards us.

"They've arrived!" I bellowed.

Spinning around, I clutched Holmes, pulling us both behind a stand of bramble. "Take the child and make for the carriage," I whispered. "I shall create a diversion."

"Watson, wait . . . "

"Do not fret," I interjected, my voice bearing an uncharacteristic sternness that brooked no disagreement. "Simply ensure the child's welfare. Holmes . . . "

Holmes did not answer. Instead, he rose to his feet, arched his arms above his head and hollered, "Over here!"

Concealed from view, I was momentarily taken aback. Holmes was the embodiment of reason, yet this course of action bordered on the precipice of insanity. As if in response to my silent query, he cast a glance downwards.

"Rest assured. Owing to your heroic efforts, Watson, the child is safe," he declared. "Scotland Yard is at hand."

To my relief, a constable was already present, deftly relieving me of the small child and assessing her pulse.

"Is she . . . " The constable's gaze met mine, heavy with trepidation.

"Merely unconscious, it appears," I assured him. "Perhaps sedated."

His features relaxed noticeably. "God be praised, she lives." He cradled the tiny form close to his chest.

At that moment, I became acutely aware of my trembling hands.

"If our duties here are fulfilled, I propose we return to our abode," I suggested to Holmes. "A hot cup of tea would not go amiss."

A soft chuckle emanated from Holmes, his eyes reflecting a cocktail of mirth and fatigue.

"You can have your tea, Watson," he conceded. "Afterward, however. We ought to report to Scotland Yard, ensuring the child's appropriate care. There will be no early rest for us this night."

I nodded, recognizing the still lengthy night ahead.

As we ambled towards the carriage, my thoughts veered to Miss Morgana's chilling rationalizations and I related her appearance to Holmes. How could any sane individual endorse the sacrifice of a child as a resolution?

Observing the unconscious child ensconced in the constable's arms, I remained confident of our course of action. Her life had been spared; this fact was paramount.

In unison, Holmes and I boarded the carriage, sinking into the cushioned seats as we journeyed back towards Baker Street. The rhythmic clip-clop of the horse's hooves reverberated through the tranquil streets, eliciting a sense of relief that our ordeals were concluded.

My thoughts were consumed by the tiny life we had rescued from the ritual. We had taken the only appropriate course of action. She was safe now, and that brought immense satisfaction.

But I couldn't suppress my concern for her future.

As if attuned to my thoughts, Holmes reciprocated my sentiments, his countenance unyielding. We journeyed back to our lodgings in mutual silence, unable to disregard the mental images of the child on the sacrificial altar, or the haunting echo of Miss Morgana's words. The concept of child sacrifice as a resolution was utterly incomprehensible to me.

Upon arriving at our flat, I promptly headed towards the

kitchen to boil the kettle. Holmes, maintaining his somber demeanor, followed suit.

"I remain incredulous at the horrors we witnessed," I confessed while preparing the tea. "How could any individual stoop to such monstrous depths as to exploit a child as a sacrificial pawn?"

Holmes paused, his gaze distant. "It's not my inaugural encounter with such beliefs," he confessed. "There are those who harbor convictions that a new world order can be ushered in via blood sacrifice. It's a perilous and erroneous belief, but one that some will pursue relentlessly."

I shuddered at the memory of the child on the altar. Such a horrifying reality was beyond my capacity to comprehend.

"But how could people be convinced that a ritual sacrifice can shield them from impending doom?" I exclaimed. "It's lunacy!"

"It is indeed a fallacy, Watson, yet compelling and beguiling to some. The potency of ritual has a considerable pull," Holmes murmured, his gaze distant. "There was a period, a younger, less discerning period of my life when I might have been tempted by such notions."

I gawked at my friend, taken aback by his confession.

"Yet I have grown to put my trust in the scientific method," he elaborated, a steely determination infusing his tone. "In the logical analysis of empirical data and rational observation of the world around us." He paused, then added, "I have never found solace in the notion of rituals or ritual sacrifices."

I glanced at my tea, its steamy wisps curling up, lost in my own thoughts just as ephemeral.

"My relief is profound at having been able to liberate that child," I said, offering Holmes his cup of tea. "It heartens me to think our task is complete."

Holmes shook his head, a faint frown etching lines into his forehead. "Our task, my dear Watson, is far from over. As long as there are those who hold these misconceived notions of ritual sacrifice and its potential for effecting change, there will be those determined to act on them."

My jaw slackened, my words stammering out, "But the child . . . certainly they wouldn't . . . "

Holmes's visage was grim, his eyes foreboding. "The child is indeed safe now. However, there are those who won't be appeased until a new victim is procured. As long as such beliefs persist, there will be those seeking to implement them."

The memory of the ritual sacrifice and our role in preventing the child's death sent a shudder down my spine.

"We must accept, Watson, there are those who are yet to have their fill. Such horrors do exist, and continue to persist," Holmes continued. "They demand a victim, and in the pursuit of their beliefs, they are willing to sacrifice even a child."

But I knew that we were equally determined to make any sacrifice to protect the innocent from such monstrous acts. Ignorance will persist in some, their steadfast belief in their actions unshakeable. Yet others will hold on to the conviction that the child was spared for a purpose.

"Surely, we can't do anything about such perceptions," I said.

Holmes sighed. "Perhaps, Watson," he said. "But can we afford to ignore them when the lives of children are at stake?"

"But how?" I questioned. "How can we stop it?"

Holmes sighed again. "The first step is always investigation, Watson. We probe rumors or reports of ritual sacrifice, follow the trail to its source. We gather evidence and ensure those responsible face the consequences of their actions."

In silence we shared our tea, each lost in his own reflections. Despite the comforting moment, I found no solace in the knowledge that our task was far from finished. There were those in the shadows, harboring misguided belief in the efficacy of ritual sacrifice, unyielding in their determination.

As the last sips of tea passed our lips, we stood up, our wearied bodies preparing for the journey to Scotland Yard to report our findings. Our night had been fraught with danger and exhaustion, yet we couldn't permit ourselves respite until we were certain the child we had saved was indeed secure.

As we ambled towards Scotland Yard, my mind was haunted by the image of the rescued child and the malevolent forces still prowling. A shudder crawled up my spine at the thought of the catastrophe we had averted. It was a sobering reminder of the brutal world we inhabited.

Upon entering Scotland Yard, we made our way to Lestrade's office to relay our findings. His countenance betrayed shock as we detailed the gruesome ritual we had interrupted.

"This is deeply perturbing," he murmured, disbelief resonating in his voice. "We must delve deeper to gather more intel on these ritualists."

Holmes nodded, a grim determination on his face. "I propose we investigate any reports of missing children or suspicious activities in the vicinity. We need to unveil the faces behind these horrific beliefs."

With that, we left Scotland Yard, eager to finally rest. We had rescued one child, but there were others out there, still vulnerable. These thoughts were in my mind when we returned to Baker Street.

Upon entering our rooms, an unexpected sight greeted us. Seated by the fireplace was Miss Pamela, her ebony hair cascading in gentle waves around her face. She looked up as we entered, her eyes meeting mine.

"Apologies for the intrusion," she began softly. "I have withheld important information from you, but I assure you I had good reason."

Holmes and I exchanged wary glances. Despite the gentle desperation in her voice, we had to tread with caution.

"What information?" I asked.

Miss Pamela hesitated momentarily, her eyes flitting between Holmes and me. "I must confess. I was forced into collusion with this cult knowing of their intent to resurrect a dark savior within a child. I only complied as they held my own child hostage, assuring his return if I obeyed their command."

"And why do you reveal this now?" Holmes queried.

A hint of fear clouded her eyes as she stood, ready to flee. "Because I was there earlier tonight. I witnessed your intervention. Now, I plead for your help to rescue my son. I am ready to reveal everything."

Holmes and I shared a glance, pondering the unexpected turn of events.

"Please, be seated," I gestured towards a nearby chair. "Tell us everything."

Taking a deep breath, the woman began, "I myself was ensnared by The Order of the Black Hand. They believe a second savior will rise up and free the world from sin. They believe the savior will be reborn in a child's body and are prepared to go to any lengths to fulfill this prophecy."

As her tale unfolded, my heart sank. Miss Pamela had deceived us, but she was also a victim, manipulated into joining them with her child's safety hanging in the balance.

"How did they manipulate you?" Holmes asked, always the seeker of details. His face was a mask of concentration as he listened to her account.

"They kidnapped my son," her voice trembled. "They threatened to harm him if I didn't comply. They sent me a lock of his hair and his lucky stone. I had no choice but to obey."

Holmes nodded, his face severe. "And what were their demands?"

"They wanted me to find a child who met certain criteria," Miss Pamela explained. "They told me that this child would be the host for their savior and that they needed her to complete their ritual. I have pretended to be in support of this, to share their beliefs, in hopes I may locate my son."

A chill ran down my spine as I absorbed her revelations. The thought of innocent children ensnared in such a horrific plot was unbearable.

"And did you find this child, meant to be the savior?" I asked, my voice barely audible.

Tears streamed down Miss Pamela's face as she nodded. "Yes. It was the girl you rescued tonight. I served as her nanny for the preceding weeks. I am eternally grateful to you for saving her. But now, my son's life is at stake. Please . . . " Her voice trailed off, a silent plea in her eyes.

"I believe I know where your son may be," Holmes declared. "Stay here, you'll be safe. Mrs. Hudson will take care of you until we return."

Holmes glanced at me, his gaze sharp and resolute. "Watson, we must first seek assistance from the authorities. We shall require a team of armed men to accompany us. Then, without delay, we shall proceed to the modest shack by the wharf."

I nodded in agreement, and we swiftly departed from our lodgings. As we traversed the streets of London, an overwhelming sense of urgency permeated the air. Our mission to rescue the endangered children and dismantle this perilous cult demanded immediate action.

We made our way to the wharf, its wooden planks echoing with the sound of lapping waves. In the distance, the silhouette of a small shack came into view. As we drew closer, muffled cries reached our ears, filling the atmosphere with tension.

Without a moment's hesitation, Holmes forcefully kicked down the door, leading the way with an unwavering resolve. The armed officers followed closely, prepared for whatever awaited them within the dimly lit interior. There, standing over a frightened child, stood a figure that left me stunned—it was none other than Mr. Brackenbury, the man we previously believed to be the mild-mannered owner of the print shop!

A chill coursed through my veins as the realization struck, my mind racing to connect the dots. The very man presumed friend now held an innocent child captive, casting aside the boundaries of reason.

"Cease your actions at once!" Holmes's commanding voice reverberated through the shack, cutting through the stale air. "Your deceit has been exposed."

Startled, the man looked up, his expression a mixture of surprise and malevolence. "I am but a chosen member," he spat with venom. "We shall usher in the savior, and your feeble attempts to impede us are futile. You think you can halt our progress? It is too late. The sacrificial ritual was accomplished last night. The savior is already among us. I only wait for word to do away with this boy and return."

Unperturbed, Holmes stood his ground. "Fortunately for you, your understanding is flawed," he stated firmly. "Surrender now."

A derisive laugh escaped the man's lips, tainted with a hint of desperation. "You fail to comprehend. The ritual is complete. The new savior is here, and she shall bring about the demise of this world."

An icy shiver coursed through my spine as I absorbed his words. This man truly believed in the twisted dogma of his cult, their distorted beliefs weaving a web of darkness around him.

Stepping forward with unyielding determination, Holmes locked eyes with the man. "Release the child," he commanded calmly. "There is no escape."

For a fleeting moment, the man hesitated, but then he pulled a knife toward the boy's exposed neck. The cacophony of gunfire erupted within the confined space as I pulled my pistol without thinking and fired. The man fell lifeless to the ground, his sinister intentions forever silenced.

We rushed to the child, who trembled from the ordeal but remained unharmed and I tenderly cradled the young boy in his arms, providing solace and reassurance.

As we retraced our steps to Baker Street, a lingering sense of foreboding clung to my thoughts. The man's proclamations about the sinister savior of the world lurking among us and the impending apocalypse continued to echo in my mind. I realized that our task was far from over; we could not rest until this malevolent group was eradicated once and for all.

Holmes observed my unease.

"We have achieved a great deal today, Watson," he assured me, his voice steady and composed. "Tidying up the remnants shall be a straightforward matter. Clearly, their plans have already been hindered. The man himself was unaware that their plot had been foiled earlier this night, with the girl saved."

Curiosity and confusion stirred within me, compelling me to seek answers. "I must inquire, Holmes. How did you discern the whereabouts of the boy? And why was he not intended to be the sacrifice? Is it not more logical to assume a second coming of a savior would be male?"

"It was the sight of the child's garments hanging on the line during our earlier visit here that led me to surmise that he might be found in that very shack. After all, it served as a workman's refuge on the wharf, a spot for respite during a fisherman's lunch break, rather than a dwelling fit for a young boy. As for why it was a female chosen to be the savior instead of a boy, let us continue after we return the child."

We had arrived at 221B Baker Street and Mrs. Hudson greeted us at the door. Relief swept across Miss Pamela's countenance as she rushed inside, finally reunited with her son. She took him upstairs to make a fuss over him in private.

Mrs. Hudson handed Holmes a folded paper. "This came for you just now, moments before you arrived. It slipped beneath the door."

Holmes opened the paper to find another tarot card, in the same style as the others. He held it up for me to see. On it, a knight lay on his back, a series of blades hanging over him in a threatening manner. The knight himself lay as if in a state of death. His arms were crossed over another sword resting on his chest, a red rose nestled against the blade. The bright splash of crimson on the otherwise subdued card felt threatening, a reminder of a heart bleeding outside the mortal cage of bone that normally housed such things. The card was named FOUR OF SWORDS.

"Horrible, Holmes! Will we never be free of this?" I asked. Fatigue from the recent events had set into my core, making my temper short.

"You can relax, Watson. This is a message, as all the tarot are. It means rest. This crisis is over, for now. I suspect, however, we will have dealings with Miss Morgana again in the future." He examined the paper to find his name written in the shaky script of the elderly.

"I will trust you on that, and gladly. And why, Holmes, do you believe they selected a girl to bring about the second coming, rather than a boy? The latter seems the more obvious choice."

Holmes handed his hat to Mrs. Hudson with a wry smile.

"Ah, my dear Watson, how peculiarly biased your assumption is. Why should a savior not be a female, dark or otherwise?"

Stammering and somewhat embarrassed, I attempted to clarify my thoughts. "Considering the philosophical and historic nature, one would presume . . . well, most individuals would assume a dark savior to be male."

"Ah, Watson, you underestimate the power of duality," Holmes mused, his eyes glinting with insight. "In this case, it is only elementary that the antithesis of a savior would manifest as a female—a reverse mirror image, as it were."

"Exactly, Doctor. How perfectly gauche of you to just assume a savior must be male," Mrs. Hudson added.

My mouth opened to respond, but I swiftly closed it as the truth crystallized before me. Mrs. Hudson chuckled mirthfully as she took hold of my hat and gloves.

"There you have it, Watson," said Holmes. "It is wise to withdraw while you still can. Never underestimate a woman, especially one as remarkable as Mrs. Hudson."

Clearing my throat, I acquiesced, knowing that further discussion would prove futile. "Indeed, Mrs. Hudson. Your point is well taken, particularly in your case. I consider myself wiser."

"Indeed, a wise man you are, my dear Watson," said Holmes.

The Riddle of the Red Tower

Naching T. Kassa

1: The Ghost

A dense fog had settled over London that icy October of 1890. The kind which lends itself to the aid of dark villains and evil deeds.

A desperate plea, in the form of a young boy, had sent me out into the gloom. He had led me into the East End and the cobbled streets of Whitechapel, under the flickering gaslit street lamps. Here, I considered the fiend who had once prowled the alleys and byways, the Ripper who had never been caught. And I must confess that every scream of laughter, every shout, sent a chill to my very marrow.

The boy, one who seemed strangely familiar, led me to a shabby lodging house and a room on the second floor. There I found a man lying upon a thin mattress. Clad in beggar's rags, his beard and hair unkempt, the fellow struck me as one of those poor indigents so plentiful in the East End. Imagine my surprise when he took my hand and called me by name.

"Do you know me, Watson?" he asked. "I'll warrant you do not. It has been a long while since our time at Blackheath."

I leaned closer to the man. Large, blue, feverish eyes peered up at me from a pale face. And though his hair had prematurely grayed, I recognized him immediately.

"Ponsonby? Jonathan Ponsonby? Dear fellow!"

"Good old Watson. When I learned you were a doctor, and I had need of one, I sent the boy to you right away. Give him this coin, will you? I promised it to him if he would fetch you."

Ponsonby handed me a gold sovereign, and I gave it to the lad. He tipped his hat and hurried from the room.

"You are ill, my friend," I said. "Let me fetch someone and—"

He shook his head, and a spasm of coughing overcame him. When it finally passed, he lay gasping upon the mattress.

"No, Watson, there is no time. You know I am dying." He turned his gaze to the ceiling. "And I know he will not come here."

"Who?"

"A dead man. A ghost."

I pressed my hand to Ponsonby's brow. He chuckled, and another spasm of coughing overcame him.

"I am not delirious, old man. Not yet," he said at last. "There is a ghost. He followed me for months until I hid here among the beggars. It seems he is a particular spirit."

"And this, a strange mystery," I replied.

"Which is why I sent for you. I am in need of your friend, Mr. Sherlock Holmes. It seems I am to have no peace in life, and only he can grant it to me after death. You must bring him at once."

"There is no need," a voice called from the doorway.

I turned to find a tall man dressed as a workman entering the room. Ginger hair protruded from beneath his soft cap. My guide, the boy, stood at his side. I rose to my feet, positioning myself between the intruder and Ponsonby, but before I could say a word, the workman removed his cap and wig. Sherlock Holmes stood before me.

"Hello, Watson," Holmes said, smiling at my astonishment.

"Holmes! What are you doing here?"

"You remember Smith, here, do you not?"

I peered at the boy, who had seemed so familiar, and at last the memory came to me. "Why he is one of your Irregulars!"

The boy, one of the many ragamuffins which served as the ears and eyes of Sherlock Holmes in the London streets, winked.

"He has been watching Mr. Ponsonby since yesterday," Holmes continued. "When the gentleman sent him to fetch you, the boy came to fetch me first."

"You were looking for me?" Ponsonby asked.

Holmes crossed to the dying man and knelt beside him. "Your wife has commissioned my services. She fears for your safety."

"As I fear for hers. I can never go back. He will kill us both if I do." Ponsonby tried to rise, but the effort drained the strength from him and sent him into another fit of coughing. He pressed a soiled handkerchief to his mouth. It came away stained with blood.

"He cannot remain like this," I said to Holmes in a low tone. "He is suffering from consumption and is in dire need of a hospital."

"No!" the dying man cried. "No, he will find me there, and if he cannot extract the secret from me, he will punish her. He swore he would. He warned us all."

"All?" Holmes said, leaning forward. "Who is this man and whom did he threaten?"

"He knows we've taken it. He searches for it, and if he cannot find it, he will kill those who know of it." He moaned then, a piteous sound, and reached into the pocket of his filthy coat to withdraw a parcel wrapped in a silk handkerchief. "This will explain all that I cannot. It contains a secret, one the ghost covets. Do not tell anyone I gave it to you. Let him think I died with it. Let him believe it lost . . . forever."

Ponsonby gave a great shuddering breath then, one which rattled in his chest. Once a large and boisterous man, he lay pale and shrunken in death.

Holmes took the parcel from his hand and slipped it into the pocket of his coat. He then reached beneath the mattress and removed Ponsonby's purse. "I shall return this to Mrs. Ponsonby. No doubt she will need it for the undertaker. Will you accompany me, Watson? I must inform the lady of what has transpired, and I would find your company most helpful."

"I should be happy to."

Holmes took the key from the lock, and we stepped out. I took a last look at the rooms of the unfortunate man and sighed. "Poor Ponsonby. We were great friends when we played rugby at Blackheath. It was sad to see him so . . . haunted."

"The human mind is far more frightening than any ghost," Holmes replied, shutting and locking the door. "Other than your time at Blackheath, what do you know of him?"

"You would not expect it of such an athletic chap, but he was a fine artist. I believe he became a painter. Though it seems he was somewhat unsuccessful."

Holmes smiled. "Do not judge him by his current circumstances, old fellow. A few months ago, he resided in Hampstead and his paintings sold well."

We descended the stairs and stepped out into the fog-swirled street. It seemed the world had grown darker and colder since I'd entered the lodging house.

Holmes hailed a hansom cab, and we soon found ourselves on the way to Hampstead and the former home of Jonathan

Ponsonby. When we arrived, it was past nine o'clock. Holmes knocked upon the door, and a stout woman carrying a lantern peered out.

"Mr. Holmes?" she asked. She eyed me with apparent mistrust. "And who is this gentleman?"

"This is my friend and colleague, Dr. Watson, Mrs. Tolliver. I have news for your mistress."

Her expression grew grim. "Is it bad news, sir? It must be if you're here at this late hour. Well, best come in. I'll let the lady know you're here."

The housekeeper took our coats and led us to the drawing room, where a small fire burned upon the hearth. Two chairs sat before it. I took one of them and Holmes the other. He gazed into the dying flames whilst I studied the room. It was not what I had expected.

Holmes had assured me of Ponsonby's wealth, but the state of the man had led me to believe him close to destitution. The drawing room dispelled all such notions. A rich Persian rug covered the floor and paintings, many by masters, adorned the walls. A photograph of three children, two girls and a boy, occupied a place of honor on the mantel. All of the furnishings denoted wealth and taste—a far cry from the man who now lay in a rundown lodging house in the East End.

The housekeeper had departed but returned not a moment later. She was accompanied not by the lady, but by a middle-aged gentleman with short-cropped hair, dressed in a dark coat and silk hat. His gaze settled upon Holmes, and his thin face grew pale.

"Forgive me," he said. "But are you Mr. Sherlock Holmes?"

"I am he," my friend replied, rising. "Though I am afraid you have the advantage of me. Other than the fact that you are right-handed, are a doctor, are at times forgetful, smoke cheroots, and have visited Mrs. Ponsonby this afternoon, I know nothing of you."

The fellow's eyes grew wide. "H-However could you know that?"

"You've written reminders to yourself on the cuff of your left sleeve and forgotten to remove your stethoscope from round your neck. This speaks to the fact that you are both forgetful and a doctor. Since the writing is on your left, you are right-handed."

"But how did you know I had been here this afternoon?"

"As I mentioned before, you smoke cheroots. I can tell by the tobacco stain on the middle finger of your right hand. Cigarettes do not leave this particular stain. I also discovered a half-finished cheroot in the fireplace. Mrs. Tolliver is a conscientious housekeeper and would never allow the fireplace to go a day without cleaning. Therefore, you had to have come this afternoon and not the day before."

The gentleman smiled as though relieved. "For a moment, I thought myself in the company of yet another clairvoyant."

"Another?"

"My . . . patient said you would be here and that I should go to see you. Though he has astonished me on many an occasion, I was positively floored by his prediction this evening."

"Patient?" I asked. "Then, you are a doctor?"

"Where are my manners? It is as you said, Mr. Holmes, I am quite forgetful. My name is Dr. Cyril Clemmons. I am the Deputy Superintendent of Broadmoor Criminal Lunatic Hospital."

"Dr. Clemmons," said I. "You were trained by Dr. Seward of the Seward Asylum."

"That is correct, sir," Clemmons said. "You have heard of me?"

"Only in the pages of *The Lancet*."

The smile faded from the man's lips. "You are a doctor?"

"I am Dr. John Watson, yes."

"Mr. Holmes' biographer? Were you a friend of Jonathan Ponsonby?"

"I was."

"Then it is true. It's all true." He withdrew a folded page from his pocket, all the while swaying as though he might faint. I rushed to his side and helped him to a chair.

"I must apologize," Clemmons said. "I have been under a great strain of late. I have never believed in the supernatural, until now, and it has left me a bit shaken."

Holmes glanced up at me, then at the superintendent. "You spoke of a clairvoyant when first we met. Perhaps you could elaborate?"

"It would seem I have no choice."

Before another word could be said, Mrs. Tolliver arrived with the lady of the house. Mrs. Ponsonby was a tall, graceful beauty with hair the color of jet. She wore a dress of claret hue and it pained me to think that she would soon trade it for widow's weeds. Dr. Clemmons and I rose as she entered. He stepped forward and took her by the hand.

"I did not expect you until tomorrow, Cyril," she said.

"I am sorry, Emma. It was not my intention to come so late. I . . . I was told I should come." He handed her the folded page.

The lady did not unfold, nor peer at what he'd given her. Instead, she turned to my friend. "You have news for me, Mr. Holmes? Have you discovered the whereabouts of my husband?"

"I have."

Clemmons reached for her arm. She clutched it with her free hand. "And?"

"He is no more. He succumbed to consumption not an hour ago."

Though tears filled the lady's eyes, she did not waver as Clemmons had earlier. "I feared as much. Where is he?"

"In Whitechapel."

"I'd hoped he'd go to Southsea. It would have been far better for his illness." She turned again to the doctor. "This page. Did it come from Roger?"

Clemmons nodded. "He said you should have it tonight and open it in the presence of Mr. Holmes and Dr. Watson. He said if you show them, they might believe."

"Who is this person of whom you speak?" Holmes asked.

"He is a patient of mine," Clemmons replied. "His name is Roger Thomas."

The lady crossed to a nearby table and unfolded the sheet with some care. She set it upon the surface and stepped back.

A charcoal drawing had been sketched onto the white page. The reader should know that I am not an authority on art. And that Holmes, a descendant of Vernet's sister, might find my assessment plebeian at best—though even his evaluation of the Dutch Masters is somewhat crude. However, when I laid eyes upon Thomas' sketch, I found it to be the finest I had ever seen. The scene had been depicted in such careful detail that were it not for the strokes of charcoal, I might have believed the picture to be a photograph instead of a sketch.

At the center, a bearded man lay upon a thin mattress, clad in a worn coat. Two men attended him.

"Holmes!" I whispered.

"Yes, Watson," Holmes replied. "It is Ponsonby. And we are standing above him."

2: A Spectral Visitation

"Roger Thomas drew this before I returned to Broadmoor," Dr. Clemmons said as we continued to study the drawing. "One of the attendants watched him in the room as he worked. When I returned to the hospital, Thomas asked to see me and placed it in my hand himself. I do not know if it has convinced you of his clairvoyance, but it has certainly convinced me."

I am not ashamed to say that a chill crept over my skin as the doctor spoke. Only Smith, the boy, had been with us in the room. No one else could have observed the scene, let alone described it to an inmate.

"He was not always clairvoyant," Dr. Clemmons said. "Once, he was a simple artist. Nothing special, mind you. He was known for his landscapes and seascapes, but little else. Those he attended university with far eclipsed him, including Basil Hallward."

"The painter?" Holmes asked. "The one murdered by his model this past July?"

"The same. Thomas and Hallward were close friends for many years and might have remained so if Thomas had not been accused of murder. Poor man, he was always a jealous fellow, prone to fits of melancholia. His fiancé, Annie Wilkinson, was killed while he was in just such a condition. He does not remember the event and swears he did not do it, but the evidence said otherwise. He experienced a complete breakdown in the courtroom, claimed her ghost had told him who the true murderer was. That is how he came to Bethlem Royal Hospital. He attempted suicide there on several occasions, and it was decided he should come to Broadmoor where he could practice his art. It was here he met the painter, Richard Dadd, and everything changed."

"How so?" Holmes asked.

"Dadd was a talented painter but known for violent fits of madness—he stabbed his own father to death because he believed him to be the Evil One. We had been vigilant with him, and he gave us little trouble, preferring to stay in his room and paint. You should've seen his miniatures. Wonderful paintings of beautiful fairies. So lifelike, it was as though he'd actually seen them."

"Dadd and Thomas were courteous when first they met, and things only grew better the longer they knew one another. Dadd spoke rather incoherently to those of us in charge, but Thomas seemed to understand him. He became a teacher to the younger man and Thomas learned much at the feet of such a master. Then, one day, it all ended. Dadd turned on Thomas while they painted in the garden. He demanded that Thomas 'pick up his mantle and accept the duty given to him' and when Thomas refused, he knocked him to the ground. Near strangled the life out of him. It's a wonder he didn't die.

"Dadd never felt remorse for his actions. So, it was quite surprising when he asked an orderly to deliver an envelope to Thomas on his behalf. The young man wept when he opened it. I suppose he was quite touched by the action."

"You did not open the envelope yourself?"

"At Broadmoor, we try to give the inmates a certain amount of privacy and trust. We even pay them for work. I could never read such an exchange."

"Did he tell you what was in the envelope?"

"Unfortunately, his larynx was crushed in the attack, and he could not speak. It has healed somewhat in the four years since, but he has never spoken of the envelope."

Holmes raised an eyebrow as Clemmons continued.

"Thomas healed within a month, but he did not see Dadd again. The man died during his convalescence. Thomas began the sketching soon after. They were small pictures at first and concerned rather mundane situations. The strange thing about them was—well, the actions within the sketches were coming true."

"Coming true?" I asked.

"Once he sketched a rainstorm mere moments before it took place. There hadn't been a cloud in the sky and yet the rain came. An inmate broke a drinking glass two minutes after he sketched the scene. I know it may seem like simple coincidence, but when these things start to add up, one begins to take notice. This year, the strange things began. The things which have convinced me of his power."

"The frightening things," the lady murmured.

Clemmons nodded. "It all began in January, the seventeenth of the month, to be exact. It was when Thomas sketched a place he never could've seen. A place outside of Broadmoor.

"You must understand. Thomas was sentenced to Broadmoor over six years ago, and he spent two years in Bethlem before that. For a total of eight years, he has been an inmate. He has had no visitors. Not even Hallward had come to visit him. He had no contact with anyone outside of the hospital, and yet . . . and yet he sketched the murder scene of Alex Trevelyan as though he were witness to it."

A silence fell over us, a pall not unlike that of a graveyard.

"I know of the case," Holmes said. "He was shot in the doorway of his study. The murderer was never apprehended."

I too knew of the Trevelyan case. It had been one of Holmes' few failures and, like all of them, had never been solved.

"Thomas drew the scene of the murder down to the minutest detail and had included some things not included in the newspaper report. When I showed it to the inspector at Scotland Yard, he was most impressed. He would've arrested Thomas had we not convinced him that the man had not left the hospital or our sight."

"Who was this inspector?" Holmes asked.

"He had a rather odd name. Lestard? Lestrad?"

"Lestrade?"

"Yes, that's the one! He confiscated the sketches and has kept them ever since. Said it was important evidence."

A smile played about Holmes' lips. "It seems we shall have to visit the good inspector when time allows, eh, Watson? Were there other sketches?"

"Inspector Lestrade has most of them, but there is another. Thomas drew it but a day ago, but he will not show it to me. To be honest, he's been asking after you. He drew the sketch tonight, hoping to convince you."

"I would very much like to see this sketch."

"I would be happy to show it to you. Could you visit Broadmoor tomorrow?"

"I could not come until after noon. There is another case which requires my attention."

Clemmons frowned. "Is there no way you could come earlier?"

"I am afraid my schedule will not allow it."

"Very well. I suppose I shall see you on the morrow." He turned to the lady and once again took her by the hand. "My deepest condolences on your loss, dear Emma. If you will allow me, I shall make all the arrangements for the collection of poor Jonathan's body."

"It would be a great comfort to me if you did."

"Amelia will be round tomorrow. I imagine she will wish to stay with you during this difficult time."

The lady nodded. "Thank you, Cyril."

"I will engage the undertaker right away."

Holmes stepped forward and handed him the key to Ponsonby's room. "You will have need of this then, Dr. Clemmons. Ponsonby can be found at No. 34 Dorset Street. The room is on the second floor near the stairway."

"Thank you, Mr. Holmes," Clemmons said.

"I too am grateful, Mr. Holmes," the lady said, when he had gone. "You have accomplished what the police could not."

"I only wish my news had been happier," Holmes said, reaching into his coat pocket. He withdrew Ponsonby's purse and the parcel wrapped in silk. "I recovered these few things. The purse is yours. I have no need of a fee. I would, however, be grateful if you allowed me to keep this parcel. There are one or two points of interest left to me in this case and I believe it may hold the key to why he passed as he did."

"You said he died of consumption."

"And so, he did. However, I would like to discover what drove him into hiding and away from his family."

"Then, of course, you may have it. I would be interested to know what you uncover from it."

"And I would be pleased to inform you."

We took our leave and Mrs. Tolliver showed us to the door. Holmes led me once again into the cold darkness of a fog-shrouded London. A quick peek at my watch revealed that the eleventh hour had come and gone. Midnight had crept upon the world.

We had left the cab waiting and boarded quickly. The horse's hooves echoed over the cobblestones as we traveled from Hampstead to Baker Street. When we arrived, Holmes paused before alighting.

"Will you come to Broadmoor tomorrow, Watson?"

"Certainly. By a lucky chance, I've no appointments."

"Capital. Come to Baker Street and together, we will embark for the hospital."

He left the hansom and hurried up the steps to the door. I knocked on the roof of the cab and continued on to Kensington High Street and my home.

The driver left me at the curb and vanished into the fogbound street. As I mounted the steps which led to my front door, a familiar feeling overcame me. I felt as though I were being watched.

Many times, in Afghanistan, I had experienced the sensation of an unseen observer. It had served me well and saved my life innumerable times. And though it had dulled somewhat since my return to England, I heeded it whenever it arose. Now was one of those instances.

The feeling grew stronger as I approached the door. I did not glance about, for I did not wish to alert the watcher to the fact that I sensed him. As I slipped the key into the lock, I happened to look up into the brass plate behind the doorknocker. There I saw a reflection that stilled the breath in my chest.

Like Marley in that oft-told tale of Christmas, I recognized a face reflected in the plate, the face of a man I had never seen. Malevolent eyes glared at me from the pale and bearded countenance. Bushy, black brows gave the face a wild and primitive aspect.

I spun around, expecting to find the fellow behind me. To my shock, no one stood there. The street lay quiet beneath the flickering streetlamp.

The sense of being watched remained.

I quickly unlocked the door and entered, shutting it behind me. Once inside, the feeling faded, and I breathed more easily. My mind, however, whirled with what I had seen, and Ponsonby's warnings about a ghost seemed to ring in my ears.

The last time I had felt such unease, had been while I lay wounded on the battlefield at Maiwand, the bone of my shoulder struck by one Jezail bullet and my leg by another. In those moments before Murray had thrown me over a packhorse and taken me to safety, I had feared my life might end at the hands of the treacherous Ghazis. I had heard their fierce cries in the distance and for a time, even after my escape, my dreams had been haunted by those selfsame shrieks. I had woken in a sweat, unsure of where and when I was. It had been years before the dreams faded. I had never expected to be gripped by such a fear again and yet here it was.

Time is a healer of all wounds and with time, it is easy to evade the ghosts of the past. But how does one escape the specter which marks you at your door?

The darkness gave no answer.

3: Sketches of Murder

I awoke the next morning in my bed, autumn sunlight streaming through the window. The memory of the previous night lay fresh in my mind, but the fear had dampened. Without the impairment of such an emotion, I could consider the matter with a clear head. And I endeavored to see the problem as Holmes would—with logic and reason.

I began by eliminating the impossible.

The reflection could not have belonged to a ghost. It could only belong to a man of flesh and blood. Of course, if the culprit had been behind me, I would have seen him when I turned. I was forced to admit the one improbable truth that remained. I had imagined the whole thing.

It is not an easy thing to admit that your senses have failed you, and as a doctor, it distressed me greatly. However, it was far easier to accept this than the presence of an apparition. My face burned with shame, and I resolved not to speak of the incident to Holmes.

I dressed quickly and descended the stairs. My wife had gone to stay with a school companion in Sussex and the house seemed quite empty without her. I would've taken my breakfast quite alone if the knock hadn't come upon the door.

My maid, Mary Jane, seemed to be nowhere in sight, and though I called to her, she did not reply. I hurried to the door and opened it myself. Holmes stood upon the doorstep.

"It seems you did not receive my telegram," Holmes said with a slight smile. "Or you would not be so surprised."

"I'm sorry to say I did not. Would you come in? I've not yet eaten breakfast."

"No, no, old fellow. I'm on my way to Scotland Yard, and if you are to accompany me, we must forgo breakfast."

"Then I shall fetch my hat and coat."

I retrieved my things from the hook and while doing so, discovered the telegram Holmes had sent. It lay upon the floor near the door. I quickly pocketed it and stepped out, locking the door before entering the cab.

"I did not think I would see you so soon, Holmes," I said as the hansom rattled over the cobbles. "I thought I was to meet you at Baker Street later in the day."

"The case which occupied me has been solved, and I am free to investigate the matter at hand. It seems Lestrade has taken a valuable piece of the Trevelyan case into his custody, one he did not mention to me."

"Do you believe it details the crime, as Clemmons said?"

"It is a capital error to theorize where data is absent. I believe the sketch is important to Lestrade or he would not have kept it. That is why I wish to see it."

After our arrival at Scotland Yard, we visited the office of Lestrade. He greeted us as we entered and bade us sit in the two wooden chairs before his desk.

"What brings you here, Holmes?" the ferret-faced man asked.

"I was told you'd discovered something which may shed some light on the Alex Trevelyan case."

The smile faded from his lips. "Where did you hear such a thing?"

"The Deputy Superintendent of Broadmoor Hospital."

Lestrade reached into his desk and withdrew a sheaf of papers tied in black ribbon. He stared at it for several seconds before handing it to Holmes.

"The man who drew these is a madman," he said, as Holmes untied the ribbon. "He has never left Broadmoor, and he did not know Trevelyan."

"So the Deputy Superintendent said," Holmes replied. He turned the first page of sketches, as I peered over his shoulder.

Once again, I marveled at the expertise of the artist. Alex Trevelyan stared up at us from the page. He stood on the threshold of his study, dressed in a smoking jacket, his empty right sleeve pinned to the shoulder. It seemed strange to see him alive. I had only observed his face in the pale grip of death.

Holmes set the first sketch on the desk and turned to the next. This sketch featured a dark, almost shadowy figure in the foreground. Trevelyan appeared to be in earnest conversation with this person. There was not a hint of surprise on his face, no sign of fear. The next page showed otherwise.

In my time as a doctor, I have seen many expressions on the faces of those close to death. The worst, and the one that comes closest to mind, belonged to the villain, Dr. Grimesby Roylott. The expression on the face of Alex Trevelyan exceeded even this horror. Never have I seen an artist capture the abject terror and agony a man must experience at the hands of his murderer. As for the figure, we still could not see his face, but he no longer lurked in the gloom which had shielded him. Details of his clothing and hair had become visible. He possessed dark hair, cut quite short, and the suit he wore was of a fashionable cut.

"Hello," Holmes said under his breath. He withdrew his glass from the pocket of his coat. "What's this?"

He trained the glass upon the man's neck. A small scar, white, and in the shape of an "L" marred the skin. Holmes glanced up at Lestrade. "If I am not much mistaken, this sketch has given me the solution to this case. I know who murdered Alex Trevelyan."

"You do?" Lestrade said, rising from his chair. "Who?"

"You will find that Trevelyan's cousin, Alastair Jago, has just such a scar upon his neck. I noticed it during the inquest."

"Jago? It couldn't have been him. He was in Paris when the murder occurred."

"So he would have us believe. Do you remember the actor? Cambridge Jones? No, of course not. His death caused little fanfare in the Parisian papers and *The Times* did not carry news of it at all. However, were I to show you a picture of the man, he could easily pass for Jago. It was he who traveled to France. And when he was no longer of use, Jago had him killed."

"But what would Jago gain from such a plan? He had been cut from the will."

"He may have been excluded, but Miss Elizabeth Trevelyan was not. I believe she is his ward now, is she not?"

Lestrade's brow furrowed. "I will look into this immediately."

Holmes revealed the next picture, which was as detailed as the last. In it, two men strolled through an area easily identifiable as Hyde Park. I recognized both from their pictures in the paper some months back.

"Lord Allenby and his son, John," I said. "Standing in the very place where patricide occurred."

Holmes turned to the next page, and I gasped in disbelief. His expression grew grim.

"Now I understand why you did not tell me of these drawings, Lestrade."

An unknown man, his back once again toward us, stood with a knife raised above the bloodied body of the Lord. His son, John Allenby, lay in the grass nearby, apparently senseless.

Lestrade lowered his eyes. "By the time Dr. Clemmons delivered these to me, John Allenby had already met his fate on the gallows. There was nothing I could do to help him."

"You could have restored his good name," Holmes replied drily, "by capturing the man who murdered his father."

"And if I had shown you these sketches, as Clemmons insisted I do, would you have believed me?"

Holmes didn't answer. Instead, he turned to the next page.

The subject of this last drawing was somewhat mundane. An elderly woman with a kind face stood in a kitchen, garbed as a maid. Before her was a tray and on it sat a pot of tea, a cup, and a small plate of biscuits.

"Strange," Holmes muttered.

"Odd," I replied. "Perhaps this picture was added by mistake."

"What makes you think so, Watson?" Holmes asked without looking up.

"It seems to be a portrait of a servant. I see no murder here."

"It would seem so. Would you mind much if I were to borrow this sketch, Lestrade?"

"If you like. Though I don't know why you would. As you've said, it has nothing to do with murder."

"It provides its own little mystery for me," Holmes replied, folding the sketch, and placing it in his pocketbook. "I trust you will keep me informed as to the Trevelyan and Allenby cases?"

"I will, though there's precious little to go on in the Allenby murder."

"On the contrary. Though Thomas has not given us the identity of the murderer, he has provided us with a wealth of information. Look here, at the murderer's clothing. Though he is dressed in a rather shabby overcoat, the attire beneath speaks of a gentleman. No tradesman would wear such expensive boots or trousers. And the knife is notable in itself. The blade is long and comes to a thin point, much like a dagger."

Whilst Holmes instructed Lestrade, I had been studying the man in question. My gaze strayed from him to the victims and then to the trees beyond. It was then I noticed something which turned the blood in my veins to ice. Behind the trunk of a great elm, a figure lurked.

The man's face had not been visible to me before, or if it had, I had not noticed it. I could not mistake him. It was the same man I'd seen reflected in my doorknocker the night before.

The sight of him robbed me of my speech. I simply could not believe it was he, but there it was, the bearded face, the beetling brows. How had he come to be on the page?

Before I could say a word, Holmes returned the other pages to Lestrade and bade him good day.

I followed Holmes from the Yard in somewhat of a daze, and it took several moments under the autumn sun to shake me from it.

Holmes decided that we should not delay our visit to Broadmoor another minute, and so we boarded a cab bound for Paddington Station. To my great relief, Holmes did not speak during the journey. Instead, he sat deep in thought, his chin sunk upon his breast and eyes shut, leaving me to brood over what I had seen.

After Holmes had telegraphed Clemmons to inform him of our imminent arrival, we settled into our railway carriage. Holmes immediately withdrew his pocketbook and unfolded the sketch. He placed it upon his knee and, withdrawing his glass, studied it for some time. At last, he gave an exclamation of triumph and handed it and the glass to me.

"Look here, Watson," he said. "There is murder after all."

I took the page from him and gazed upon it, striving to see what Holmes had. It was then I saw it. In the cracked window, behind the maid, the same strange man peered in. There was no mistaking those features. Once again, I could not speak.

"Come, Watson," Holmes said a trifle impatiently. "You're a medical man. What do you see?"

I knew I could not hide my agitated state from him and would have confessed all, had he not leaned forward and pointed to an object near the teacup. It was an uncorked bottle, lying upon its side.

"An empty bottle?" I said.

"Take a look at the label, Watson. Thomas' detail, like his mentor's, is quite extraordinary."

I did as he bade me and, to my horror, read the word, "Arsenic."

I glanced up, eyes wide. "By Jove, Holmes! You're quite right. She's poisoned someone."

"Or means to. I am not convinced this murder has taken place."

"You are not? How could you know? Most poisonings by arsenic occur over time and mimic the symptoms of a stomach ailment. The victim could have passed months or even years ago."

"You see, but you do not observe, Watson. Have you not marked the calendar on the wall behind the maid? The year is 1890 and the month October. Observe how the dates have been crossed out, and the last day in such a condition is but a day hence."

"Then you are correct. The murder has not happened. We may yet have time to stop it."

"If we find the kitchen," Holmes said, withdrawing his cigarette case from his pocket. He lit a cigarette, leaned back in his seat, and lapsed into silence.

We arrived in Crowthorne at a quarter of twelve. Clemmons had sent a carriage to meet us and the transfer to the conveyance was a quick one. Within moments, we were on our way.

I shall never forget the first time I saw Broadmoor. The red-brick building was an imposing one, and even beneath the light of the noonday sun, appeared full of menace. It sat upon a high, pine-covered ridge, gigantic towers flanking either side of the gate. They stood as grim sentinels, better suited to watching over a dragon rather than a populous of madmen and women.

Clemmons awaited us within, and he led us to what was known as "The Privilege Block," a section of the asylum reserved for the least dangerous of the inmates. I was somewhat surprised to see that these men resided in single rooms instead of a dormitory.

"We will find Thomas on the terrace," Clemmons said. "He often sits there when conditions allow. The light is good today and the weather unseasonably warm. Ah! There he is."

We stepped out and looked onto a terrace which sloped down toward a stone fence below. From here, one commanded quite a view of the beautiful and sprawling countryside. A few yards from the doorway we had just passed through, a thin man sat on a stool, an easel before him. From a distance, he seemed young but, upon closer inspection, his sandy-blond hair showed streaks of gray, and the lines on his face became clearly visible. He did not glance up as we approached.

"Hello, Thomas," Clemmons said. "I've brought you some visitors."

The artist grumbled a reply but continued to ignore us. He

chose a paintbrush from the table nearby, dipped it into his palette and continued his work.

"He is often like this," Clemmons remarked. "Once, he painted for two days with nary a break for food, drink, or sleep. He is very like a machine until he has finished. Then, he tends to collapse and cannot be roused for days on end."

Holmes cast me a sideways glance, but I pretended not to recognize the similarity between him and Thomas. Nor did I mention it.

"They have come from London to see your sketches," Clemmons said, addressing Thomas once more. "This esteemed gentleman here is Mr. Sherlock Holmes. The other is Dr. John Watson."

At the mention of my friend's name, the artist ceased mid-stroke. He looked up at Holmes for the first time, and I thought I saw something like hope kindle in his eyes.

"Holmes?" the man rasped, his tone a little above a whisper. He slid off the stool and hurried over to my friend, whom he clasped by the hand. "Only you can save me!" he cried.

4: The Secret in the Bookshelf

Thomas stared at my companion with seeming desperation, grasping at his hand and then tugging at his sleeve.

"Now, now, Thomas," Clemmons admonished. "Do not treat Mr. Holmes in this manner."

The artist glanced about, quivering and shaking. "We must go to my room. He is coming. He is near."

Clemmons set a hand on his shoulder. "Very well. We shall go to your room. But you must behave yourself, or I shall have to ask Mr. Holmes to leave."

Thomas released Holmes at once. He lowered his head and nodded.

We retraced our steps down the hall and entered a room, one

much larger than the rest. Paintings and sketches lined the walls, some portraits, others incredibly detailed landscapes. To my left, an easel stood. On it was a large canvas covered by white cloth. A simple bed stood off to the right side, and a small table and chair to the left. Sunlight streamed through the high, barred window before us.

"Gaslight?" Holmes said, pointing to the lamp ensconced on the wall. "I did not notice such a luxury in the other rooms we passed."

"It is why the Superintendent arranged this room for him. At one time, it belonged to Dadd. He used the gaslight to paint in the evenings and now, Thomas does as well."

Thomas had not entered the room with us. Instead, he had remained outside, glancing back and forth with some trepidation. Only when he had entered the room and shut the door, did his demeanor change. For the first time since our arrival, he grew calm. He approached the table and began to rummage about, knocking a candlestick to the floor as he did so. At last, he turned to us with a sketchbook in hand. The cover was worn and stained with paraffin wax. Holmes' eyes grew eager as he looked upon it.

"Look," Thomas croaked and pushed the book into Holmes' hands. "He is coming. He will be here soon."

"Who is coming?" I asked.

Thomas glanced about once more. "He will kill her if I tell you."

"Kill who?"

Thomas motioned to the book. "Me. Save me."

Holmes opened the volume to the first page. Once again, we were privy to the most amazing work I'd ever seen. It was the face of a lovely young woman rendered in watercolor. Chestnut hair, whose beauty exceeded even that of Miss Violet Hunter's, lay stylishly piled upon her beautiful head. And, though she would never rival my wife, I could not help but admire the small nose, the coquettish lips, and the deep brown eyes.

Clemmons seemed even more affected than I. He stared with wide eyes and shook his head.

"Why, that is my wife," said he. "My Amelia."

"Sorry," Thomas replied in an odd and emotionless tone. "So sorry."

Holmes turned the page. At the sight of it, Clemmons nearly dropped to the floor.

Clemmons' wife lay at the base of a great oak, beneath a full moon. A red ribbon of blood coursed from her pale and lovely throat.

Clemmons had gone ashen, and it was all I could do to keep him on his feet. I walked him to a straight back chair near the table and he dropped rather unceremoniously into it. Thomas watched us with that strange, flat expression, and then yawned.

"My God, what shall I do?" Clemmons said softly. He glanced up at my companion. "Please, Mr. Holmes, you must save her."

"Save me," Thomas echoed.

Holmes turned his attention back to the painting. "I will do my best. But you must do exactly as I say."

"I am entirely in your hands."

"The first thing you must do is send a telegram to your wife in London and tell her not to leave the Ponsonby home."

Clemmons blinked. "How on earth did you know she was in London?"

"You mentioned that she would be coming to see Mrs. Ponsonby last night. They are sisters, are they not?"

Clemmons' eyes widened. "Yes."

"Then be quick, man! Her very life may depend upon it."

Clemmons leaped to his feet and hurried from the room, leaving us alone with Thomas. The artist stared after him. When the Deputy Superintendent had gone, he hurried to a bookshelf and withdrew an issue of Lippincott's, opened the magazine, and then returned it to the shelf. He did this several times, the last time with his gaze directed toward Holmes. Then, he returned to the table where we stood and sank into the chair Clemmons had recently occupied.

"Thomas?" Holmes said gently. The artist looked up at him. "What can you tell me about this painting?"

Thomas pointed to the woman. "Me. You must save me."

"And what of the tree? Where is the tree?"

Thomas studied the picture for several seconds but said nothing.

Holmes set the sketchbook on the table and reached for his pocketbook. He unfolded the sketch he had taken from Lestrade and handed it to Thomas. "What can you tell me of this?"

Thomas stared at it and then shrugged once more.

"Do you know this woman?"

"She does not know it, but she's one of his. She kills for him."

"For whom, Thomas?"

This time, the impassive mask fell away, and terror shone in Thomas' eyes. "He will kill me."

"Tell me who he is, and I will save you."

"No, not me. *Me*. He will kill *me*."

Holmes paused for a moment, then said. "Give me his name, and if you cannot, describe him to me."

"He is a ghost."

The sunlight faded as he said these words, and a chill filled the air. I shivered and glanced up at the window. A cloud had passed before the sun. Thomas' voice dropped to a whisper. "He is a ghost. He is killing them one by one. He wants the secret. The secret of his soul. He—oh, God! I have said too much! He is here!"

Thomas, his face twisted in terror, stared at the window. I followed his gaze, and upon looking up, caught sight of the same bearded man who had haunted me the night before. He glowered down at us, gnashing his white teeth like some wild beast. I stood transfixed, unable to move.

"What is it, Thomas?" Holmes asked, and I realized he had turned his gaze to the window as well. "I see nothing there."

5: The Red Tower

The man vanished as suddenly as he had appeared. I continued to watch the place where he had been, my heart pounding in my chest, and Holmes' words in my ears. My friend had not seen what I had. The vision had been shared by myself and Thomas alone.

A single thought repeated in my mind. Either I was going mad, or I had truly seen a specter from the other side.

Holmes' voice broke me from my reverie. He called my name, and I turned to him.

"Look to Thomas," he said. "He is in need of your aid."

I quickly examined the artist. Once again, he had adopted that strangely detached manner. Only this time, he would not respond, no matter how we cajoled him. I took his pulse and snapped my fingers before his vacant eyes, but he simply stared ahead, lost within his own mind.

"An escape," Holmes said. "He has fled in the only way he knows how."

"Like Ponsonby," I muttered.

Holmes did not hear my words, for he had already crossed to the bookshelf. "There is method in madness, Watson," Holmes said, withdrawing the magazine which had so occupied the artist. "I believe Thomas wished to tell me something. Keep watch for Clemmons, will you? He should return from the village at any moment and, knowing his respect for the privacy of his inmates, I doubt he will approve of my activities."

I was only too glad to step out the door. The room had suddenly grown stifling. I glanced down the hall and back toward the terrace. A dark figure stood in the aperture there but moved on the moment I turned toward him. Part of my mind wondered if it was the same bearded man. I silenced such frightening thoughts.

Footsteps drew my attention to the other end of the hall, and I saw Clemmons approaching. When I returned to the room to warn Holmes, I found that he had left the bookshelf and returned to the sketchbook on the table. I met Clemmons in the doorway.

"Thomas has had an attack," I said. "He saw something in the window."

Clemmons entered and quickly examined the artist. He shook his head. "He is prone to such attacks and has been since the incident with Dadd. It took nearly six weeks for him to recover from the last one. I have no idea when he will reemerge from this."

The very thought of sharing Thomas' fate sickened me. I could not imagine living with such fear, nor of retreating inward to escape it. I would rather stare into the end of my revolver than—

The thought chased all such notions from my head. I resolved then and there that I would tell Holmes of the ghost. He would have a logical explanation, a reason for my visions. I need only wait until we reached our railway carriage. For, though Clemmons seemed a good fellow, I did not feel it wise to reveal the state of my sanity to him.

Since there was nothing to be done for Thomas, Clemmons sent for an orderly to care for his needs until he regained conscious thought. We left the room with Clemmons at our side.

"I have telegraphed my wife," he said. "Though my duties kept me from waiting for a reply, the answer should arrive within the next few hours."

"The moon will not be full for a day or more," Holmes said. "Mayhap, we will capture the culprit before this tragic event takes place."

"What more can I do to help?"

"Inform me should Thomas awake. He may be of aid to us."

"Though it is doubtful, I will do so."

Clemmons clasped each of our hands and we returned to the carriage, and thence to the train. I had intended to tell Holmes of my dilemma the moment we were underway but, once the train had begun to move, found myself at a loss for words. How could I tell my friend of what I had seen? He would think me mad, or worse, superstitious.

My decision to reveal everything was thrust to the side when Holmes reached into his coat and withdrew a well-worn envelope.

"This is the object Thomas wished me to see," Holmes said. "It is the last communication he ever received from his mentor, Richard Dadd. The missive which affected him so."

Holmes opened the envelope and withdrew not a note, or letter, but a tarot card. He handed it to me.

The card was The Tower from the Major Arcana, but unlike most tarot cards which depicted medieval castles, I recognized the red brick, peaked roof, and arched windows of the towers which stood to either side of Broadmoor's gate. Two persons appeared to be falling headfirst from one of the tower windows. They were clad in strange robes, but I could easily recognize one of them. It was Roger Thomas.

As on other occasions, Holmes easily deduced my thoughts. "The other man is Dadd," Holmes said. "His picture appears in one of my commonplace books. As for the robes, they are Egyptian. The kind worn by priests. This card means danger, destruction, and release if you believe in such things. Look at the back of it."

I turned the card over and found a list of names. The top name was Robert Dadd, followed by Alex Trevelyan, Henry James, and Wilson Collins. Galen Gladstone, Amelia Clemmons, Lord Geoffrey Allenby followed, while William Bisgrove had been written rather childishly and in red.

"This last name, Holmes, it's written in—"

"Crimson paint," Holmes affirmed. "The name is a recent

addition, within the last fortnight, at least. The first four names are written in the same hand, one I am certain belongs to Dadd, and Bisgrove belongs to Thomas. I am uncertain of the other three."

"The other three?"

"You must've noticed that Allenby, Mrs. Clemmons, and Gladstone are also in a different hand from the first four," Holmes said and lit one of the cigarettes he had taken from his case.

"I believe the original four are part of the list Richard Dadd composed shortly before he was apprehended. It was lost after and no one remembered who was on it, save his father, who he brutally murdered. He must've copied it down from memory here. There is a vague mention in my commonplace books regarding this list. Apparently, it was one given Dadd by the god Osiris, and is a list of those who had betrayed him and should die. Thomas was Dadd's protégé. Dadd must've known he was dying and needed a successor to carry on his work."

"He wished Thomas to kill Collins, James, and Trevelyan, then?"

"It would seem so. As you remember, Clemmons said Dadd demanded that Thomas 'pick up his mantle' and when Thomas refused, he attacked him."

"But what of the other four names?"

"Those few were added later. I am uncertain as to why. We know now that Allenby was murdered by an unknown assailant. Perhaps, these names were set here to threaten or frighten Thomas into revealing a secret."

"And he added this Bisgrove? To what end?"

"Data, Watson," Holmes reminded. "I am in need of data and I have sent a message to my agents in London to collect just that."

Holmes pulled the silk-wrapped parcel from his coat pocket and uncovered it. It proved to be a sketchbook, covered with stains of paraffin wax.

"Is that . . . "

"One of Thomas' sketchbooks."

"How did Ponsonby come by it?"

"That is the question, Watson. One I cannot answer without further evidence. At any rate, it is a strange text. I do not believe I've ever read stranger. The ravings of a madman set down and put to paper. Long passages about a captured soul and the one who will kill to retrieve it. There are sketches too, mostly of a tree with a large cross upon it and a specter, dressed in a hood. You'll recall Ponsonby's last words regarding a ghost?"

I shifted rather uncomfortably in my seat. "I do. He said it would not pursue him into Whitechapel, that he was quite safe there. He said it sought the secret within that book. Do you suppose that is the secret? This captured soul?"

"There is no supernatural element to this case, Watson," Holmes chided. "If there is a secret, it is one of this world and not the next. You would do well to remember that fact."

After Holmes spoke these words, I lost my nerve. Not only would he find my spectral visitations to be superstitious twaddle, he would think me a coward. I could not have that. Though it caused me pain, I told him nothing of the ghost.

6: The Figure on the Battlefield

The train arrived at Paddington Station twenty minutes later, and we engaged a cab back to Baker Street. Upon reaching 221 B, we found Wiggins of the Baker Street Irregulars waiting at the curb. Holmes' eyes grew bright at the sight of the boy, and before the cab could stop, he leaped out.

His exchange with the boy took but a few seconds, and before I could alight from the cab, he met me at the door.

"I'm on the scent, Watson," said he. "And the game is afoot. Unfortunately, this is a path my Boswell cannot follow. Will you meet me here tomorrow at nine o'clock? I warrant there will be much to tell you."

"Of course."

The moment I gave my assent, he dashed away, and hurried up the steps with Wiggins close behind.

The sun had begun to sink from the autumn sky, and tendrils of gray mist filled the street. Soon, the gloom of autumn would usurp the light of day. I thought of the ghost, its bestial face and gnashing teeth, and a subtle dread filled me. I had no wish to be out after dark.

The cab took me home. Once again, the house seemed lonely

and shrouded in shadow. I unlocked the door and, once inside, locked it again.

With the click of the key in the lock, a sudden sense of ease overcame me, and a pang of hunger reminded me that I had not eaten breakfast nor anything else that day. I made my way to the kitchen.

The house lay quiet before me. The gas had not been lit, and every fireplace I passed was cold and dormant. When I entered the kitchen, the stove stood in much the same condition.

I called for Mary Jane once more but received no reply. Apparently, the girl had been gone the whole day. My home had become a silent tomb.

After stoking a small fire within the stove, I prepared a pot of tea and a few cold sandwiches. These I carried to my study, where I lit the gas and started a fire before sitting at my desk to eat.

Once the room had warmed, I removed my coat. Something rustled in the pocket, and I removed it. It proved to be the telegram I had thrust into my pocket that morning. I had believed it came from Holmes, but upon closer inspection, I realized I was mistaken. It was not a telegram, but an envelope with a note inside. The message had been hastily scrawled across a sheet of foolscap.

Dear Dr. Watson,

I know you will think me foolish, but I must give notice. Your house is haunted.

Last night, a man stood in my doorway staring at me all night long. Only with the light of morning did he finally vanish.

Please forgive me, doctor. I cannot work here a minute longer.

Mary Jane Howell

I read the note several times, my heart growing lighter with every word. Here, in my hand, was proof that I was not mad. Someone else had seen the phantom. Not a madman. A sane young woman.

I decided to leave my house and return to Baker Street. With this new bit of evidence, I could speak to Holmes with confidence.

It mattered little whether he was home or not. I would await his return. I pulled on my coat and turned toward the door. Something outside of it drew me to a halt. In the shadows, just beyond the gaslight which flooded the hall, I had glimpsed movement.

I squinted into the darkness, my heart thundering in my chest, and approached the threshold. Something moved near the floor, and I realized a figure was crawling toward me. It moved with a strange, jerking movement, as though an invisible puppeteer pulled its strings.

I did not call out, nor did I move. I simply stared down the hall as the figure grew closer and closer. Only when it had reached the edge of darkness, where shadow met gaslight, did it halt. Here, it revealed its bearded face and grinned at me with sharp, white teeth. As it rose to its feet, I took a quick step forward, and grasping the door, slammed it shut.

The moment I had done so, the specter crashed into it, thumping against it, trying to break it in. I turned the key in the lock, but the creature continued its assault. One, two, three times it threw itself against the door.

Then, just as suddenly, it stopped.

An expectant hush filled the air.

Several minutes passed with no sound from the other side of the door. I remembered how Mary Jane had described her encounter with the ghost, how it had not faded until morning light. No doubt my experience would be the same.

What kept the fearful specter from the room, I did not know. Perhaps it had an aversion to light, for each time I had seen it, it had somehow been cloaked by darkness. Knowing that I had a way to repel the creature bolstered my spirits. All that I need do was test my theory.

I took the box of matches from my desk and, with one at the ready, headed for the door. The key turned silently in the lock, making only the briefest *click*, but I waited before opening the door. When no noise was forthcoming, I turned the knob and peered through the crack.

Moonlight filled the window, lighting the hallway with its soft, silvery glow. No one stood outside my door.

With great care, I crept into the hall, my match and its box in hand. It seemed my theory had been correct. The light had chased the creature away. A lamp was ensconced on the wall but a few feet away. I reached up to turn the switch and, to my utter horror, discovered it would not turn. Worse than that, the lights in the room behind me guttered. Only the dim firelight remained.

I rushed back toward the room, only to have the door shut before me. Plunged into such sudden darkness, I was forced to light the match in my hand. As the little flame flared to life, I saw the specter glide toward me, its eyes wide, teeth bared. I thrust the match at it, and it vanished like a puff of smoke.

Deep and unnatural laughter echoed about me. Something jostled my elbow, and I nearly dropped the matchbox. I continued to thrust the match forward. When it burned down to my fingers, I dropped it upon the carpet, stomped it, and lit another.

The laughter grew steadily louder and higher until it had become nothing but a shriek. A shriek not unlike the ones I'd heard at Maiwand. I fell to my knees, and the matchbox tumbled from my grip.

A sweet and cloying scent enveloped me. It reminded me of something I should know, should recognize. It stifled me and I crawled toward the only light I could see, that of the moon.

The world became a nightmare. The hallway of my home dissolved. Wood became dirt, walls opened onto the battlefield of Maiwand. Bloodied hands reached for me from the darkness and tugged at my clothes. Shrieks sounded off in the distance. I kept my eyes on the moon.

"Watson?" a voice called.

"Here, Murray!" I cried. "I am here!"

The moon floated above me, illuminating the battlefield. Corpses lay still upon the bloody ground for what seemed like miles. Within their number, a few yet lived, and something dreadful flitted among them.

A hooded specter stood in stark relief against the moonlit sky.

A wounded man moaned several yards away from me. He held up his hand, and the specter glided forward. It paused by him and knelt, but instead of treating him, it fell upon him and, in a fit of fiendish glee, cut his throat.

Another wounded soldier called out, and the specter darted toward him. It fell upon him, laughing.

The terrible shade continued its work, searching for the wounded and dispatching them without remorse. As it grew closer, I knew it would soon reach me.

Cold and clammy hands seized me by the wrists, and a shard of fear pierced my heart. But it was not the specter which held me. Nor was it Murray. Roger Thomas dragged me away from the field and laid me against a rock wall.

"You are the only one who knows, Watson," said he. "You have all the pieces and only the master can decipher them. But first, you must be free."

The wall against which I leaned grew luminous and cold. Thomas nodded to it, then rose and stepped away.

The fiend which roamed the battlefield must've heard our exchange for it came barreling toward me. Though its face was hidden beneath its hood, I knew, somehow, that it was the bearded ghost which haunted me. I clenched my fist and struck the wall with the back of my hand. When I pulled it away, I saw blood upon the knuckle and for some reason, there was no pain.

I breathed in the air. It was cold and fresh.

7: The Maid and the Mesmerist

When I opened my eyes, the battlefield had gone, and I now sat near the window. A crisp autumn breeze flowed through the broken pane. I looked down at my hand, and the dark, scarlet stain which covered it.

Darkness no longer shrouded the hall. The lamp blazed forth with welcoming light. It appeared the ghost had gone at last.

I rose to my feet, the world turning slightly before righting itself. Once I had regained my senses, I made for the bedroom and my gladstone bag.

The cut was not a bad one. I found no shards when I dressed it, and though it ached somewhat, it did not hamper my movement.

When I left the room, I heard a knocking upon my door. A voice called my name. Holmes' voice. I would have rushed down the stairs, but the world spun, and I was forced to slow my descent.

"Holmes?" I cried upon opening the door. "How did you come to be here?"

"I have need of your services as a doctor, old fellow," Holmes said. "Can you come? You are far more qualified than the police surgeon and closer by."

"I will come at once. Let me fetch my bag."

I turned to ascend the stairs once more and nearly collapsed against the banister. Holmes caught me by the shoulder.

"Are you quite all right?"

"A bit dizzy. The night air will clear my head."

"Stay here and I will bring your bag."

I nodded. "Very well. It is in the bedroom, on the bed."

Holmes glanced down at my hand, and in that moment, I knew I could no longer keep my secret.

"Holmes, there is something I must say."

"If your tale is a long one, it would be best if you related it in the cab," Holmes said. "Wait there for me. We have not a second to lose."

I did as he bade me and hurried out to the cab which awaited us. The night air did much to improve my state of mind. By the time Holmes had rejoined me, the dizziness had fled.

"Driver, back to 23 Weymouth Street," Holmes called. "A sovereign if you get us there within five minutes."

The cab lurched forward.

"We have a few moments," Holmes said as the cab rushed along. He leaned back, legs stretched before him, and fingers steepled. "Tell me your tale."

I told him everything, the words rushing from me in a torrent. From the moment when I had first seen the ghost to Mary Jane's experience, and finally, to my recent visitation. When I had finished, the cab had slowed, and we had arrived at our destination. Holmes said nothing as we stepped out. He paid the driver his sovereign and sent him away, then led me up the street toward a home ablaze with light.

"When I returned to Baker Street," Holmes said, "I found a telegram waiting. It was from Lestrade, and it confirmed my suspicions regarding Alastair Jago. Lestrade went to see him shortly after our visit. The fellow confessed the moment he set eyes on the inspector."

"Then, Thomas' sketch—"

"Though it was correct, I would hardly call it evidence of precognition. It is entirely possible that another observed the details of the murder and then relayed them to Thomas."

"But why?"

"To create a reputation. Or enforce a belief. Which brings us to your tale. Though a trifle dramatic, it is not without its merits. You say you've seen this so-called ghost in Thomas' pictures?"

"In two of them. I did not think to look at the others."

"Then you did not see it in the sketch in which Mrs. Clemmons features so prominently?"

"No."

"I have taken great liberties where Thomas is concerned. Rest assured, I shall return his property when the case has been solved. The watercolor lies within my pocketbook, and you shall see it when the night's work is done." He rubbed his hands together. "While you've been grappling with ghosts, I have been searching for Galen Gladstone and William Bisgrove. I sent a message to Wiggins and the Irregulars from Paddington with hopes that they could locate the former. Their investigation was quite efficient. They located him before I arrived at Baker Street. It seems he was a showman at one time—a mesmerist, to be precise. This is his door."

"And what of Bisgrove?"

"According to Lestrade, Bisgrove is dead. He was drowned nine years ago."

A constable with a large mustache opened the door upon Holmes' knock.

"Mr. Holmes, thank heavens you've returned," he said.

"What is it, Brown? Has Gladstone taken a turn for the worse?"

"No, sir. He is as he was. It's Miss O'Hare. I fear she's done herself a mischief."

Without a word, Holmes strode into the house with the constable and me at his heels. We passed through the foyer, the dining room and into the kitchen. I was not surprised to find that it resembled the sketch Thomas had created, from the cobwebs in the corner of the ceiling to the woodgrain in the table. Nor was I shocked to find that Miss O'Hare, an elderly maid, was the subject of the picture. She sat in the glow of a nearby oil lamp, her gaze unblinking.

"She's been this way since you stepped from the room, Mr.

Holmes. Just like a figure from Madame Tussaud's. I tried to rouse her, but she wouldn't move."

"She said nothing before she was overcome?"

"Not a word. Though she did gasp a little. It was almost as though she'd seen something. Fair gave me the frights. I couldn't see anything there."

I examined the woman carefully. "Her condition resembles that of Roger Thomas. There is little I can do. We should send for Clemmons."

"I am sure Lestrade will see to that detail," Holmes said, his brow furrowed. "Come. We shall find him upstairs with your other patient. Remain here, Brown. Alert me if her condition changes."

We left the kitchen and mounted the stairs. Holmes led me into a rather sumptuous bedroom, where an elderly man lay upon a large, ornate bed. Lestrade stood at his side, and I joined him.

"Glad you've come, Dr. Watson," Lestrade said. "Have you been to see Miss O'Hare?"

"I have. She is suffering from a condition of the mind. I can do nothing for her."

"We've had her like before, villains who won't speak or feign madness. I believed her to be one of those." He shivered. "But I pricked her hand with a pin, and she didn't even blink. Suppose I'll have to call someone up from Bethlem or Broadmoor."

"May I suggest Broadmoor's Deputy Superintendent?" Holmes said. "He is well-versed in such conditions."

"I will have a wire sent right away."

As Lestrade left the room, I turned to my patient.

"Will he live, Watson?" Holmes asked.

"His skin shows several lesions, but it has not adopted the dark color which portends death. If he is no longer exposed to the poison, he will live. How did you do it, Holmes? How did you stop her?"

"Once the Irregulars had discovered the house, I entered it in the guise of a tradesman looking for work. Miss O'Hare admitted me quite readily when I told her I was a glazier. Did you note the cracked window which appears in Thomas' sketch?"

"I did. It was that very window that the ghost peered through."

Holmes frowned and continued his story.

"While I worked in the kitchen, she prepared the tea for Gladstone, whom she said was unwell. I watched her pour a few drops of arsenic into the cup—she was quite brazen about it—and prepare to take it upstairs. Under the pretense of chivalry, I offered to take it up for her and when she tried to dissuade me, I knocked the cup upon the floor. With a profuse apology, I hurried to the door where Lestrade waited outside. I told him what I had seen, and the arrest was made. Miss O'Hare protested, of course. She said that the bottle was purely medicinal, prescribed to treat the old man's gout. Lestrade and I left her with Brown and found Gladstone as you see him now."

"Do you believe her story?"

"I don't believe a reputable doctor would do such a thing. A disreputable one, however . . . "

Gladstone stirred then, and his eyelids fluttered open. He looked up into my face. "Who are you?" he asked.

"I am a doctor. My name is John H. Watson."

"Watson? Are you the companion of Mr. Sherlock Holmes?"

"I am. He stands at my side."

The elderly fellow squinted at Holmes. "Why have you come to the bedside of a sick old man?"

"During a separate investigation, I learned your maid was poisoning you," Holmes replied. "We came to stop her."

"Moira? She would never do such a thing."

"I wish I could say it was not so, but I saw her put the arsenic in your tea myself."

Gladstone shook his head. "No. She's loyal as the day is long. She would never try to kill me. If she wanted to, she would have done it long ago."

"How many years has she been of service?" Holmes asked.

"Service?"

Holmes raised an eyebrow. "Ah. It is as I thought. All for appearances. You wished to live together under the same roof."

The old man glanced up at Holmes, his eyes wide. "What? How?"

"You do not wear a ring and yet, there are several feminine items in this room. At the moment, I have counted no less than three—five with the stockings under the bed."

The elderly man sighed. "It is true. Moira is not my servant. I am, unfortunately, married to a woman who will never grant me my freedom. This was the only way Moira and I could be happy. It's been thus for over thirty years. That is why I cannot believe this of her. Where is she? She'll soon put everything right."

"She is unwell," Holmes said firmly.

Gladstone grew pale. "Unwell? She has not harmed herself, has she?"

"No, she is unhurt but deeply afraid. So afraid, she has retreated from the world."

The old man covered his face with both hands. "Again? It's happened again? She has not had a spell in years." He tried to rise from the bed. "I must go to her."

"You must rest," I said. "She will be well cared for."

"Cared for? They will send her to Bethlem or worse, Broadmoor. I will not have it!" He fell back, wincing.

"You must not overexcite yourself in this weakened state," Holmes said. "You will be of no use to her if you remain ill."

"You are right," Gladstone said. "But something must be done. Can you aid us, Mr. Holmes? Perhaps, with your reputation—"

"I will do what I can," Holmes replied. "A word or two will keep Miss O'Hare from the institutions you have mentioned."

"Bless you, sir. Bless you."

Holmes moved toward the door, and I followed. He paused in the doorway and turned back to Gladstone.

"If it is any consolation, Mr. Gladstone, the lady did not mean to poison you. She said the arsenic was medicine, prescribed by a doctor."

"What?" Gladstone said. "Prescribed? Dr. Vestman would never provide such a thing."

"Are you speaking of Dr. Emil Vestman?" I asked.

"The same."

"It is true," I said to Holmes. "He is well respected in our circles."

"What would possess Miss O'Hare to say such a thing?" Holmes asked. He suddenly turned to Gladstone. "Mr. Gladstone, you were a showman, were you not?"

"One of the best, if I do say so myself. Sold out every show I ever put on. Had them lining up round the corner at Piccadilly. I was the greatest mesmerist of my age."

"Then you are a giant among your peers. You must know all the tricks of your trade. Tell me, were you ever able to hypnotize someone into doing something criminal?"

"It is impossible," Gladstone replied. "No one will break their own moral code, not even while in such a trance. However . . . there are ways to circumvent it."

"By telling someone they are administering medicine when they are actually poisoning? I see by your expression that my deduction is correct. Now, then. I have one other question for you. Gladstone is the name you use on the stage, a play on that of a doctor. What is your true name?"

The elderly man grew quiet. At last, he said, "My name is Bisgrove. Henry Bisgrove."

"You had a son, born of your first wife, did you not?"

"A most unhappy man. His name was William. I made the mistake of sharing my knowledge with him."

"It is as I thought. Have courage, Mr. Gladstone. I will do all that I can."

I followed Holmes out the door and into the hall. We met Lestrade upon the stairs.

"I've sent Brown to wire Clemmons," he said. "He should return presently."

"Where is Miss O'Hare? Have you left her alone in the kitchen?"

"There is nothing to fear where she is concerned. She will not escape."

Holmes rushed down the stairs, and Lestrade and I followed. When we entered the kitchen, we found her as she had been, unmoving and unseeing. The door which led to the trade entrance, however, stood slightly ajar. Holmes hurried to it and peered into the alley. "Watson, the lamp."

I snatched the lamp from the table and brought it to my companion. The dim glow illuminated the cobblestones and the door handle.

"The lock has been forced," Holmes observed. "Rather expertly. It seems we entered the kitchen at a most fortuitous moment."

He crossed from the door to the small window which looked in upon the kitchen and studied the cobbles beneath before walking up the alley to the street.

"Square-toed boots," he mused upon his return. "And new ones as well. The prints show no sign of wear." He entered the house and set the lamp on the table. "Our man stood at the window for some time. He waited until Miss O'Hare was quite alone before he unlocked the door. His presence must have alarmed her greatly to send her into such a state. It is most probable that he meant her harm. Have her taken upstairs to her room, Lestrade, and have her watched at all times.”

“Why would anyone wish to kill her?” Lestrade said in a hushed tone.

“Perhaps she knows more than she should,” Holmes replied.

8: Mrs. Ponsonby’s Visit

It was well after ten when we reached Baker Street. Holmes offered me my old room for the night, and after the day’s events, I agreed. I slept, and no ghosts haunted my dreams.

When the light of dawn finally arrived, I woke to the aroma of toast and strong coffee. I left my bed and having dressed, joined Holmes in the sitting room. He stood at the window, staring out onto Baker Street. On the table lay the familiar sheaf of papers Lestrade had shown us two days before.

“I see Lestrade has been here. Any word as to Mr. Gladstone?”

“He is well enough, though Miss O’Hare remains the same. Clemmons is with her now. He has promised to come as soon as he can.” He beckoned me to the window. “It appears we have a visitor.”

I looked down as a woman dressed in black stepped from her carriage. Mrs. Ponsonby gazed up at the window before approaching the door. Mrs. Hudson admitted her and brought her upstairs to the sitting room.

“Please forgive me for visiting at such an early hour, Mr. Holmes,” Mrs. Ponsonby said, attempting a smile. Sorrow cast a shadow over her face, however, and it seemed that at any moment she might weep. “It is my sister. She left my home yesterday and has not yet returned. I have had no word from her, and I am sick to think what might have happened.”

“Calm yourself, Mrs. Ponsonby,” Holmes said. “Give me every detail you can remember, no matter how trivial. Was your sister disturbed when she came to your home?”

“She was aggrieved by the death of my husband, but no more than I. Though . . . ”

"Yes?"

"She went up to the attic where Jonathan kept his paintings. I have kept everything in its place since his disappearance and, since his death, I have not dared to go up there. There are so many memories." She pulled a handkerchief from her sleeve and dabbed at her eyes before continuing. "We had talked of a painting Jonathan had painted for her and I told her she might have it. She went upstairs to get it, but when she came down, she seemed quite affected, I would say almost absentminded. She brought the wrong painting down with her. I pointed the mistake out to her, and she took it back up. She left soon after and did not return."

"Her husband wired her yesterday. Did she not receive the wire?"

"She left before it came. I did not read the telegram until this morning, and when I did, it frightened me dreadfully. I wired Cyril immediately but have received no reply. Oh, Mr. Holmes! Can you help me? I cannot bear to think that something might have happened to her. Cyril's telegram seemed so urgent."

Holmes rose and paced the room. "You must consider the next question I pose carefully and tell me the complete truth. Has your sister been to visit Roger Thomas?"

Mrs. Ponsonby shook her head. "Why would she? There is no reason."

"She does not know of his presumed precognitive powers?"

"I do not know that she does."

Holmes paused, and his expression grew stern. "I cannot be of aid," he said.

"What?"

"I asked for the truth. If you cannot reveal it to me, all is lost."

"Holmes," I cried. "This is unchivalrous of you."

"No, Dr. Watson," the lady said, holding up her gloved hand. "He is right. She has been to see him, and she does know of his powers."

"Did she speak of her visit?"

"No. She mentioned she had seen him and then she asked for the painting."

Holmes' tone grew gentle. "Thomas has a name for her, doesn't he? A pet name?"

Mrs. Ponsonby lowered her eyes. "I wondered if you would discover our secret." She rose and, wringing the handkerchief with both hands, said, "Yes. He has a pet name. When he was little, he couldn't manage the word 'Amelia' and so he called her 'Me-me.' Lately, he's shortened it to 'Me.'"

"Save Me," I whispered. "Then . . . "

"Yes," Mrs. Ponsonby said. "Roger Thomas is my brother."

9: The Face Only I Could See

"How did you know?" she asked. "How did you know Roger was my brother?"

"The photograph upon your drawing room mantel," Holmes replied. "Two girls and a boy? Since the photograph was taken over thirty years ago, they could not be your children."

Mrs. Ponsonby resumed her seat upon the settee. "Roger was such a sweet child. He was the youngest of the three, and my parents doted on him. Unfortunately, he also suffered from the deepest melancholia. The malady seemed to grow better as he grew older—and he was much improved by the time he met Basil Hallward—but the specter of it was always there. When he met Annie, we thought it gone for good. If ever a match were made in heaven, it was those two. I think all would've been well had it not been for the tragedy."

"Her murder?" I said.

"No, the drowning of William Bisgrove. He had been a chum of Roger, Jonathan, and Basil. William had trained to be a doctor, but he was of such a mercurial temperament, he'd left the profession to become an artist. They were all painters, and each modeled for the other. Basil's paintings were always rather ethereal. He believed he could capture the true essence of a man—his very soul—on canvas. Well, you know how he met his end. Poor man. It seems so strange how all have come to such unhappiness."

"And what of Bisgrove? How did he come to be drowned?" I asked.

"William and Roger had a dreadful row over Annie. William said she was his very soul and that Roger, along with Basil and Jonathan, had stolen her away from him. He had to be restrained and expelled from my brother's house. He vanished after that and next we heard of him, he was dead. No one knows for sure, but there is a belief he drowned himself.

"I never met William, and have only Jonathan's word as to his character, but he seemed a very unkind fellow. Still, I do believe Annie blamed herself for his drowning. Soon after, she too was murdered."

"You do not believe your brother responsible?"

"Oh, Mr. Holmes, he is not capable of murder. Certainly not where Annie was concerned. It was the conviction and the imprisonment at Bethlem that drove him insane."

"If he was not insane before Bethlem, why was he sent there?"

"He was deeply melancholic following Annie's death and became extremely disconsolate. He would neither speak nor eat. Cyril had come into our lives then—he'd begun courting Amelia—and he used this condition to have him committed. His intentions were good, and they saved Roger's life, but they did not save his sanity. Amelia, Cyril, Basil, Jonathan, and I have worked tirelessly to have him released to us, so that we might care for him."

"Hallward believed in his innocence?"

"Deeply. He engaged Lord Allenby as Roger's barrister. He and Jonathan thought they might have discovered something which could exonerate Roger. I suppose we shall never know what it was."

"Perhaps we shall. May I call on you in an hour's time, Mrs. Ponsonby? I have a few inquiries to make, but I believe I may be able to shed some light on the disappearance of your sister. As to Dr. Clemmons, he is in London and should be here soon. I will tell him of his wife then."

"Thank you, Mr. Holmes. The telegraph office was my next destination."

When she had gone, Holmes took a pinch of shag tobacco from the Persian slipper on the mantelpiece and filled his Cherrywood pipe. "We have learned an interesting fact, Watson," said he.

"That Thomas is the lady's brother?"

"No, I'm speaking of Lord Allenby and his connection to Thomas."

"He was his barrister. Do you believe that is the reason why he was killed?"

Holmes nodded. "He wished to prove Thomas innocent. Just

as Amelia Clemmons does." He took the watercolor of the lady from his pocketbook and spread it out on the table.

"I did not wish to cause Mrs. Ponsonby distress," he said. "That is why I did not unfold the page in her presence. I believe, however, that there is a clue to Mrs. Clemmons' whereabouts on this page. We have only to find it."

I studied the picture, and while Holmes searched for clues, I searched for the ghost. My gaze roved over the tree and, for the first time, I noticed a cross cut into the trunk. I was about to reveal this detail to Holmes when my previous efforts were rewarded. I saw the ghost standing at the end of a trail in what seemed to be an archway.

"Here is my ghost, Holmes," I said, indicating the spot.

Holmes trained his glass upon the figure. "Where?"

"He is just there. Beneath the archway."

"What does he look like?"

Fear dropped like lead into my stomach. I pressed my finger to the page. "You cannot see him? He wears a dark suit, his hair is curly and black and he wears a heavy beard. His eyebrows are thick and meet above his nose."

Holmes glanced up at me sharply. He unfolded the sheet, which depicted Miss O'Hare in the act of poisoning. "And here, you said he was in the window? Is he still there?"

"Yes. He is glaring in at her."

Holmes pulled the portrayal of Lord Allenby's murder from the sheaf. "And again, where is he?"

"Behind the tree."

"The same man."

"Yes."

"And here, where is he here?" He asked, pointing to the picture of Alex Trevelyan.

I looked the picture over several times. "He . . . he is not here."

Holmes nodded. "I do not know why I cannot see him, and you can, Watson. Perhaps it is some sort of suggestion you have been given. But the description you have given me is identical to that of the drowned man, William Bisgrove."

10: The Ghost Revealed

"The ghost is William Bisgrove?" I asked.

"I would hesitate to call it a ghost," Holmes said. "But, for want of a better word, the term shall suffice."

"Why did I not see him in the picture of Alex Trevelyan?"

"For the same reason that there are no sketches corresponding to the murders of Robert Dadd, Wilson Collins, and Henry James."

"They are from the original list."

"Well done, Watson. Thomas' sketches depict murders from the second part of the list which was not written by Dadd."

"But . . . if Trevelyan's murder is not part of this, why did Thomas sketch it?"

"Mayhap to ensure belief in his precognitive powers. Or to ensure my aid in discovering . . ."

He grew quiet.

"I have been a dolt, Watson. A prize idiot. Should Clemmons arrive before I return, have him wait for me and we shall all go round to Mrs. Ponsonby's together." With these words, he pulled on his coat and rushed out the door.

Clemmons arrived shortly past nine. He was pale and drawn and it was clear he had not slept. When I relayed the news regarding his wife, I thought he might faint, but with more courage than I gave him credit for, he remained on his feet.

Holmes returned a few minutes after ten and we all set out for Hampstead. Mrs. Tolliver admitted us to the Ponsonby home with her usual surly manner and showed us into the drawing room where Mrs. Ponsonby waited. At Holmes' request, the lady led us to the attic where Ponsonby had painted.

A set of steps led to the attic room and Clemmons followed Mrs. Ponsonby with Holmes and me in tow. The door opened onto a spacious room filled with canvases, paints, and easels. All the windows were covered with heavy drapes, and only one had been swept aside. This illuminated the room, which was rife with the odor of linseed oil.

"Forgive me, Mr. Holmes, but how will looking at paintings aid in finding my wife?" Clemmons asked, his voice echoing throughout the room.

"Something she saw in this room forced her departure," Holmes said. "We must find what it was. Mrs. Ponsonby, the painting Mrs. Clemmons brought downstairs. Where has it gone?"

"It is here," she said, indicating one near the door. "It was not one of Jonathan's. Roger painted it a few months ago. He gave it to my husband on his last visit to Broadmoor."

Holmes snatched it up and took it to the window.

An enlarged version of Dadd's tarot card had been painted on the canvas. It was identical, with two exceptions. The man falling on the left was no longer Dadd. It was William Bisgrove. Below him stood an oak. A cross had been carved into its trunk.

Holmes frowned as he examined the painting and it occurred to me that what I had seen might be invisible to his eyes. This was confirmed when Clemmons said, "Why, this is the tarot card Dadd gave to Thomas. I would recognize him anywhere. He is the man on the left."

"And the man on the right is Thomas," Holmes said.

The fact that neither man had seen what I had, forced me to keep my own counsel. I decided to reveal it to Holmes later, without the Deputy Superintendent in attendance.

"An odd painting, to be sure," Clemmons continued, shaking his head. "I don't ever recall seeing Thomas paint it."

"I believe you were in London at the time," Mrs. Ponsonby said. "It was a month or more after poor Basil's passing. Jonathan seemed quite taken with it."

Mrs. Tolliver entered at that moment, with a message in her hand. She handed it to Mrs. Ponsonby and then hurried off.

"It is for you, Cyril," Mrs. Ponsonby said. "From Scotland Yard."

Clemmons opened the envelope and quickly read the missive inside. "I am needed at the Gladstone home. Miss O'Hare has begun to stir. I must go at once."

"Do what you may for Miss O'Hare," Holmes said. "Watson and I will continue the search for your wife."

"But Mr. Holmes—"

"Miss O'Hare's information may be invaluable," Holmes said. "And we are quickly losing time. The moon will be full tonight."

Clemmons nodded. "I shall go immediately."

"Good man," Holmes said, reaching out to shake his hand. "If you learn anything, send word to Baker Street."

We did not remain long in the presence of Mrs. Ponsonby. When Clemmons had been gone a scant five minutes, we hurried from the Ponsonby home and into the street.

"What did you see, Watson?" Holmes asked. "You were wise to hold your tongue, but I would not advise you to take up the American game of Poker. Your face is an open page where secrets are concerned."

"It was not Dadd falling from the tower. It was Bisgrove. And he was falling toward a large oak tree."

Holmes quickly engaged a cab. "Baker Street," he said. As the hansom rolled away from the curb, Holmes glanced out the window and into the street behind us.

"We must hurry, Watson. I have set the bait, but there is no guarantee the quarry will take it. I shall stop at my rooms and collect my loaded hunting crop. And since we cannot stop in Kensington, you will have to make do with my revolver."

"You expect danger?"

"Our opponent is a clever one and has killed on more than one occasion."

"Where are we headed?"

"To Crowthorne and thence to Broadmoor. I have wired Dr. Nicholson and asked to see Thomas' room. He has agreed."

"What do you hope to find there?"

"A secret which has lain buried for nearly ten years. One which is the source of so much tragedy."

We made a brief stop at Baker Street and then were once again on our way to Paddington Station. Holmes glanced over his shoulder many times and when we boarded the train, took one of the compartments closest to the engine. He said little during our journey, so focused was his ever-watchful eye on those who passed our compartment. More than once, he rose to peer out the door into the corridor. When the train stopped in Crowthorne, we were the last to leave. Only when we had stepped from the train and observed the empty platform, did he seem at ease.

Dr. Nicholson had sent a carriage to meet us and again, we found ourselves propelled toward the looming presence of Broadmoor. When we arrived, we were shown to the Superintendent's office. Nicholson, a balding rather jovial man with a great walrus-like mustache, greeted us with a hearty handshake. He told us Clemmons had apprised him of the situation regarding Thomas, and that he would show us to Thomas' room himself.

"The poor fellow is in the hospital wing now," Nicholson said, as we traveled the long corridor. "Hopefully, he will recover. Some of them don't you know. Some of them just . . . waste away."

"I suppose it is their way of escape from this world," Holmes said.

"It is one way."

"Has anyone ever escaped Broadmoor?"

Nicholson took on a severe expression which, on his rotund face, seemed woefully out of place. "Unfortunately, there have been a few. But most have been recovered. Only one has escaped during my tenure. His name was Bisgrove."

"William Bisgrove? How did he come to be here?"

"He murdered one of his fellows at the mine in which he worked and was sent here after his trial. I never thought him to be insane. He was quite clever and I've no doubt he pretended his illness to escape the hangman's rope. You must excuse me, Mr. Holmes. Bisgrove is a black spot on my career. He has never been recaptured."

"May I ask how he escaped?"

"He liked to sketch; charcoal was his medium of choice. We allowed him a room on Privilege Block. One day, while taking exercise with the other inmates, he overcame one of our attendants, broke the lock on the terrace gate and escaped into the woods."

"His room, where is it?"

"By strange coincidence, it is the one beside the room Thomas now occupies."

"And Thomas' room, that belonged to Dadd, correct?"

"It was. Bisgrove spent some time with Dadd before he escaped." He stopped before Thomas' room. "If you gentlemen do not mind, I shall leave you here while I return to my office." He called an attendant over. "When you wish to leave, Jenkins will take you."

Thomas' room had not changed since our last visit. I glanced up at the window, half-expecting to see the ghost of Bisgrove peering in.

The thought unnerved me to such a great degree that I took a step backward, and into the covered canvas on the easel. The white cloth slipped off, revealing the painting beneath. It was the portrait of a rather studious gentleman. He possessed a large forehead, sunken eyes, and the austere expression of the academic. He reminded me of a professor or a math tutor.

Something about the man filled me with dread. It was as though his future and mine might somehow be intertwined. I recovered the painting, just as Holmes called out to me.

"Do you remember the bell rope in Helen Stoner's bedroom, Watson?"

"The false one? I do."

"And Thomas' sketchbooks. Do you remember anything odd about them?"

"Both were covered with paraffin wax."

"Thomas is mad, but not so mad that he would use candlelight when a gas lamp is so readily available."

Holmes took the chair from the table, set it below the lamp and climbed upon it. "It is as I feared. This lamp has not functioned for some time. Not in the way it was intended, anyway. Hello . . . there is a hose within this sconce. No doubt it leads through the wall and into the next room."

A faint scent filled the air. It jarred my memory and reminded me of the night I had received my own spectral visitation.

"I have been a fool," I said.

"Eh, Watson?"

"It was ether. Ether all along."

"The anesthetic?"

"It can cause hallucinations. I have smelled its sweet odor each time I've experienced a visit from the apparition." I shook my head. "There is no ghost."

"Bravo, Watson," Holmes said, and applauded me. "I have wondered what the substance was. You have found your way at last. And in so doing, you have provided me with a piece of the puzzle."

Holmes stepped off the chair and began a further examination of the room. He searched the bed first, both above and under, then the bookshelf and finally the table. When he lifted the cloth on the canvas of the academic's portrait, his eyes widened, and for a moment, I believed he might have recognized the fellow. He moved on, however, pausing at the center of the room to draw a cigarette from his case. Something must have caught his eye, however, for he replaced it and hurried back to the bookshelf.

"He has hidden the secret in plain sight, Watson," Holmes said, plucking the issue of Lippincott's from the shelf. He opened it and, after paging through it, handed the magazine to me.

"The Picture of Dorian Gray?" I read. "This is the chronicle of Basil Hallward's death."

"Yes," Holmes replied. "And it also holds the secret that Bisgrove covets. Yes, Watson. Bisgrove is not a ghost. He is very much alive. You met him but a few days ago when he brought us the sketches Roger Thomas had drawn. He hoped we would believe in the man's clairvoyance and, in doing so, would find that which he seeks."

"Clemmons?" I cried, aghast. "He is William Bisgrove?"

"Did you not mark his boots when we climbed the stairs this morning, Watson? They were new and square-toed, just as the prints outside the window of the Gladstone home were. A home which happens to belong to Henry Bisgrove. Lestrade did not visit my rooms this morning, as you incorrectly deduced. I went to see him at Scotland Yard. There, he told me the story of Bisgrove and the murder at the mine. He also told me of the killer's eventual incarceration at Broadmoor, his escape and drowning. Since the drowned man had been in the water for some time, his face could not be identified. A tailor's mark in his clothing is what led the police to believe he was Bisgrove. This morning, when I so hastily left you to await Clemmons, I wired Seward's Asylum and asked for a description of him. I learned he is a medium-sized fellow with brown hair and weak eyes. He is very concerned with his health and never smokes, not even the occasional cheroot cigar. This led me to believe that it was Clemmons who drowned, and that Bisgrove adopted his persona. Bisgrove took up his position at Broadmoor and contrived to have Thomas committed to Bethlem, once he had murdered the man's fiancé."

"All because she did not love him?"

"No, Watson. While Mrs. Ponsonby's story is quite romantic, it is, I'm afraid, far from the truth. You'll remember Bisgrove's claim that his friends had stolen his soul? That is why he hunts them, why he has weaseled his way back into their midst. Is that not true, Mrs. Clemmons?"

I turned to the doorway and, for the first time, saw a woman dressed in violet, standing there. She lifted the dark veil and revealed the lovely face of the Deputy Superintendent's wife.

"Yes, Mr. Holmes. It is true. Would that it were not. I have shared six years of my life with that monster, six years which cannot be returned."

11: Amelia

"Do you know where they have hidden it?" Holmes asked as the lady stepped into the room.

"Until yesterday morning, when I visited Roger, I knew nothing. He showed me a watercolor—"

Holmes removed the page from his pocketbook and handed it to her.

"Yes, that is the very one. He told me I would die but was too afraid to tell me the name of my murderer. Instead, he sent me looking for a painting in Jonathan's attic. I could not believe it when I saw it. There was a face there, one I have only seen in his pictures. I did not know I had been looking into it every day for the past six years."

"You saw the face of Bisgrove?" I said.

She stared at me with her magnificent eyes. I fancied I saw hope within them, the same hope I now felt.

"You saw it too? You saw his face within Roger's painting? And the oak tree—with the cross?"

"I did. I have."

"No one else has seen the face. Only Jonathan, me, and Roger who put it there."

"Bisgrove is the son of a mesmerist. He has likely given a suggestion that you see it," Holmes said. "He has used ether to cause hallucinations and created his spectral visitations that he may frighten you into revealing the location of the portrait—the one painted by Basil Hallward."

The lady pressed a gloved hand to her forehead. "I knew he searched for it. Has he learned it is here near Broadmoor?"

"He has. Mrs. Clemmons—"

"Please, do not use that name. I cannot disservice a man I do not know by carrying his name, nor will I carry the name of a murderer who once wormed his way into my heart. Call me Amelia."

"You are in grave danger, Amelia. Can you tell us where the painting can be found?"

Amelia stared at the picture, her face quite pale. At last, she looked up. "All of this began so innocently. It was a jest Annie wished to play on William. She was always teasing him. They did not know he would take it so seriously, that he would believe Basil had stolen his soul and placed it in the painting. It was William who murdered Annie and placed the blame on Roger. I know that now.

"Jonathan knew it from the first. He did not think Bisgrove would return to Broadmoor once he had escaped the place. It was he who hid the painting in Crowthorne Wood beneath—"

"The oak with a cross carved into its trunk," Holmes said.

"Yes. He did not tell me nor my sister what he'd done—there was no need. As I told you, I only learned of it yesterday. Jonathan did not know Bisgrove would become Cyril Clemmons, or that he would torture Roger into madness to recover the portrait. I certainly did not suspect him of such things. When I met Cyril, I saw only his charm. I married him out of vain foolishness and brought the devil among us. He's driven Jonathan to his death and now seeks to murder me, for if he cannot possess the painting himself, he will destroy all who know of its existence." She sighed. "My sister and brother are no longer safe, and it is my doing. All of it."

"You must not blame yourself," I said.

"There is no one else left to blame." She turned her gaze on Holmes and nodded. "I will make you a bargain, Mr. Holmes. If you allow me to aid you in your quest to capture Bisgrove and find the painting, I will show you where the tree is. I know where it is. I've been there many a time with Jonathan and Emma."

12: Crowthorne Wood

The sun was at its zenith when we entered Crowthorne Wood, bearing the shovels we had procured from Broadmoor's gardening shed. Amelia led the way over the trail with Holmes and I close behind. We could just see the road between the trees, and a great clamor drew our attention to it. A carriage came rattling down toward the asylum, black horses covered in sweat, the driver cracking the whip above their heads. Amelia halted as they passed.

"It is Bisgrove," she said, shivering.

"He has no doubt discovered that it was I who sent the message this morning and not Scotland Yard. Yes, Watson, that was my other destination before he arrived at Baker Street." He took Amelia by the arm. "He cannot see you among the trees, Amelia, and he is a man of flesh and blood, not a spirit. He cannot reach you now." He led her back up the trail, clutching the shovel in his right hand. I slipped my hand into my pocket and gripped the revolver.

We hurried up the trail and deep into the wood, past large and stately conifers. In treeless patches, heather grew in golden abundance. Oak and elm, touched by October, wore their autumn robes. I might have been inspired by the beauty of the place, had our quest not been an urgent one.

At last, we reached an older part of the forest, filled with mighty oaks. The smallest of these grew in the center of a clearing and bore a cross upon its trunk. Amelia rushed toward it.

"This is the one," she said.

Holmes and I set to digging. It did not take long to dislodge the soft soil, and after twenty minutes, our shovels struck what proved to be a black steamer trunk. Together, we pulled it from the earth.

We had no key for the lock, but a few blows from Holmes' shovel soon struck it off. He threw it open. Inside was a large canvas wrapped in coarse cloth. Holmes removed it and we looked upon the handiwork of Basil Hallward.

It had been painted in oil, and though the body and background were beautifully rendered, the face was the most hideous thing I had ever seen. How can I describe the twisted features, the wide and lidless eyes? If ever evil had a face, it was captured here in Bisgrove's portrait.

Amelia looked upon it with a shudder. "Basil has done it," she whispered. "He has set Bisgrove's soul onto the canvas and trapped it there."

Holmes covered the painting with the cloth and took it from the trunk. The sun, which had filled the clearing with warm light, seemed to grow dim as he did so.

"We should destroy it," Amelia said. "Burn it right here and let the wind take the ashes."

"If we do, we will fail in capturing Bisgrove," Holmes replied. "We can only garner his confession if we keep it."

The wood seemed to grow silent as we began our journey from it. Neither we nor the lady spoke, as we strained to hear any sound that might be out of place. We knew that Bisgrove had returned to Broadmoor, but we did not know whether he had intuited our intentions when he discovered Holmes' ruse.

The trail seemed longer than when we had first trod it, as though several miles had been added to its length. And as it grew longer, time seemed to move along more quickly. The sun dipped toward the horizon, allowing purple shadows to pool within the forest.

When we reached the last stretch of the trail, a sense of being watched passed over me. I looked toward the trail's end, where the branches of the trees had formed a natural archway, and saw a figure standing there. I could not make out the face, but I knew it to be Bisgrove.

Holmes had seen the figure as well. He halted, and Amelia and I followed suit.

The figure stood still for several moments before darting off to the left.

Amelia took one of the shovels, freeing my right hand so that I might withdraw the revolver from my pocket.

"Let us move off the trail and into the opposite side of the wood," Holmes whispered. "I fear that this way leads only to ambush now."

We followed his lead, moving slowly in the underbrush and pausing often to listen. Not a sound issued from the opposite side of the trail as the rapidly setting sun created more places for our opponent to hide.

I shall never forget those moments as we moved away from the trail and further into the wood. The silent air grew colder around us as we struggled to keep as silent as Bisgrove. Once, I heard the crack of a twig behind us and I whirled, ready to meet a charging foe, only to find no one. I quickly lowered my gaze to the brush which covered the forest floor but, thankfully, nothing crawled within it.

We halted upon reaching the edge of the forest and peered into the field. Twilight had crept upon the world while we'd been in the wood and a few lights had sprung up within far off Broadmoor.

"The moon will not rise for some time," Holmes said. "The darkness will hide us as we cross the field. We've only a few minutes to wait."

I looked back into the dark wood, searching for a sign of our opponent. An icy breeze moved among the trees and their leaves and boughs soughed, but nothing else moved. I could not help but wonder where our opponent had gone.

We waited until night had fallen before venturing out into the field. Using Broadmoor as a guide, we began our trek through the waist-high grass. Holmes moved beside me.

"I do not think our quarry is in the wood, Watson," he whispered. "He would've made some attempt by now, but like a spider, he waits for us to leave the trees and come to him. Take Amelia to the road and wait there for me. I shall join you anon."

"Where are you going?"

"I am headed back to Broadmoor with the painting. Given a choice, I believe Bisgrove will follow me and not Amelia."

"You take too great a risk, Holmes. We should go on together."

"I have endangered the lady long enough, Watson. It is time to eliminate her from the equation and dispense with the scoundrel. Go now. I entrust her to your care."

He veered away from me and into the darkness. I hurried to Amelia's side.

"Come, Amelia. We will make for the road," I said, my tone hushed.

"Where is Mr. Holmes?"

"He has gone on to lead the villain away from us. We shall wait for him by the road."

We pressed on, the tall trees waving before us in the cold wind. We were nearly to the road when a sickly sweet odor filled the air.

I tried to pull the revolver's trigger, but it was too late. The figure rose from the grass before us and pulled us into its dark embrace.

13: The Ghost Returns

When I opened my eyes, Bisgrove was gone, as was the revolver. I was once again on the battlefield of Maiwand.

In the distance, men screamed, and the hooded figure I had escaped before cackled. I looked across a sea of corpses, watching as it robbed another man of his life.

"This isn't real," I said aloud.

The specter moved to the next unhappy soul, the blade in its hand gleaming. I shut my eyes and turned away as he shrieked. His cries grew quieter and soon he made no sound at all.

I gritted my teeth and tried once more to banish the vision from my mind. But when I opened my eyes, it still remained. The specter moved from one wounded man to another, stabbing and slashing. I knew I should stop him, should save these men, but I could not. My leg and shoulder, both injured by the Jezail bullets, lay useless at my side. I could not move.

Another scream filled the air, not a man's cry this time, but a woman's. I glanced up. Amelia stood near me, her face a mask of fear. The specter had seen her and was gliding across the dead toward her, bearing down on her.

She did not belong here, not in this world of the past. She did not belong among those I had abandoned to death when Murray loaded me upon the packhorse and carried me away.

I knew then I would not fail her. I *could* not fail her.

I pushed myself up, my leg and shoulder no longer pained by the ghostly injury of so long ago and launched myself toward the specter. To my surprise, he did not vanish nor turn to smoke between my fingers. I caught hold of cloth instead, and together we fell to the ground.

Maiwand disappeared the moment I touched him. The rising moon revealed a face wrapped in a thick scarf. When I pulled it away, the face changed before my eyes. One moment, it belonged to Clemmons, then to Bisgrove, then to the twisted thing that inhabited the painting of Basil Hallward.

The features of Clemmons returned, and he struck me across the chin. I fell to the side, dazed, as Amelia screamed once more. When I looked up, I saw him pursuing her. I scrambled to my feet and staggered toward them. Bisgrove caught her, and upon throwing her to the ground, lifted his hand. A knife gleamed within it.

"Stop!" a voice cried out.

At the sound of such a masterful tone, Bisgrove froze, the knife above his head. A match-light flared up in the darkness, and in its dim light, I recognized the face of Sherlock Holmes.

"Release her," Holmes said. "Or I shall destroy this painting and with it, your soul."

Bisgrove did not move. He continued to hold Amelia down.

"Very well," Holmes said. He lifted the canvas and brought the match to it.

"No! No!" Bisgrove cried.

"Then step away," Holmes said.

This time Bisgrove obeyed my friend. He allowed Amelia up and to her feet. She rushed to Holmes' side.

I had lost the revolver, but it took little effort to relieve Bisgrove of his knife. I was not surprised to see that it was the same knife the murderer had used in Thomas' sketch of Lord Allenby. I pressed the point against the villain's back.

"What have you done to it?" Bisgrove said, his voice no longer that of Clemmons, but a deeper, gruffer one. "Why does it look like that? Why does my soul look that way? It didn't look that way before. It was beautiful before."

"Did you think your soul would not suffer from all that you have done to it?" Amelia asked. "Did you truly believe it would remain pristine?"

"You did this!" he cried. "How long have you known where it was? How long have you lied to me?"

His eyes grew wide and wild. "You've used me, haven't you? Used me to kill your friends and in so doing, you've ruined my soul!"

"You alone are responsible for your actions," Holmes said. "The lady played no part in your evil deeds."

"She betrayed me. Just like Annie did. Like they all did. They trapped my soul, and they wouldn't give it back. I warned them they would die if they didn't give it back."

"You killed Annie!" Amelia cried.

"And I would do it again."

"You will pay for those actions," Holmes said. "You and you alone."

"No, Mr. Sherlock Holmes," Bisgrove replied. "You shall pay. With the life of your friend."

Bisgrove turned, but I was ready for him. I slashed his forearm with the intent to wound, and to my horror, saw the knife pass *through* it. He reached for my throat and grasped hold.

Holmes had dropped the canvas to the ground and lit another match. He cupped it in one hand, protecting it from the breeze which swirled about us.

"Drop the match, Holmes," Bisgrove demanded. "And hand the painting over or I shall squeeze the life from your friend."

I clutched at Bisgrove's hands but could not touch them. They seemed as insubstantial as those of a ghost.

Holmes stood for several moments, his gaze on Bisgrove. He shifted it to me.

Holmes has always been a man of strange habits, a genius, an impatient fellow who does not make friends easily. But for all his faults and all his strengths, I knew two things: he was my friend, and I had entrusted my life with him. I nodded my head to his unspoken inquiry.

"Very well," Holmes said. "I shall drop the match."

It fell from his fingers.

"No!" Bisgrove cried. He released me and dove forward. The match plummeted. I thought it might be extinguished by the wind, but the minute Holmes released it, all fell still. When the flame touched, the canvas burst into flame.

Bisgrove screamed in agony, and for several minutes it seemed as though *two* voices rang out. The howl lasted only as long as the painting burned, then it died away. Bisgrove lay upon the grass where he had writhed in agony, his visage not unlike that which had once looked out from the painting of Basil Hallward.

14: An End to it All

I saw little of Holmes after our adventure at Broadmoor. He was soon engaged on an important case and with my wife's return and my own flourishing practice, I had little time. Though I did see him in November, the circumstances of the dramatic affair he had been investigating—one which nearly killed him—drove the incidents at Broadmoor from my mind. It would be December before I received a message from him, inviting me to Baker Street.

"I do not understand it, Holmes," I said as I warmed myself before the cheery fire. He stood by the mantel, staring at Dadd's tarot card. "Why did Clemmons come to Lestrade and to you with the sketches? Wouldn't it have served him better if he had hidden or destroyed them? They revealed his part in the murders."

"To you, Amelia, and Jonathan Ponsonby, they did," Holmes replied. "Somehow, he had suggested the clues to you and the others through mesmerism and hidden them from himself. As to why he wished the good inspector and me to see them, I believe he hoped they would interest me in the case. He wanted quite desperately to find the portrait, and he needed my help to do it. Think of it, Watson. If you were a murderer and you wished to hire the foremost consulting detective, how would you go about it? You cannot ask him straight out. You need to appeal to his interests and involve him in something beyond the realm of the ordinary. First, Clemmons took Thomas' drawings to Lestrade, hoping the good inspector would bring them to me. He was careful to include the murder of Lord Allenby only after John Allenby had been hanged for his father's death. Otherwise—"

"You would find him to be the murderer."

"Precisely. But Lestrade, knowing of my distaste for the supernatural, and embarrassed by his incompetence, did not inform me. Bisgrove then turned to you, following you and hoping you might lead him to me. He had been searching for Ponsonby, as Ponsonby had hidden the painting and possessed the sketchbook, and you unwittingly led him to him."

"That is why he was so eager to fetch the undertaker. He wished to take charge of Ponsonby's body and thereby, recover the sketchbook Thomas had given Ponsonby."

"Yes. Ponsonby must've come by the sketchbook the same day he visited Thomas, when Thomas told him of the tarot card painting. Bisgrove then used Ponsonby's story of the ghost to 'haunt you' as it were. You, like Lestrade, did not wish to tell me of your supernatural visitations, and so Bisgrove had to find another method of involving me."

"Gladstone and Miss O'Hare."

"Excellent, Watson! Yes, he tried to kill two birds with one stone by murdering his father and his father's lover. He took a great risk there, for these murders would reveal the fact that Clemmons did not exist, and Bisgrove was still alive. Miss O'Hare might have revealed it to us had she not fallen into one of her fits when he forced the lock on the door. You'll recall, he possessed such skills. He used them to escape Broadmoor when he was imprisoned there. She confirmed this fact for me when I visited her and Mr. Gladstone last month.

"It is also obvious that Bisgrove had no alibi that evening, for both Lestrade and Mrs. Ponsonby wired him and received no reply.

"He thought he had escaped unscathed from his failure at the Gladstone home, but what he did not know was that Thomas had disclosed the tarot card to us and, by adding Bisgrove's name, revealed that he was alive.

Also, as I suspected, Bisgrove had added the other names and used them to frighten Thomas. I deduced this because Bisgrove claimed to have never seen the card and yet, when we saw Thomas' tarot card painting, he said he had. The handwriting on the card also matched the reminders Bisgrove wrote upon his cuff. I realized this when I shook his hand upon leaving the Ponsonby home.

"Do you believe Lord Allenby had discovered this fact, and that is why he was killed?"

"He may or he may not have. Bisgrove added him to the list because of his investigation into the murder of Annie Wilkinson. In his misguided way, he may have believed Allenby also knew where the portrait was."

"What of Mary Jane? Why did Bisgrove appear to her if his intention was to frighten me?"

"It is far easier to frighten someone when they are alone than when someone else is in the house. He also stayed in the dark so that you could not recognize him, even by chance."

A knock sounded on the door, and Mrs. Hudson entered the room. She carried two cards on a silver salver. Holmes read the cards and then waved her toward the door.

"Please, show them in Mrs. Hudson."

Mrs. Hudson retreated and soon returned Mrs. Ponsonby and Amelia, once Clemmons and never Bisgrove, entered.

"We had to come at once, Mr. Holmes," Mrs. Ponsonby said. "We are so grateful."

"It was your statement that has freed Roger," Amelia added. "He has been vindicated and will be released from Broadmoor by week's end. We must reward you. This purse of gold—"

"I am glad to see justice done," Holmes said, raising a hand. "That is fee enough."

"You are a most remarkable man," Amelia said. "And though you may refuse us, please accept this from Roger. He sketched it for you."

Holmes accepted the page offered him. He gazed at it for several moments and then nodded his thanks.

"Roger and I are going to live with Emma," Amelia said. "The countryside has not been kind to us, and it seems a change is in order. We've also arranged for Dr. Clemmons to be buried under the correct marker instead of that of Bisgrove. It is the least we can do for the poor man."

"And what of Bisgrove?" Holmes asked.

"He has been buried in the Broadmoor Cemetery under his true name. I think it will be a lonely grave."

"As it should be," Mrs. Ponsonby said. "We do apologize for the short visit, Mr. Holmes. But we must be on our way. There is much to do before Friday."

"Before you leave, Amelia, can you answer a question for me?"

"Certainly."

"Do you know why the portrait was not destroyed in the first place? It seems to me much would have been saved if it had."

"I suppose the simplest answer is the best, Mr. Holmes. None of us wished to be a murderer."

"An interesting answer," Holmes said. He held the tarot card out to Amelia.

"No," she said. "You may keep the card, Mr. Holmes. We have had enough destruction in our lives. It is time for release."

With that, the ladies took their leave and once their tread on the stair had faded, I turned to Holmes.

"How did you know destroying the painting would kill Bisgrove?"

"I told you, Watson. No ghost is as potent as those which exist in the human mind. Bisgrove's belief in the portrait convinced him its destruction would kill him. Just as the suggestion given by Bisgrove to you, Amelia, and Ponsonby convinced you his ghostly image appeared in the sketches. He also suggested he was a ghost to you that night in the field, and that is why the knife went through his arm."

"He used my fear to deceive me," I said, lowering my gaze to the floor. "I have shown the white feather."

"No, Watson. You are no coward. You have shown great courage in this matter. Who else could have faced their greatest fear, plumbed the depths of insanity and returned to tell the tale? I know of no one, not even I."

Such praise from Holmes left me speechless.

"Speaking of the tale, what of this case?" Holmes asked. "Will you publish it?"

"Though Amelia gave me permission to write it, I think I will consign it to the tin dispatch box instead. The ladies have endured enough. When they have passed from this earth, I shall."

A sudden thought came to me. "Holmes, if Jago was responsible for Trevelyan's death, how could Thomas have drawn it? How could he have drawn any of them in such great detail? You said yourself, Bisgrove was forgetful. How could he have conveyed these details to Thomas? And he was in London when Ponsonby died, he had no time to return and collect the sketch of him."

"You'll recall, Bisgrove was also an artist who excelled in charcoal and he knew Dadd."

"But if he was there, he would have seen Ponsonby hand you Thomas' sketchbook. He would have pursued you and not Ponsonby's body."

Holmes lifted the sketch Mrs. Ponsonby had given him and passed it to me. Once again, the artist had drawn the man with the ascetic visage. The man I had dubbed "professor."

"I suppose, Watson," Holmes said. "Some things shall remain a mystery."

Subscribe to Crystal Lake Publishing's Dark Tide series for updates, specials, behind-the-scenes content, and a special selection of bonus stories
- http://eepurl.com/hKVGkr

The End?

Not if you want to dive into more of the Dark Tide series.

Check out our amazing website and online store
or download our latest catalog here.
https://geni.us/CLPCatalog

Looking for award-winning Dark Fiction?
Download our latest catalog.

Includes our anthologies, novels, novellas, collections, poetry, non-fiction, and specialty projects.

WHERE STORIES COME ALIVE!

We always have great new projects and content on the website to dive into, as well as a newsletter, behind the scenes options, social media platforms, our own dark fiction shared-world series and our very own webstore. Our webstore even has categories specifically for KU books, non-fiction, anthologies, and of course more novels and novellas.

About the Authors

John Linwood Grant is a professional writer/editor from Yorkshire. He writes strange fictions, contemporary and period-set, with some ninety stories published in the last few years, including in award-winning anthologies, a Victorian murder/mystery novel, *The Assassin's Coin*, and several novellas. His second collection, *Where All is Night, and Starless* (Journalstone), was a Shirley Jackson Award nominee, and his third and fourth collections are due in 2024. He edits various weird fiction anthologies, including the *Sherlock Holmes & the Occult Detectives series* (Belanger), as well as *Occult Detective Magazine* (Cathaven). He can be found regularly on Facebook, and his eclectic website http://greydogtales.com/blog/

Angela Yuriko Smith is an award-winning poet, author, and publisher with experience as a professional writer in nonfiction. Publisher of Space & Time magazine (est. 1966) and two-time Bram Stoker Awards® Winner. She shares Authortunities, a weekly calendar of author opportunities at angelayurikosmith.com.

Naching T. Kassa is a wife, mother, and writer. She's created short stories, novellas, poems, and co-created three children. She resides in Eastern Washington State with her husband, Dan Kassa.

Naching is head of Talent Relations and Audio Division Manager at Crystal Lake Publishing. She is a member of the Horror Writers Association, Mystery Writers of America, The Science Fiction and Fantasy Writers Association, The Sound of the Baskervilles, The ACD Society, The Crew of the Barque Lone Star, The Beacon Society, The Sherlock Holmes Society of London and The John H. Watson Society. Naching was a recipient of the 2022 HWA Diversity Grant.

Readers . . .

Thank you for reading *Sherlock Holmes and The Arcana of Madness*. We hope you enjoyed this 11th book in our Dark Tide series.

If you have a moment, please review *Sherlock Holmes and The Arcana of Madness* at the store where you bought it.

Help other readers by telling them why you enjoyed this book. No need to write an in-depth discussion. Even a single sentence will be greatly appreciated. Reviews go a long way to helping a book sell, and is great for an author's career. It'll also help us to continue publishing quality books. You can also share a photo of yourself holding this book with the hashtag #IGotMyCLPBook!

Thank you again for taking the time to journey with Crystal Lake Publishing.

Visit our Linktree page for a list of our social media platforms. https://linktr.ee/CrystalLakePublishing

Follow us on Amazon:

Our Mission Statement:

Since its founding in August 2012, Crystal Lake Publishing has quickly become one of the world's leading publishers of Dark Fiction and Horror books in print, eBook, and audio formats.

While we strive to present only the highest quality fiction and entertainment, we also endeavour to support authors along their writing journey. We offer our time and experience in non-fiction projects, as well as author mentoring and services, at competitive prices.

With several Bram Stoker Award wins and many other wins and nominations (including the HWA's Specialty Press Award), Crystal Lake Publishing puts integrity, honor, and respect at the forefront of our publishing operations.

We strive for each book and outreach program we spearhead to not only entertain and touch or comment on issues that affect our readers, but also to strengthen and support the Dark Fiction field and its authors.

Not only do we find and publish authors we believe are destined for greatness, but we strive to work with men and women who endeavour to be decent human beings who care more for others than themselves, while still being hard working, driven, and passionate artists and storytellers.

Crystal Lake Publishing is and will always be a beacon of what passion and dedication, combined with overwhelming teamwork and respect, can accomplish. We endeavour to know each and every one of our readers, while building personal relationships with our authors, reviewers, bloggers, podcasters, bookstores, and libraries.

We will be as trustworthy, forthright, and transparent as any business can be, while also keeping most of the headaches away from our authors, since it's our job to solve the problems so they can stay in a creative mind. Which of course also means paying our authors.

We do not just publish books, we present to you worlds within your world, doors within your mind, from talented authors who sacrifice so much for a moment of your time.

There are some amazing small presses out there, and through collaboration and open forums we will continue to support other presses in the goal of helping authors and showing the world what quality small presses are capable of accomplishing. No one wins when a small press goes down, so we will always be there to support hardworking, legitimate presses and their authors. We don't see Crystal Lake as the best press out there, but we will always strive to be the best, strive to be the most interactive and grateful, and even blessed press around. No matter what happens over time, we will also take our mission very seriously while appreciating where we are and enjoying the journey.

What do we offer our authors that they can't do for themselves through self-publishing?

We are big supporters of self-publishing (especially hybrid publishing), if done with care, patience, and planning. However, not every author has the time or inclination to do market research, advertise, and set up book launch strategies. Although a lot of authors are successful in doing it all, strong small presses will always be there for the authors who just want to do what they do best: write.

What we offer is experience, industry knowledge, contacts and trust built up over years. And due to our strong brand and trusting fanbase, every Crystal Lake Publishing book comes with weight of respect. In time our fans begin to trust our judgment and will try a new author purely based on our support of said author.

With each launch we strive to fine-tune our approach, learn from our mistakes, and increase our reach. We continue to assure our authors that we're here for them and that we'll carry the weight of the launch and dealing with third parties while they focus on their strengths—be it writing, interviews, blogs, signings, etc.

We also offer several mentoring packages to authors that include knowledge and skills they can use in both traditional and self-publishing endeavours.

We look forward to launching many new careers.

This is what we believe in. What we stand for. This will be our legacy.

Welcome to Crystal Lake Publishing— Tales from the Darkest Depths.